Ple

Secrets, SCHEMES & Sewing Machines

For my wonderful family – every last one of them

STRIPES PUBLISHING
An imprint of Little Tiger Press
1 The Coda Centre, 189 Munster Road,
London SW6 6AW

A paperback original
First published in Great Britain in 2015
Text copyright © Katy Cannon, 2015
Cover copyright © Stripes Publishing Ltd, 2015
Cover photography copyright © Alister Thorpe, 2015
Black and white illustrations courtesy of www.shutterstock.com

ISBN: 978-1-84715-514-6

Printed and bound in the UK.

10 9 8 7 6 5 4 3 2 1

Secrets, SCHEMES & Sewing Machines

KATY CANNON

Stripes

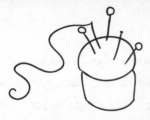

ABOUT THE
SEWING PROJECTS

The sewing projects in this book, much like the recipes in *Love, Lies and Lemon Pies*, are meant as a jumping-off point for your own sewing adventures and I've tried to include something for everyone.

The projects range in difficulty from the really simple (Needle Book) to the rather more tricky (Drop-waisted T-shirt Dress) with a lot in between. Some are easier with a sewing machine, but most can be sewn by hand.

If you've never sewn before, you'll need to learn some basics before you jump in. The internet – not to mention your local library – is there to help you. There are endless sewing websites with detailed descriptions of how to sew the stitches or techniques included in the projects, often with very helpful pictures or videos, too.

Once you've mastered the basics, there'll be no stopping you. So go ahead and make your own school bag, or decorate a plain canvas tote bag with sequins and buttons. Make yourself a skirt, or upcycle one you found in a charity shop. Just like Grace, you'll learn how to make your outfits, accessories, home – and life – utterly yours. Unique and special – and with added sparkle.

Katy x

P.S. Don't forget to send in photos of your creations via my website! I'd love to see them.

Here are some things you might find handy for starting off:

Sewing Kit

Needles (varying sizes)
Pins
Safety pins
Cotton thread
Embroidery thread
Tailor's chalk
Measuring tape
Paper for patterns
An iron
Fabric glue
Fabric scissors
Pinking shears
Ordinary scissors
A sewing machine with needles
and bobbins (optional)

Basic Stitches

Running stitch
Back stitch
Whip stitch
Blanket stitch

CONTENTS

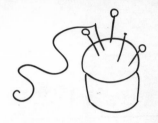

WHAT YOU NEED TO BEGIN

A needle.

Thread.

Fabric.

And a pattern.

Sewing is more than just a hobby. Learning to sew
means you can create outfits, accessories and looks
knowing that no one else will ever have something
exactly the same. You will always be unique and true
to yourself. Whichever pattern you follow,
make it your own.

My dad told me to always have a plan. Doesn't matter if the plan changes or shifts a little, as long as you have one. "Fail to plan, Grace, and you plan to fail!" he'd say. "I want you to plan to succeed."

So I got ready to start sixth form with a plan – to be a star. To matter. After the disappointment of coming in second to Lottie Hansen in pretty much everything that happened during my GCSE year, I needed to win at Year Twelve. After all, it wasn't like I had had a baking apprenticeship and a fortnight in Paris to keep me busy over the summer, like some people. I didn't even have the hot boyfriend.

All I had was a plan to prove myself – to my parents, my friends and even to me. But it all went out of the window the night before term started, the moment Faith knocked on our front door.

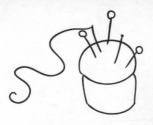

NEEDLE BOOK

What you need:

2 pieces of card, 15 x 10cm
1 piece of fabric, 20 x 26cm
2 pieces of felt, 13 x 20cm

What to do:

1. Lay your fabric out in a landscape orientation with the pattern (the right side) facing down and the back of the fabric (the wrong side) showing.

2. Place your pieces of card in a portrait orientation, side by side on the wrong side of the fabric, with a 1cm gap between them and a border of fabric around the edges.

3. Glue the card in place, then fold and glue the edges of the fabric neatly over the card.

4. Glue one piece of felt over the card that's still showing, to give you a neat finish, then fold in half to make the needle book cover.

5. Mark the middle of the felt inside the book, and the middle of your second piece of felt – this will be your spine.

6. *Lay the second piece of felt inside the book so the marks match up, then sew in place with a line of running stitch or back stitch using embroidery thread in a complementary colour up the spine, from top to bottom. Now you have the pages of your needle book.*
7. *Store your needles in the pages by feeding them through the felt and back out again.*

My breath burned in my lungs and, for the first time in the three weeks since term started, I was actually grateful that we still had to wear school uniform in sixth form, and that high heels were not allowed. I didn't dare waste time checking my watch, I already knew I was late. Not just for school, but for something far more important.

I was late for the *auditions*.

And it was all Faith's fault. Her fault I hadn't had time to run my audition speech in the mirror enough times yesterday. As if some "family dinner" in a restaurant was suddenly more important than my actual life.

"Since when do we have family dinners?" I'd asked Mum, but she'd just given me the sad eyes and gone back to talking to Faith. Again.

Then, back home, there had been the photo album from my parents' wedding and embarrassing stories about me as a child. I'd escaped to my room to call Yasmin, relieved to talk to someone who didn't make everything about Faith. Mostly because she didn't know Faith existed. Then it had been late and I must have forgotten to set my alarm because suddenly it was morning and I was running late before I even got out of bed.

I rounded the last corner before the school gates at high speed, grabbing hold of a lamppost to spin myself around in the right direction. Other sixth formers were still sauntering through the gates behind a crowd of younger kids, so maybe I still had a chance. Maybe the bell hadn't rung yet. Maybe I could make it…

I cursed Mr Hughes and whatever stupid timetabling issue meant he'd had to hold the auditions *before* school this year, instead of after school or even at lunch.

"I don't want to waste any time," he'd said at our last Drama Club meeting, the first I'd actually managed to make that year. "We've had a few weeks to get familiar with the material and I think you're ready. My vision is for something really special – different from the traditional versions of Shakespeare we've done before. I'm going to need real commitment from everyone, starting with the auditions. I want each of you to prepare a two-minute speech – a monologue from any play you like – and I'll be keeping time. The auditions will be held on Monday morning at 8 a.m. sharp in the school hall."

And now it was almost nine.

Shoving my way past a few slow-movers, I raced down the path towards the main doors and veered left into the school hall, just as the bell clanged out over the speakers to signal the official start of the school day.

"Thanks for coming today, everyone. I have a really good feeling about this show." Mr Hughes beamed at the group of people on stage, who all looked unbearably pleased with themselves. Then, realizing they were running the risk of being late for registration, they started to scatter.

I had bigger worries than missing registration.

"Mr Hughes." I sidled up to his chair, still trying to catch my breath. "I'm so sorry I was late today. Bit of a family crisis, I'm afraid."

His gaze unnerved me. It felt like he was studying me, analyzing me, like a character in a play. "Another one, Grace?" he asked. "Wasn't that the excuse you used when you missed Drama Club the first week we came back? And the second, actually. Is it something you'd like to talk about?"

My smile froze. No, actually, it really wasn't.

"It's been an ... interesting summer," I told Mr Hughes, aiming for wry understatement in my voice. What I actually felt was disbelief, confusion and just a tinge of despair, but I figured he didn't need to know that. "I'd still really like to audition for the play. You know how much I love Shakespeare." Total lie, but teachers always liked to hear that sort of thing. "And how much time and energy I've put into Drama Club over the past five years." A little reminder that I'd paid my dues and worked my way up.

This year's play, after the roaring success of last year's *A Midsummer's Night Dream* (featuring yours truly as the fairy queen), was *Much Ado About Nothing*. As far as I'd been able to tell from the film clips on YouTube, it was about two people who argued all the time to hide the fact they were secretly crazy about each other.

I was the queen of banter. Nobody in the group could pull off a flirty argument like me. I was born to play Beatrice. This was my year to take the lead. That was the plan!

Mr Hughes studied me a moment longer, then got slowly to his feet. "I think, Grace, that if you were really as invested as you claim, you'd have managed to make it to Drama Club more than once this term. And you'd have been on time this morning."

My breath was back, but my palms were sweating now. He wasn't actually being serious, was he? "Mr Hughes, really, you don't understand—"

"I think I do. You have stuff going on in your life," he interrupted me. "But the thing is Grace, *so does everyone else.*"

Heat rose up to my cheeks and I knew I was blushing. He had no idea about my life and I didn't see why I should have to tell him.

"Oh, come on," I said, anger and embarrassment throbbing in my chest. "I'm the best actress you've got in this club. You're not seriously going to leave me out because I was late? Just let me audition, please. I'll come to the drama room at lunchtime, or after school. Whenever."

But Mr Hughes shook his head. "I'm sorry, Grace. I need a cast I can rely on to show up on time, and for every rehearsal, not just when it suits them."

"But wait..." I darted in front of him to stop him reaching his files. "You're not being fair."

"Auditions aren't about being fair, Grace. And they're not about who's been here the longest, or who thinks they deserve what. They're about choosing the right person for a role."

"*I'm* the right person," I insisted. "Who else are you going to cast? Sara? Violet? They're not a patch on me and you know it."

"They did the most important thing, though. They showed up."

Mr Hughes sidestepped me to gather up his files. "I'm sorry, Grace. Auditions are closed."

And with that he left the hall, with me staring blankly after him, wondering if that had really, truly happened.

The sound of a chair scraping on the wooden floor made me spin round, as I realized that my latest private humiliation hadn't been private at all. There by the door, stacking up chairs, was a guy I didn't recognize. Taller than me by half a foot, and with sandy hair he brushed back from his face with his fingers, he didn't look like anything special. But then he glanced up and his pale blue eyes caught mine, and I got the uncomfortable feeling that he could see right through me.

I blinked. "What are you doing here?" I snapped, embarrassed. He was in uniform, and looked about my age. New student, I guessed.

My eyes narrowed as he raised an eyebrow at me and pointed at the chairs, a smirk spreading across his face. "I thought it was kind of obvious."

"So, what? You were auditioning?" He was cute enough to make a passable Benedick, I decided, once I'd persuaded Mr Hughes to let me play Beatrice. The irritating smirk would be perfect for the banter. Not to mention those eyes...

But the new guy shook his head. "I'm more of the backstage sort. Looks like you might be, too, by the sound of things."

"Not a chance," I said. "I just need to convince Mr Hughes to let me audition. He'll come round."

"I don't know, he seemed pretty decided." The new guy boosted the last chair on to the stack, before lifting the whole lot as if they weighed nothing and carting them over to the other side of the hall. "And he's not the sort of man who changes his mind easily."

"You clearly haven't seen how persuasive I can be," I told him. "Besides, how would you know? You're new, right? You can only have been at this school for, like, five minutes."

"True." He grabbed his school bag and swung it up on to his shoulder, fixing me with that cool blue stare. "But I'm Connor O'Neil. Mr Hughes is my stepdad. I'm not just helping him backstage – I'm the stage manager. Which in this case means I'm helping with the casting, too. And, to be honest,

I can see exactly why we wouldn't want you in the play. Far too high maintenance."

Connor sauntered out of the hall, leaving me alone for real this time. Which was a good thing, since I was gaping slightly. High maintenance? Who did he think he was, acting like he knew all about me?

He knew as little about me as I did about him, anyway. Mr Hughes's stepson. How had I missed that? I leaned back against the stage and replayed the whole exchange with him and Mr Hughes in my head. Damn it. The one guy I could have used on my side, to help me convince Mr Hughes to give me the part, and he thought I was a teenage diva with an ego problem.

Not the best start to my bid for stardom.

The bell rang again and I realized I'd missed registration completely. I grabbed my bag and dashed out of the hall to my first class of the day – history. Fortunately for me, I shared the lesson with Jasper. Maybe he'd know enough about Connor O'Neil to help me win him over, convince his stepdad to give me the starring role, and get my sixth-form plan back on course.

After three weeks of studying Russia and communism, I already knew our history lesson was going to be a snoozefest. The only slight relief from the boredom was the fact that the teacher, Mr Edwards, was slightly deaf, and didn't always notice when Jasper and I were chatting. We'd teamed up at the back of the classroom on the first day, and I had promised to prod Jasper with a sharp pencil whenever he started to snore.

"How were the auditions?" Jasper asked, before yawning. "God, Mondays."

"I hear you." Dropping my bag beside my seat I smoothed down my skirt and sat down quickly, before Mr Edwards arrived. My skirt was just a smidge or eight above regulation length and although Mr Edwards might not be able to hear well, there was nothing wrong with his eyesight. This day really didn't need a trip to the head of sixth form and a lecture about appropriate dress. "I overslept. Missed the auditions."

Jasper winced. "Bad luck. Does this mean you're in an even worse mood than normal for a Monday?" He studied me, a little frown appearing across his forehead. "Hang on, why are you smiling? Is there some evil scheme afoot to maim or injure whoever gets the lead so you can step in and save the day?"

I gave him a Look. It was still kind of hard to believe that I was actually friends with Jasper.

I mean, who actually uses the word "afoot" these days? But over the last year I'd realized that Jasper was more than "that weird goth kid". And after his girlfriend, Ella, left town last Easter to live with her mum up North, Jasper had needed distracting, so we'd ended up hanging out together quite a bit. Then this summer, with Yasmin away and Mac and Lottie in Paris, it had mostly just been him and me.

"No schemes." I turned my attention to the front of the class, where Mr Edwards had just walked in. "I don't need schemes to be a star. I just need the chance to actually audition."

Jasper rolled his eyes and I knew he was thinking, *Same old Grace.*

Well, fine. I had a plan and I was sticking to it. Yeah, home might be kind of crazy right now, and I wasn't stupid enough to think I could hide something as big as Faith forever, but I didn't want to let it change me or my plans for the year.

Speaking of which… "Actually, you might be able to help me. What have you heard about this new guy – Connor?" Jasper always had the best gossip. I guessed it came from his irritating habit of asking endless questions all the time.

He gave me a sideways look. "Why? What's he to you?"

I shrugged, playing it cool. "Nothing. But he's stage managing the play, apparently. I met him this morning after the auditions." I paused. "Oh, and it turns out he's Mr Hughes's stepson."

"Yeah, I heard that. Poor guy. So what? You're hoping he can help you score a special audition?"

"Wouldn't hurt to try," I admitted. Maybe Connor and I *could* be friends, since we would have to work together on the play anyway. And friends helped each other, right?

"OK, so what have you heard already?" Jasper half turned towards me in his chair. We were whispering now, since Mr Edwards was wittering on about Stalin.

"That's pretty much it."

"Well, all I really know is that he transferred here from a school over on the other side of London." So, about forty miles from our leafy little suburban town.

"That's it?" I asked, surprised. Usually, Jasper had a lot more on people.

"Yeah. I mean, I chatted to him a bit the other day – he's in my English lit class. He seems nice. Friendly." Jasper shrugged. "I don't know – we didn't really get on to sharing our deepest secrets or anything."

"Huh." I frowned. "Why not?"

Jasper laughed, loud enough to attract a glare from Mr Edwards. We both ducked our heads behind our books again.

After a moment, I asked, "No, seriously. Why not?"

"Because I didn't know you'd be quizzing me later?" Jasper said. I shot him a look. "OK, fine. I assumed he didn't really have any. Like I said, he's a nice guy. People like him."

"People? Which people?"

"I dunno. He doesn't seem to have been hanging around with anyone in particular, I don't think."

"Then how do you know people like him?"

Jasper stared at me. "Seriously, what's this about?"

Warmth hit my cheeks and I looked away. "Nothing. Really. I just … when I met him this morning, he was all smirk and attitude. I guess I thought he might be more of a Mac type – well, Mac before he found Lottie and baking and salvation, or whatever." Troublemaker, generally considered Bad News. Probably on his last chance. The kind of guy who might be persuaded to help me.

But from what Jasper said, I'd read him wrong.

Jasper groaned. "Of course. You're sizing him up as boyfriend material, like when you had a thing for Mac last year. And you're not interested in him unless he's a bad boy, right? Poor old Connor O'Neil is out of the running for winning your affection, just because he never set fire to anything."

"I didn't have a thing for Mac. He was a lost cause the moment Miss Lottie fluttered her fan at him, or whatever it was she did."

"I think it was probably the chocolate chips," Jasper said, unhelpfully.

I prodded him with an extra-sharp pencil.

The next big setback to my Get An Audition plan came the following morning when I arrived at school, perfectly on time even though I only had a study period first thing, and found the cast list for *Much Ado About Nothing* pinned to the noticeboard by the hall.

My name wasn't on it. At all.

I scanned through the list again, checking over my shoulder to make sure that no one else was watching me. Nothing. Not even Third Maid From the Left, not that I'd have taken it if they'd offered. It was Beatrice or nothing for me.

And it was looking alarmingly like nothing.

I shook my head. There had to be a mistake. I knew Mr Hughes had wanted to make a point the day before, but I hadn't honestly believed he wouldn't let me be in the play *at all*. Maybe this was the understudy list, or something. That would make sense. Why else would Violet Roberts be down to play Beatrice? I mean that, right there, was the clearest sign ever that someone had screwed up here. Violet didn't have a flirty bone in her body.

I stalked out of the hall and headed towards the drama room, a small classroom round the back of the hall, with easy access to the stage. I needed to straighten this out with Mr Hughes immediately, before too many other people saw that list and started asking questions.

"Ah, Grace." Mr Hughes looked up as I opened the drama-room door, a tight smile on his face. Connor was sitting at a desk at the front of the classroom, and he turned those knowing pale eyes on me as his stepdad said, "I was sort of expecting you."

And I knew, right then, that the list wasn't a mistake.

My body flushed hot with embarrassment, then cold and clammy as the reality of the situation settled. I wasn't Beatrice. I wasn't the star. In fact, I wasn't *anything*.

But I was still Grace Stewart. Prettiest girl in my year (officially – there was a vote back in Year Nine).

Epic party thrower (until the police and my parents gatecrashed that one time). And yeah, maybe I hadn't won that baking apprenticeship to Paris last year, and maybe Mac had chosen Lottie when he could have, maybe, had me.

But I had stuff going for me. I made killer cupcakes, for a start.

A year ago, I might have thrown a hissy fit at Mr Hughes, far worse than the one Connor had witnessed the day before. In fact, the resigned expression on Mr Hughes's face told me that was what he was expecting. But there was too much at stake right now to risk it. I needed this part any way I could get it. Otherwise, what was the point? My whole plan this year was to succeed – to make my parents proud. If I didn't get Beatrice, it was all ruined.

Of course, there was another reason to hold back the diva trip. Connor thought I was too high maintenance to play Beatrice? Well, I could prove to him right here and now that he was wrong. My dad always told me I could be anything I wanted, if I wanted it badly enough. And I wanted to play Beatrice so much it burned.

Besides, while Dad talked about making plans, Mum always told me, "you catch more flies with honey than vinegar."

Time to test that theory out.

Closing the door behind me, hearing its quiet click, I took a deep breath and made myself smile a non-confrontational, friendly smile. When I turned back, Mr Hughes's resigned expression morphed into wary uncertainty. Even Connor was watching with interest. It made his eyes look warmer.

Perfect.

"I just saw the cast list for *Much Ado About Nothing*." I approached the desk, still smiling. "I think it'll be really interesting to see what Violet does with the role of Beatrice."

"Look, Grace. You missed the auditions. And Violet actually did a very decent version of one of Beatrice and Benedick's exchanges with Ash. I think—"

"And like I say, I can't wait to see it," I interrupted. He was dragging me off-plan. "I just wanted to ask, since I won't actually be on stage for this production, if there's anything else I can do to help out." Light, airy, unconcerned.

Because I was damned if I was going to let anyone else know how much I hated not being Beatrice.

Mr Hughes blinked slowly, his mouth slightly open. "Anything you can do … to help?"

I nodded. "That's right." God, seriously, was it

that much of a shock?

"Well…" He grabbed a file from his desk and flicked through it. "Um, we could do with some help on the costumes. Are you any good at sewing?"

I'd made a needle case and a pin cushion with my gran when I was about seven. "Absolutely! And I'm sure I can pick up any new techniques I need." Like, you know, how to actually sew or fix costumes.

"Great." Mr Hughes still sounded pretty uncertain. "Um, the Sewing Club are going to be organizing most of the fittings during rehearsals. Maybe you should talk to Miss Cotterill about joining them for their meetings."

"Of course!" I kept my smile fixed, even though Miss Cotterill was about a hundred and eighty and I suspected that Sewing Club would consist of four Year Sevens trying to learn to thread their needles. "Well, I'd better get to class. Thanks, Mr Hughes!"

"OK. Um, first proper rehearsal is on Friday. See you there?"

"Wouldn't miss it." I paused. "There's no Drama Club after school today, then?" When we were working on a play, we often had rehearsals twice a week, on Tuesdays and Fridays.

"No, just… Well, just a read through for the main parts, actually."

The smile grew painful at this point. I'd never really noticed, but not everyone was there for all the rehearsals. Just the people who were needed. I'd always been needed before.

"Of course. That makes sense. Bye, Mr Hughes." I had to get out of there and vent, somewhere people couldn't see. But as I turned towards the door, Mr Hughes stopped me.

"Wait, Grace." When I looked back, he was standing, studying me, like he was weighing up his options. Finally, he said, "I haven't actually cast the understudies for the lead roles yet. If you wanted, I might be persuaded to find time for one more audition."

Yes! I loved it when a plan came together. "That would be brilliant, Mr Hughes. Do you have time now?" Understudy wasn't the lead, but it was a chance to show him – and Connor – what I could do.

He checked his watch. "I have a few moments. Tell you what..." He reached behind him and grabbed two scripts from the desk. "Why don't you and Connor have a go at a Beatrice and Benedick scene together? I'd like to hear what you make of the exchange on page six."

Connor didn't look too pleased at the prospect

but he didn't say anything. Annoyance bubbled up in me. Did he really dislike me so much on one meeting that he couldn't even read a few pages without being miserable about it? Or was he still convinced that I was too much of a diva to understudy? Either way, I needed to change his mind if I ever wanted to win back my lead role.

I needed to truly rock this audition.

I flicked to page six and scanned through the text. It was Beatrice and Benedick's first meeting in the play, and perfect for showing off my biting banter. I grinned to myself and looked up to find Connor's glare turned on me.

"Start from 'I wonder that you will still be talking'?" I asked, and Mr Hughes nodded.

I took a breath, trying to think myself into Beatrice's head. A woman mocking a guy who was cute but annoying. I glanced at Connor. That should be easy enough.

As long as I could get my tongue around the language. Shakespeare was worse than Jasper. Still, at least I had the advantage of having watched plenty of video clips and listened to it spoken. I bet Connor hadn't even read the script yet. This was going to be far harder on him than me.

"I wonder that you will still be talking, Signior

Benedick: nobody marks you," I read, trying to inject plenty of disinterest into the words. Then I watched Connor, waiting for the comeback.

"What, my dear Lady Disdain! Are you yet living?"

I couldn't tell if the absolute dislike in Connor's voice was acting or not. I decided it didn't matter. So what if he hated me? I had the audition I wanted. As long as Mr Hughes cast me as Violet's understudy it was only a short step to the lead. Sooner or later it would become clear to everyone that Violet simply couldn't do the part justice.

I'd expected Connor to trip over the words but he didn't, which was even more annoying. Why did he have to be good at this, when he obviously didn't even care about it? In fact, he barely glanced down at the script before giving each line, every one with the same distaste and mockery that Benedick's words should have. Was it just acting?

We read to the end of the scene, Connor flipping his script closed before I'd even finished my last line. He tossed it back on to the desk but I clung to mine, waiting to hear Mr Hughes's comments. This might not matter to Connor, but it sure did to me.

"What do you think, Connor?" Mr Hughes

asked. He was smiling, which I took as a good sign.

Connor shrugged. "She's OK."

"Such praise," I muttered. "Really, stop, you're embarrassing me."

Mr Hughes laughed. "Oh, I can see it's going to be fun working with you two this year. OK, Grace, you win. That was great; you can understudy Violet for the role of Beatrice."

I let out a little squeak of excitement, but Connor just rolled his eyes.

Mr Hughes obviously caught the movement, because he turned to his stepson and said, "And I'm considering roping you in as understudy for the role of Benedick, actually. That was really good, Connor."

"It's just words." Connor got to his feet. "I'm more use to you backstage, trust me."

I clenched my jaw. Just words? What was he even doing helping out with the play if that was how he felt about it?

Mr Hughes laughed again. "Such appreciation of our literary heritage." He shook his head. "Go on, you two. I'm sure you're supposed to be somewhere else by now – and I have to cover a class in the English department."

"I've got a study period," I admitted. "But

actually, I might go and see Miss Cotterill first. Sort out the Sewing Club side of things." I didn't want him thinking I was going back on our agreement. I knew I'd only been given the chance to audition because I'd given him something first.

"Good plan." Mr Hughes was looking very pleased with himself, as if he had somehow single-handedly rehabilitated my entire character by denying me the lead in a play. Honestly. Teachers.

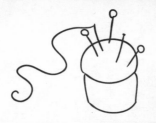

HEART PINCUSHION

What you need:

Coloured felt
Stuffing

What to do:

1. Draw a heart the size you want your pincushion to be on a piece of paper and cut out.
2. Fold your felt in half, and pin the paper heart to it, making sure the pins go right through both layers.
3. Cut around your heart and then unpin the paper, leaving two identical felt hearts.
4. Pin the hearts together again to stop them slipping as you sew.
5. Beginning at the bottom and starting your thread between the two layers of felt, stitch around the outside of the hearts with three strands of white embroidery thread, using whip stitch or blanket stitch, removing the pins as you go.
6. Stop when you have just 4–5cm left unstitched, unthread your needle and remove any remaining pins.

7. Fill your heart with stuffing until it's nice and plump.
8. Thread your needle again and finish sewing the rest of the way around the heart.
9. Stick your pins into the cushion to keep them safe until you start your next sewing project!

"How long are you going to keep this up?" Connor asked, as we stood outside the drama room, watching Mr Hughes walk off.

"Keep what up?"

"Pretending that you're actually going to be any help with the costumes," Connor said. "No, never mind, I reckon I know. Until Violet gives in and lets you play Beatrice, right? I bet you've got the whole scene sorted in your head. You come into rehearsals one day and Violet's off sick, and you have to step in. Everyone sees how fantastic you are and Violet willingly steps aside to let you take the lead. The whole of Drama Club cheers. Am I close?"

I wriggled my shoulders a little uncomfortably. He was a lot nearer to the truth than I'd have liked. I didn't want this guy to know me – or to even think he did. Because there was a hell of a lot more to me than one school play.

"Not even on the same continent," I lied.

"I want the play to be a success, yes, and I enjoy acting. But I'm happy to be involved in any way that helps. And, actually, I'm really interested in learning about costumes."

"Really." How did he manage to put so much disbelief into one word?

"You've met me twice. We've read one scene from a play together. Don't start like you know everything about me. For all you know, I might want to be a wardrobe mistress in the West End when I leave school."

"You might," Connor said. "But I doubt it."

"Why?" I asked crossly. I couldn't help it. The guy was getting to me.

"Because I saw how much you wanted that part."

For once, I didn't have an argument. So, instead, I headed across the corridor towards the textiles classroom, my mouth tightening in annoyance when he followed me again.

"You don't actually have to come with me to make sure I go, you know. I'm not your responsibility."

"I know." He didn't move though. "Maybe I need to see Miss Cotterill, too."

I didn't argue. If he was determined to drive me crazy, he was going the right way about it. But there was no reason to let him know that.

"Fine," I said. "Maybe I'd like the company."

For some reason, he laughed at that. A real, amused laugh. And in among all my frustration and annoyance and everything, I couldn't help but notice that he had a nice laugh.

False advertising, I decided. It was probably things like his laugh that made Jasper think he was nice. Friendly, even.

When clearly he was annoying as hell.

The textiles classroom was close to the drama room, but it wasn't somewhere I'd spent a lot of time before – not since my last textiles class in Year Nine. I had a horrible feeling that Miss Cotterill was probably still going to remember the hideous stuffed whale thing I made in that class. I just hoped she wouldn't mention it in front of Connor.

"You want to join Sewing Club?" Miss Cotterill peered over her tiny glasses at me. "Are you sure?"

Connor was silently laughing behind me. I couldn't see him, but I just *knew*.

"Very." I tried out my best "I know what I'm doing" smile. It had worked for Mr Hughes. "I'm going to be, um, wardrobe and props mistress for the school play, so it's important I join you here while you're all working on the costumes."

Miss Cotterill didn't look particularly impressed by my made-up title, but at least she didn't snort with amusement. Unlike Connor.

"Fine," she said, turning back to her desk, where a queue of Year Sevens was forming, all with tangles of thread and fabric. "But I warn you, costumes are tricky. It's going to be a lot of work, and if you want that fancy job title I expect you to earn it. So I hope you're ready to work hard, and that you have some idea what you're doing."

"My gran taught me to sew when I was little," I told her, a little stung that she so obviously didn't think I was up to the job. "I'll be fine."

"Hmm," she muttered, probably remembering the stuffed whale. She handed back a detangled felt heart to the first Year Seven. "We'll see. And what about you, young man? What's your job here?"

I moved aside to let Connor take centre stage. He shrugged. "Jack of all trades, really. I'm going to be the stage manager on the play, so I just wanted to introduce myself."

That she looked approving of. "Good. I'm sure you'll be kept busy, and that we'll be seeing a lot of you. Now, I have a class to teach. Grace, I'll see you in Sewing Club on Monday."

We were dismissed.

"Wardrobe and props mistress?" Connor asked, the moment the classroom door swung shut behind us.

"I'm in charge of the costumes. What else would you call it?" Picking up speed, I skipped down the steps back to the hall and headed for the sixth-form common room.

"Delusions of grandeur," Connor replied, following me. "Guy— I mean, Mr Hughes just said you could help with the costumes, remember, princess."

I pulled a face. "Don't call me that."

Connor raised his eyebrows. "If the shoe fits…"

"Then I'd be Cinderella," I shot back. Stopping outside the common room, I leaned against the wall and watched him. "Tell me. Why are you even bothering being stage manager if you don't care about the play."

He looked right back at me with those cool blue eyes. "I never said I didn't care."

"You said it was 'just words'."

Connor's smile was slow, like he knew something I didn't. It made my insides itch. "Well, it's true. Until the cast get up on stage and breathe life into it, it's nothing but words."

His tone made me pause. Maybe he did really care about this play. But not half as much as I did.

"Well, they're going to need costumes for that, aren't they? So it's just as well you have me."

"A wardrobe mistress who knows nothing about costumes. We are truly blessed."

I glared at him as I grabbed the door handle to the common room. Any moment now I'd be free of Connor and all his questions and assumptions about me. "Trust me. I'm going to make sure this whole play is brilliant." *Especially once Violet gives up on playing Beatrice and lets me play the lead,* I added silently.

"We'll see," Connor said, sounding far too much like Miss Cotterill for my liking.

"Yes, we will," I said, making sure to get the last word.

Now I just needed to remember how to sew.

That afternoon I left school at the usual time, walking the long way round to wander past the drama room. It was still warm for late September, and through the open windows I could hear laughter and chatter as the cast ran through the script together for the first time. I wrapped my blazer tighter around me to ward off a chill that had nothing to do with the weather.

I almost imagined I could make out Connor's laugh amid all the noise. Because *of course* he'd be there. He *mattered* to the play – and to Mr Hughes. Benefits of having relatives in the right places, I supposed.

But that was *my* place. Where I was supposed to be. And until I won it back, I had to go home – a place that felt less like mine every time I walked through the door. A house that had relatives in all the *wrong* places.

Home was a ten-minute walk from school, fifteen if I dawdled. I made it in twenty, pausing at the end of the double driveway when I clocked the older, cheaper car parked there. Not something either of my parents would drive.

Faith's car. Again.

Sucking in a deep breath, I soldiered on up the drive, fishing my keys out of the front pocket of my school bag as I went. It was fine. I'd just tell them I had homework, so I couldn't get involved in looking at old photos or wedding planning or whatever it was they were doing today. Thirty seconds of polite chit-chat and I could be alone in my room again. At least that still felt like mine.

"Grace?" My mum's voice rang out the moment I turned the key and pushed the door open. "We're in the kitchen, sweetie."

I dumped my bag by the coat rack and slipped my arms out of my blazer, taking rather more time than was strictly necessary to hang it up. Then I padded

42

through the hall towards the kitchen.

I'd expected to see the wedding-planning file spread out over the counter, or maybe more wedding-favour samples – chocolates or packets of wildflower seeds or something. Instead, I walked in to find my mum and Faith dolloping cookie dough on to lined baking trays. The KitchenAid was out on the side, dough hanging from its mixer attachment, and a few chocolate chips had escaped across the counter. As I watched, Faith picked one up and popped it into her mouth.

"You're just in time!" Mum said. "These will be ready in a few minutes. We can all sit and have coffee and cookies together!"

"You're ... baking?" I mean, yes, the evidence spoke for itself, but still, I needed to be sure. After all, I didn't think my mum even knew we owned a mixer. The interior designer had picked it because it matched the tiles when we had the kitchen redone a couple of years before. Lottie had been the first person to use it, when we were practising for the School's National Bake-Off last year.

In the eight years we'd lived in that house, I'd never seen my mum bake *anything*. A stir-fry, or pasta with sauce from a jar, was a culinary achievement for her. My mum was the anti-housewife. She always said she worked hard so that she could pay other

43

people to cook, clean and all that stuff.

But now Faith was here, and she was making chocolate chip cookies like it was perfectly normal.

"I hear you're quite the baker," Faith said, a small smile on her lips. With her neat blonde bob and her blue eyes, she looked like a younger version of Mum. An older, shorter version of me, with worse hair. "Maybe you could take a look at these, see if they're OK?"

She tilted the tray slightly so I could see, but I glanced away. Baking was my thing, not hers. And it wasn't like Mum had shown any interest when *I* was making chocolate chip cookies. Or in anything I did other than getting good grades and perfect reports. She'd made the odd drama show, I supposed, but only if she hadn't had to work that evening.

"I'm sure they'll be great," I said. "Maybe I'll grab one later. I need to go and ... do my homework."

The corners of Faith's mouth turned down just a little and I felt bad for a moment, as the reasonable part of my brain reminded me that this wasn't really her fault. She was as much a victim of the whole stupid situation as I was.

But the reasonable part of my brain didn't win a lot of arguments against my heart, or the part of my head that screamed that this was *my* kitchen, *my* house, *my* family, not hers.

"We'll see you later, then." The disappointment in Mum's eyes was obvious, but I ignored it. Even the reasonable part of my brain blamed her, at least fifty per cent, for the whole Faith thing. Apparently whatever mistakes my parents had ever made, I was supposed to be fine with them – despite the fact that they *never* forgot *any* of my screw-ups.

I wanted my parents to be proud of me, but right then, it was kind of hard to be proud of *them*.

I'd reached the top of the stairs, and was just a few steps away from my bedroom door, when I bumped into Dad.

"Gracie! How was school? Was it the auditions today?"

"Yesterday," I said, wishing he'd leave it at that, but knowing he wouldn't.

"Well? How did it go?" He leaned against the bannister, obviously settled in for a long discussion.

"Actually, I... Well, I missed them. But I persuaded Mr Hughes to let me audition today instead. For the lead understudy role. And I got it!" I hurried the words out, trying to focus on the positives.

"You missed the auditions?" Of course that was what he homed in on. "How come?"

I shrugged. "Overslept."

He gave me his disapproving face. "Well, I guess

you've learned your lesson by missing out on the lead role. I bet you'll set your alarm next time, right?"

"Right." I'd say anything if he'd just let me get to my room and be alone. I know my dad, and I know he thought he was being helpful, pointing out what he thought I'd done wrong, but all it was doing was making me cringe inside. And feel more worthless than I already did.

"So, are you really going to settle for the understudy part? It's not like you to let somebody else steal your place like that. You know, second best—"

"Is just like all the rest," I finished for him. I'd heard it often enough.

"Exactly." He snapped his fingers together as he spoke, as if I'd passed some test. "And I've always known you were born to be more than just another follower in the herd."

I managed a weak smile. "Thanks, Dad." Did he believe that about Faith, too?

"So, you're going to win your part back, then?"

I nodded, without even thinking. "Of course I am." Because that was what he expected of me. That was the plan.

"Good girl. I knew you wouldn't let anyone take your chance to shine without a fight." He pressed a kiss to the top of my head.

My heart clenched tight. He was wrong. Yes, I'd fight Violet for my part in the play, but I'd already let Faith steal my place in the family.

"I need to do my homework," I managed to mutter, as I pushed past him towards my room.

"Look on the bright side. If you still don't get the part, at least you'll have more time for schoolwork, without all those lines to learn." Dad laughed at his own bad joke, completely oblivious to how I was about to crumple up into a ball if he said one more thing. "We'll definitely be expecting straight As in your exams now, right?"

As if they weren't already.

I dived into my room, letting the door swing shut behind me, and sank down to the floor.

He didn't mean to pile on the pressure, not really. That was just his way. He didn't understand when I got upset, couldn't see that every word made me feel ... inadequate.

As Mum always said, "it's just how he is."

But he was right. I did deserve that part and I *should* fight for it.

After a few moments, I calmed down. No point losing more time obsessing on my dad's comments – I had too much work to do. I hadn't even told him about the costumes and Sewing Club. Not that it would mean anything to him anyway – it wasn't the lead.

Switching on my laptop, I set my music playing. Then, when I was sure no one was going to show up brandishing cookies, I went digging under my bed.

There, tucked behind a box of old scripts and a bag of clothes I'd meant to give away, I found it. My gran's sewing basket, perched on top of the books she gave me, back when she first tried to teach me to sew.

My gran died when I was ten. She'd left me her sewing basket and I'd kept it, more as a keepsake than a hobby I ever intended to pick up again. I tugged it out and blew the dust off the top before delving inside.

In among the threads and fabric and pins and tape measures, all neatly coiled and piled and sorted, I found two things that made my chest ache. The first was a tiny, folded fabric case, filled with needles of every possible size. The second, a faded red pincushion in the shape of a heart.

I'd made those for her and she'd kept them. No, not just kept them, she'd used them. She'd made them part of her sewing basket.

Suddenly, the image of her sitting there in her floral-patterned chair, sewing basket at her side and project on her lap, was so strong I had to close my eyes to stop myself crying, I missed her so much.

I pulled out the top tray and there, underneath

all the bits and bobs, were stacks of fabric squares, all neatly cut out but not yet sewn together. Gran's last patchwork quilt. She'd made quilts for all her grandchildren – I still had mine on my bed. She was making one for a friend's grandchild when she died.

I tucked the squares away again. Maybe one day, if I learned enough, I'd be able to finish it for her. But first, I had to learn to make costumes.

With a deep breath, I took stock. Gran was gone, Mum was baking with Faith, Dad thought I was an utter failure and Connor thought I was some sort of diva. Violet was playing Beatrice, and my plan for the year was utterly screwed up.

But despite all of that, I was determined to be the best and most brilliant wardrobe and props mistress St Mary's school – any school – had ever seen. It was all part of the new plan.

Mr Hughes wanted cast members he could trust to show up? Fine. I'd be so indispensible, helpful and low maintenance while sorting the costumes that Mr Hughes would know I could be trusted with the lead. And once he saw me play Beatrice up on stage, he'd know I was the best person for the job, not Violet.

I pulled out Gran's sewing book and turned to the first page. I just had to be patient in the meantime.

Then I'd have my chance to shine.

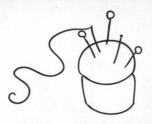

CUPCAKE APPLIQUÉ

What you need:

Felt in two different colours
One red button
Something to sew your cupcake on to!
(A canvas tote bag, an apron,
a T-shirt … whatever you like)

What to do:

1. Start by drawing a very simple cupcake shape on to some paper.
2. Cut out the cupcake case and the top of the cupcake so they are two separate pieces. Pin the cupcake case to one piece of felt, and the top to the other.
3. Cut out your shapes to create felt pieces.
4. Pin them into place on your bag/apron/T-shirt – you can overlap the felt to make your cupcake look more realistic.
5. Sew around the edges of each piece with three strands of embroidery thread, using blanket stitch or whip stitch to attach it.
6. Remove the pins.
7. Sew your button in place as the cherry on top of your cake.

I'd barely got into the food tech classroom for Bake Club and dumped my bag by my workstation before Yasmin and Lottie were both perched on the stools opposite, interrogating me.

"So, what's this about you and the new guy?" Yasmin wore her favourite green apron with the yellow and pink cupcakes on the pockets. For the first time, I found myself wondering how they'd been sewn on. Sewing Club was clearly infecting my brain. "Jasper said you were asking about him, and I saw you walking to the common room together."

I rolled my eyes. "I can't tell you any more than I'm sure Jasper already has." I glared over in the direction of his workstation, where he was chatting to Mac. Jasper waved back cheerfully. "Lottie, your boyfriend *does* realize he doesn't actually go to this school any more, right?" I said, changing the subject.

"He knows. I think he—"

"Just couldn't bear to be separated from you for

51

more than a minute?" I guessed. I'd thought that with Mac working and studying full time elsewhere, not to mention living on his own now, we'd see less of him.

"I was going to say, he wanted to see everyone. That was all." Lottie frowned, and I felt a twinge of guilt. Lottie had had an even worse GCSE year than I had, what with her mum's crazy hoarding. Although she *had* ended up with two weeks in Paris with Mac over the summer, so maybe I shouldn't feel *too* bad for her.

"And it's lovely to see him, too," Yasmin said, diplomatic as ever. "But is he allowed to just show up here?"

"The college have some sort of deal with the school," Lottie explained. "As well as his practical experience at the bakery, he's putting in some hours this year as a teaching assistant to Miss Anderson. They want him to learn to teach *others* to bake as well, apparently. Anyway, it all counts towards his final grade."

"Is he baking with Jasper today?" The boys looked like they were firmly in bromance territory, bonding over baked goods.

Lottie glanced back across at them, too. "I guess so."

We looked at each other, realizing that with Ella gone, one of us would have to bake alone. Or, worse still, with one of the new Year Tens. Lottie and Yasmin's things were already set out on the workstation across the room, and they were exchanging the sort of glances that made me think they expected me to kick up a fuss about having to share with someone new.

So I didn't. It turns out that surprising people was kind of fun.

"You guys better head over to your workstation before one of the new lot takes it," I said, shooing them away with my hands, just like my mum used to do when I was getting in her way. "I'll pair up with whoever's left over." Or, hopefully, bake alone in peace and quiet.

I was in luck. The six new Year Tens paired up happily enough on the three front workstations, and I got to hang out at the back and make banana bread with dark chocolate chips on my own, my way. No interference from the new people, no Lottie telling me I had two grams more flour than I needed, or Jasper asking me questions about Connor. Questions I had absolutely no answers to, incidentally.

It wasn't like a few conversations – OK, a few arguments – made me an authority on Connor

O'Neil. All I could tell anyone was that he read Shakespeare properly but didn't appreciate it unless it was on a stage, was Mr Hughes's stepson, and apparently saved his irritating smirk and disapproving stare just for me. Hardly an in-depth background check.

My banana bread recipe was a quick one to mix, although it took forever to bake. But it was familiar and warming – comfort food at its best. I scraped the mixture into the lined and greased loaf tin, levelled it off, and carried it over to the ovens. Then, with my banana bread baking and my timer set, I headed over to Jasper and Mac's workstation, where Mac was doing something complicated with bread dough.

"What's that?" I asked, leaning against the counter.

Mac folded the dough strands over each other, like he was plaiting hair.

"A plaited loaf," he said, tucking the ends under. "I learned how to do it in Paris."

At the word Paris he got the same misty smile on his face that Lottie did whenever anyone asked her about the trip. I rolled my eyes and ignored it, purposefully not asking any follow-up questions. I'd heard enough about Paris already. Lottie had talked about nothing else for two full weeks after they got back, and I could imagine *exactly* which memories were putting those smiles on their faces.

Jasper, however, had other things on his mind besides bread, and I'd clearly interrupted some classic male bonding. "At least you got to go *with* your girlfriend when she left town for the summer."

"It was two weeks," I pointed out, but Jasper wasn't listening.

"I barely got a couple of weekend visits with Ella over the holidays. And now she's saying she can't come down until half-term. That's weeks away!"

"Go and visit her," Mac suggested. "Girls like it when you take action. Or so Lottie tells me."

"I can't!" Jasper said. "Ella's mum says I'm only allowed up to visit once a term. And if I go up before half-term I won't be able to go at Christmas, and I've got this great plan to put together a Christmas stocking for her…"

I'd been hearing about the Christmas-stocking plan since July. It wasn't all that great that it needed six months' preparation, trust me.

"You could write to her," Lottie suggested. I hadn't even heard her come up behind me, but apparently her time limit for being apart from Mac was up again. "You know, proper old-fashioned letters."

Jasper frowned. "We Skype and message all the time. What would I say in a letter?"

Lottie shrugged. "Whatever you're thinking, I guess? Or you could send chocolate? Chocolate is always good."

Good grief, these people were hopeless. "You tell her all the stuff you'd be embarrassed to say online," I told him. "You know, the soppy stuff. How you really *feel* about her. How she makes you feel. It doesn't matter. Just the fact you took the time to write it down with an actual pen and spend money on a stamp will make her feel special. You want her to know that she's still important to you, even though things have changed. That's all." Jasper, Lottie and Mac all stared at me, open-mouthed. "Or just send chocolate," I said, with a sigh. "That probably works, too."

"Seriously, what is going on with you and that Connor?" Lottie asked. "Because that was kind of intense."

"I have had a grand total of two conversations and an understudy audition with the guy," I said. "Trust me, there's nothing going on with him. You'd know if there was." It used to be that when I started dating someone, it was the biggest news at school that day.

"But there *is* something going on with you, right?"

Yasmin said, standing next to me. "Something you haven't told us about."

"I thought we decided last year that secrets were a bad idea," Jasper said, flashing a grin at Lottie. "Especially between us."

I didn't want to tell them. Not because I thought it was a huge shameful secret or anything, although my mum and dad obviously did, or they'd have told me years ago. Like, any time before Faith arrived and screwed everything up. It wasn't even that I was embarrassed by the whole thing, even though I was, a bit. I mean, it was just weird. This kind of thing didn't really *happen* to people, did it? Except it had.

But the main reason I hadn't told them was because I hadn't decided how to spin it yet. Unless I could find a way to make the story funny, or make me look good, then finding out your parents were stupid enough to have unprotected sex as teenagers was just plain embarrassing.

The other thing was, if I didn't tell it right, I knew my friends would make it a *thing*. There'd be sad eyes and group hugs and offers to talk. And I didn't want that. I mean, yeah, I like attention as much as the next person. OK, maybe more. But not *that* sort of attention. I didn't want them feeling sorry for me, like we all had for Lottie when we found out about her mum. I didn't want my friends having secret meetings about how they could help me.

I didn't need anything from them. I just needed to get on with my life. To get my plan back on track. Was that so much to ask?

But somehow I didn't think they were going to let me get away with that.

I sighed, and my friends took it for the sign of weakness it was and moved in for the kill.

"You've been hiding out in your bedroom in the evenings more," Yasmin said. "I know, because you keep Skyping me when I'm trying to do my homework."

"And Violet told me you missed the Drama Club auditions and only just talked your way into an understudy role," Lottie said, her eyebrows knotted in a concerned sort of way. "She said you were helping out with the costumes, instead. That you'd joined *Sewing Club*."

Cue gasps from Jasper and Yasmin.

I turned to Mac. "You got anything to add?"

"You seem normal to me," he said with a shrug. God bless Mac. But then Lottie elbowed him, and he added, "But, you know. We're all here for you. Or whatever."

"So," Jasper said, resting his chin on his hands on

the counter. "You going to tell us what's going on?"

It wasn't like I hadn't planned for this moment. I'd acted it out in my head a dozen different ways. Did I want to be brave, lower-lip trembling Grace? Or don't care Grace? Or matter-of-fact Grace? Or amused, you won't believe what my parents did Grace? Or even honest, hurt and confused Grace?

In the end, I went for a combination of all of them.

"So, the thing is … it turns out I have a sister."

I don't know what sort of big reveal they'd all been expecting, but it obviously wasn't that. Lottie blinked several times, really fast. Yasmin's eyes just got really, really big. And Jasper's elbow slipped off the counter so he nearly brained himself on the edge of the formica. Almost like watching a cartoon, but more depressing because these were my actual friends.

Mac just nodded, as if to say, "Well, that makes sense." Which it didn't.

"How can you… Don't people tend to notice that sort of thing a little earlier in life?" Yasmin asked.

"Not to mention the fact that you're *clearly* an only child," Jasper said. "Just like me," he added, when I glared at him.

"What happened, Grace?" Lottie asked, in her

annoyingly sweet and concerned voice. Except even I found it hard to be annoyed at Lottie these days.

I settled down on to a spare stool. "OK, so it was the night before school started back, right? Mum and Dad were in their office, I was in my room, and there was a knock on the door. So far, so normal. Except when I answered it, there was this woman I didn't know standing there. She said her name was Faith, and she wanted to speak to Mum and Dad."

She'd looked scared, her baby blue eyes huge under her fringe. She hadn't looked six years older than me then. She'd barely looked my age, holding out that envelope with my mum's handwriting on the front.

Then my dad had come to the door, then my mum, and they'd stared, too, for a moment. Then Mum had sobbed and pushed past me to wrap her arms around Faith, saying all these things that couldn't possibly be true, my dad trying to explain things to me at the same time.

I hadn't understood anything at all. I'd just dropped back to lean against the wall because it felt like the floor was shifting under me, like the sea.

I'd felt seasick ever since.

"Turns out my parents had a baby when they were, like, our age." I shrugged, as if this kind of thing happened everyday. "They decided they were too young to bring her up themselves, so they agreed to give her up for adoption. My mum wrote to her when she turned eighteen, in case she wanted to get in touch, but she didn't. Until this summer." Giving my parents the chance to start over with a daughter who hadn't let them down yet, and making me totally surplus to requirements.

The long, awkward pause that followed was broken by the sound of an oven timer going off. We all looked up and, after a moment, Yasmin yelped, "Oh!" and dashed off towards the ovens.

"So?" Jasper always was the most impatient of the lot of us. "You can't leave the story there. What happened? Why did she show up on your doorstep?"

"She's getting married," I said. "The people who adopted her, they were an older couple. They both died a few years ago. So she wanted to find her biological parents."

"And sister," Yasmin added, returning with a plate of cookies.

"Guess so. Anyway, so that's what's going on. We've been having all these getting-to-know-you sessions and stuff. We were out for Sunday dinner last weekend and were up quite late. I forgot to set my alarm, so Mum let me sleep in the next morning because she didn't know about the auditions…"

"And that's why you missed them," Lottie finished. "Still doesn't explain Sewing Club, though."

I reached for a cookie. I wasn't ready to tell them about my plan to win back the lead role by proving myself utterly indispensible. I had a feeling that Lottie, particularly, wouldn't approve.

"I just figured that if I couldn't be *in* the play, I could probably help out another way. Mr Hughes suggested I take on the costumes, which means joining Sewing Club, too. That's all."

"Makes sense, I suppose," Yasmin said, although the look she exchanged with Lottie suggested she still thought there was more to it.

"Anyway, in summary, everything is fine. A little weird," I admitted. "But fine."

"Well, you know, if there's anything we can do…" Lottie trailed off, as if uncertain what help to offer someone whose only problem was a surprise sister.

"I'll ask," I promised. Then a thought occurred to me. "Actually…"

"Oh God," Jasper groaned. "Look at that evil grin. You're going to regret offering, Lottie."

"Hey!" I tried my best to look innocent. "All I was going to say was that I could use some help with the props and costumes. In, you know, Sewing Club."

Nothing like backup to make an awkward situation easier. Besides, I'd tried a few bits from Gran's book the night before – just some basic stitches – and, to be honest, I did need the help. Especially if I ever wanted to be good enough to finish Gran's quilt one day. Or even just learn how to sew little cupcakes on stuff.

"Sorry," Lottie said, looking genuinely apologetic. "I'd love to, but I work at the bakery after school on a Monday."

"And I babysit for my nephews," Yasmin added. "But I could help out at rehearsals on Fridays, perhaps?"

I turned to Mac, who put up his hands and said, "I don't even go to this school, remember?"

Which just left Jasper. "No," he said, then stuffed a cookie into his mouth so I couldn't press for his reasons.

"Come on, it could be fun!"

Jasper shook his head and kept on chewing.

"I really do need the help. You'd be doing me a huge favour." I tried to look desperate, but it didn't seem to make a difference.

Jasper swallowed. "No. No way."

I looked around for support, and soon Jasper was facing down three girls giving him pleading looks.

Mac gazed at the ceiling, obviously trying not to laugh.

"Oh, come on!" Jasper slumped down on his stool. "Isn't it enough that I'm already baking my way through my teenage years? Now I have to sew as well? Can't you leave me some manly pride?"

"Baking can be manly," Mac said, but no one was really listening.

Then I hit upon what I knew would be my winning argument.

"If you learn to sew," I said, leaning across the counter to look Jasper in the eyes. "You could *make* Ella her Christmas stocking."

Lottie gasped. "Jasper! That would be perfect. She'd love it, you know she would."

Jasper groaned again. "OK, OK. I give in. I'll do it."

Lottie and Yasmin high-fived and gave a little cheer.

"But I want it noted that I'm only doing this for love," Jasper yelled over them.

"Whatever you say." I smiled, as I passed him another cookie. "Whatever you say."

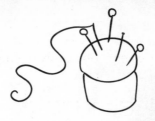

T-SHIRT CUSHION

What you need:

*An old T-shirt with a central
picture or motif
Stuffing*

What to do:

1. Iron your T-shirt and lay it out flat, right side showing.
2. Measure a square around the motif on your T-shirt just bigger than you want your cushion to be and mark it with tailor's chalk.
3. Pin both layers of your T-shirt together, then cut through both to give you two equal squares.
4. Place the pieces with their right sides together and pin in place.
5. Sew all around the edge of the cushion, leaving a 5cm gap on one side.
6. Turn the cushion the right way round, through the gap, then fill the cushion with stuffing.
7. Sew the gap closed by hand.

Friday afternoon's Drama Club meeting was in the school hall, so I met Yasmin outside her business studies classroom to walk over together. It was going to be weird enough walking into that group with everyone knowing I was only the understudy. At least this way I could prove I still had actual friends.

"This is going to be fun," Yasmin said, hitching her bag up on to her shoulder as we walked across the school campus. "I've never worked backstage on a play before. You'll have to show me the ropes."

"Sure," I replied, even though I had no idea what the ropes were, or even where they might be located. I'd never worked backstage, either. For me, it had always been about the performance. About being on stage, under those lights, with the audience staring at me.

We'd figure it out though, between us. I mean, I'd never really baked before last year, and look at me now.

First, we just needed to get through this rehearsal looking like we knew what we were doing. Especially if Connor O'Neil was watching. The last thing I wanted was to give him any more evidence I was utterly useless at the job I'd talked my way into. I could only imagine how much more irritating he'd be if he had proof of how totally out of my depth I was.

"Ready?" Yasmin asked, when I paused outside the hall doors.

I pasted on a smile. "Of course. Why wouldn't I be?"

Yasmin gave me a look that told me she knew every single reason why I might be nervous to go in there, but she didn't say any of them, which I appreciated.

"Come on, then." Yasmin pushed open the heavy double doors, and I took a breath then walked through.

The hall was filled with students, milling around like they weren't quite sure what to do yet, and all ignoring the circle of chairs set out in the centre of the room. But even with that usual first-rehearsal unease, you could see the groups forming if you looked at the scene closely.

Over by the stage, Violet was laughing too loudly at something Sara, the girl playing Hero, had said.

Violet leaned against the edge of the stage casually enough, but I knew what that lean said. It positively screamed "this land is mine". She was staking her claim as the star, safe in the knowledge that, for the next few months at least, she ruled this room and everyone in it.

Well, until I claimed it back, anyway.

Next to them were a few of the other main characters, close enough to be associated with the star, but not close enough to be properly part of the group. It would take a few more rehearsals before that happened.

Dotted around the hall itself were other smaller gangs – the bit parts and chorus, most of whom had also been cast as the other understudies in the last week, and then, at the back of the hall near the lighting desk, the tech team.

All exactly the same as every other year, except this year I had no idea where to stand. With the understudies? Or the backstage crew? Neither felt quite right.

"Lots of people," Yasmin said, gazing around the room.

"It takes a full team to put on a great show." Mr Hughes moved towards us, clipboard in hand, and smiled at Yasmin. "I assume you're here to help

Grace with the props and costumes?"

Yasmin nodded, and I said, "This is my friend Yasmin."

"Great to have you on the team, Yasmin." Mr Hughes gave her a huge smile. "Trust me, there is going to be lots and lots of work for you and Grace to get stuck into. Just wait until you hear what I've got planned... Why don't you both take a seat, and I'll try and call the rest of this rabble to order."

He wandered off towards the stage – towards the stars – and left Yasmin and me staring at the circle of chairs and trying to decide where to sit. Or at least, I was. Turns out that Yasmin was staring at something else altogether.

"I didn't know he was going to be here," she said, her voice soft.

I jerked my gaze away from the chairs to follow hers instead. There, across the room, stood Connor O'Neil, chatting to the only actor in the bunch not fawning over Violet. Connor looked relaxed, at home, in a way I hadn't expected him to. More at home than me, anyway.

"Connor? I told you, Mr Hughes made him stage manager. Unfortunately." Of course, as I spoke, he looked up and caught my eye, raising his eyebrows at me. I looked away, trying to pretend I hadn't just been caught staring, but even without looking I knew he'd be laughing at me.

He did that a lot, for someone who barely knew me. And I was pretty sure not all of it was in my head.

"Not Connor," Yasmin said, so quiet I almost didn't hear.

Which meant I had to look again. Damn it.

Resigned, I tried for a quick glance across the room to see who Connor was talking to, without looking at Connor himself. But since Connor was still staring at me that was kind of hard.

This time, he wasn't mocking. With his eyebrow raised and a small smile on his lips, he looked honestly curious, which was … unexpected. I looked away.

Back to the mission in hand, I checked out his companion. "Ash? He's playing Benedick. He's the male lead. You know him?"

"He's in my stats class," Yasmin replied, staring at her feet. "I didn't even know he was in Drama Club. I thought he just played football and stuff."

"He joined last year, I think. He worked backstage on that play, but Mr Hughes asked him to audition for this one, then gave him the lead. Not bad going, really." Sort of a reverse of my own trajectory. I turned my attention back to my friend, taking in the slight pinkness colouring Yasmin's dark cheeks. Well, now. *This* was far more interesting than Connor laughing at me again.

But before I could quiz her further on exactly where Ash sat in their stats class, and what had happened between them already, Mr Hughes clapped his hands.

"OK, everyone, time to take a seat and get to work. We've got too much to do to waste more time chatting!"

Everyone dived for the seats like a game of musical chairs, desperate not to be left standing. I slipped into a seat three chairs down from Mr Hughes, Yasmin beside me, and realized too late that Connor was sitting almost directly opposite me. Hard not to be caught staring at a guy when he's in your direct line of sight.

And Yasmin had just realized that Ash was next to him. At least her crush might make this whole rehearsal a little more entertaining. For me, anyway. Any distraction from the way Violet was holding court was very welcome indeed. And I was pretty sure Yasmin would need advice on how to win Ash over. Yasmin hadn't really dated much in the time I'd known her, and I knew she was a little shy about the whole idea. I could totally help with that. In addition to my many other talents, I definitely knew how to deal with dating. Before I joined Bake Club, boys and shopping were basically my only hobbies.

"Right," Mr Hughes said, setting his clipboard down on his lap. "Firstly, I want to say how great it is to have you all here together, and how excited I am about this production. *Much Ado* is my absolute favourite Shakespeare play and I can't wait for the chance to put together a really knock-out production of it. I think – no, I know – that all of you are going to fall in love with Benedick and Beatrice, and Hero and Claudio, just as much as I did when I was your age and acting in this play for the first time."

Well, that explained why Mr Hughes was so amped up about this one. Reliving his glory days.

I glanced across the circle again. It was like my eyes just couldn't stop themselves. Like when you're trying not to stare at the piece of lettuce stuck in someone's teeth, or the huge zit erupting out of their forehead.

Connor had one leg stretched out in front of him, his head bent down over the folder in his lap, so at least he couldn't see me watching him. His hair flopped over his forehead a little and, every now and again, he'd reach up and push it out of the way.

"Now, I want to try something new with this

year's performance," Mr Hughes went on, and I made an effort to tune in. "Last year we did Shakespeare in period costume, but I want something a little more modern for *Much Ado About Nothing*."

OK, that made me sit up straighter in my chair. Costumes were my thing this year, and if everyone just needed jeans and T-shirts that would be a lot easier than breeches and ballgowns. Had Mr Hughes decided this because Connor told him I wasn't up to the job?

"So we're just going to be wearing ordinary clothes?" Violet asked from what, somehow, seemed to be the head of the circle. I knew exactly what she was thinking: *but I wanted to look really hot in a corset*. In fairness, it's what I'd have been thinking in her spot.

"Not exactly." Mr Hughes's smile grew wider. "I want to set the whole play right at the very start of the 1920s. Just think. The war over in 1918 and the men coming home and getting demobbed only to find jazz clubs, flapper girls, the Charleston ... everything."

That didn't sound like making things easy for me, at all. But it did sound like fun... I risked another glance across at Connor. Even he had managed to raise his eyes from his folder to stare at Mr Hughes as he described his vintage vision for the play.

"If we want to pull this off, it's going to take attention to detail and a lot of work. Which is why I'm pleased we've got such a strong backstage team this year." He pointed at the lighting and sound guys first. "In addition to the tech crew, who I think most of you know from last year, we also have Grace and Yasmin running our wardrobe and props department."

A whole room full of curious eyes turned on me as Mr Hughes pointed in our direction. A room full of people who'd been wondering why I'd even bothered to show up now I wasn't the star any more.

Well, now they knew. So I met every gaze with my head held high. Even Connor's.

"We also have a new stage manager this year," Mr Hughes went on, and Connor's gaze snapped away from mine as he buried his head in his chest again. "You might not have met Connor yet – Connor, stand up?"

Despite his mutinous glare, Connor did as he was told, keeping the folder clasped to his chest.

"Now, even if you haven't met him, I'm sure most of you have heard about him – I know how gossip travels at this school. So, yes, I'm saying on the record that Connor is my stepson, and I'm very happy to have him as part of this show. But trust me, I'm going to be working him just as hard as any of you – probably harder! And I wouldn't have appointed him as your stage manager if he didn't have the experience to back it up."

Mr Hughes looked up at Connor as if he were maybe expecting him to say something about himself, but Connor took it as his cue to sit back down again, and resume staring at the floor.

With a small sigh, Mr Hughes turned back to the group. "So, does anyone have any questions before we get stuck in?"

Of course people had questions. Mostly stupid ones. But for once, I had a serious one I wanted answering.

But not before Violet had asked about what sort of dress she'd get to wear. Because obviously that was more important that the play itself. I hid a smile. The moment she got up there and fell flat on her face, Mr Hughes would know he'd made the wrong choice. And I'd be there ready to fix that.

"Well, that will be up to our wardrobe and props department," Mr Hughes said, and I gave Violet my best, innocent, "of course I won't put you in a sack of a dress", smile.

She glowered back at me.

"If the play's supposed to take place in the 1920s,

does that mean we're going to update the language, too?" Robbie, who was playing Claudio, asked, and I barely resisted the urge to roll my eyes. Had the guy never seen a non-traditional Shakespeare production in English lit?

"Sorry, Robbie, no." Mr Hughes grinned. "You still have to learn all the 'thees' and 'thous'. Now, if that's—"

"Actually," I interrupted. "I have a question."

I swear I heard Connor mutter, "Of course you do," across the circle.

"Go on, Grace," Mr Hughes said, in a way that suggested he'd heard it, too.

"You said that Connor had a lot of stage-management experience. I was just curious what sort of plays he'd worked on." If he was so comfortable doubting my abilities, it was only fair I got to question his.

Mr Hughes blinked, his eyebrows jumping up a centimetre or two. "That's a great question, Grace. Connor, perhaps you'd like to answer it?"

I smiled down Connor's glare and didn't even have to fake looking interested. He thought he knew the sort of person I was? Well, it was time for me to find out a little bit more about our new boy.

"I belonged to the school Drama Club and to

the local youth theatre back where I used to live," he said, his voice quiet but carrying fine in the now-silent room. Everyone wanted to know about Connor, it seemed. "I was assistant stage manager for two years and in my last term was promoted to DSM – deputy stage manager. I've worked on everything from musicals to Shakespeare to talent shows. That enough?"

He stared straight at me as he spoke, even though he had to know everyone else in the room was interested, too. I was just the only one who dared ask the question. And I couldn't help the irritation I felt as I realized Connor really did know what he was doing backstage. Unlike me.

"That's really interesting," I said through barely gritted teeth. "Maybe we can talk more about some of the shows you've been involved in some other time."

Connor tilted his head a little, as if he were trying to figure out exactly what I wanted. I just kept smiling sweetly.

"I think that's a great idea. After all, you're going to be working together very closely over the next few months. Right then, cast, up on stage for warm up, please!"

Everyone jumped to their feet, eager to get started.

Most raced up there, while the tech crew ambled back off towards the lighting desk. There wouldn't be much for them to do at this stage, but Mr Hughes had wanted everyone here for this first full rehearsal.

The cast were missing their Benedick though, I noticed. Ash and Yasmin stood a little way off from the stage, heads close as they talked. Yasmin had her chin dipped, but kept sneaking glances up every now and then, her hands clasped tightly together in front of her.

I really needed to talk to her about better flirting techniques.

Standing over by Connor, Mr Hughes called, "Grace?" and I hurried across to join them.

"I was just saying to Connor, while I get our cast ready for the opening scenes, why don't you two schedule in some meetings to start on the props and costumes? You've got a lot of work ahead of you, and it would help to have you both on the same page. You'll need to meet once a week, at least at the start." Connor nodded in agreement, but he didn't look happy about it. "You're welcome to use the drama room after school, or at lunchtime. Or why doesn't Grace come over to our house one evening, if you need more time? You can stay for dinner."

He clapped his stepson on the back and wandered

off towards the stage, leaving me and Connor staring at each other.

"I think we can consign that idea to the 'last resort' pile," I said, and Connor nodded. Hard.

It wasn't that I didn't like Mr Hughes, but the idea of being in his home was kind of weird. I supposed that must be how it felt for Connor all the time.

"After school, then?" Connor asked. "Which days are you free?"

"Um…" Actually, with Sewing Club on Mondays, Drama Club on Tuesdays and Fridays, and Bake Club on Thursdays, not many. "Wednesdays? Maybe?"

Connor shook his head. "No good. I'm busy Wednesday nights."

"Busy? Doing what?"

"Does it matter? Look, we'll just have to meet during study periods, or something."

"If we have any that match." The brush-off stung.

"Well, then, we'll do it at lunch, if we don't. It'll be fine. I know what I'm doing." His gaze kept jerking across to the stage, as if he couldn't wait to be somewhere else.

"Meaning I don't?" I snapped. Rummaging around in my bag I pulled out a bright pink pen. "Give me your timetable."

"Why?" Connor asked, but he was already pulling

it out from his pocket.

I grabbed it from him, and starting scribbling my own obligations over the top. As an afterthought, I added my mobile number in the corner, then handed the paper back.

"You go, check your schedule, your busy social life, whatever. Then let me know when you want to meet. Preferably at school, please."

I shoved my pen back into my bag and strode off towards the stage. Whatever Connor thought about me, I was there to work, to prove myself. And the first thing I needed to do was get a feel for the play and the cast.

And see how bad Violet really was at playing Beatrice.

Rehearsal ran over, as it always did. I'd hoped to grab Yasmin for a gossip on our way home, maybe even detour via her house for a bit and see if her sister-in-law had been cooking. But by the time we got all packed up I knew that if I didn't head straight home I'd never hear the end of it from Mum.

"I'll message you later, yeah?" I told Yasmin, as we parted at the gates. She nodded, but at that moment Ash caught up to us and I didn't have a chance of holding her attention.

"Are you going this way, too?" He pointed towards the park and Yasmin's house. "Maybe we could walk together?"

Yasmin gave him a shy smile. "I'd like that. See you tomorrow, Grace!"

I waved, but they'd already turned away. Maybe she didn't need quite so many tips on flirting, after all.

At home, Faith's car was parked on the driveway again and my spirits fell to new lows. I'd barely held it together through all the looks and whispers at Drama Club, not to mention trying to convince Connor I was actually serious about being the wardrobe mistress. All I wanted to do was curl up in my room.

I always felt like Mum and Dad were waiting for me to do something, although I wasn't entirely sure what. Welcome Faith with open arms, maybe? Tell Mum everything was fine, even though it wasn't? Say I understood, when I didn't? I *didn't* understand how this could happen. How they could have a daughter I didn't know about for sixteen years. How they could change so completely the moment Faith walked into the house. How did they go from parents who only wanted me to succeed, to prove myself, who put achievement over affection, to *Faith's* parents, who wanted to bake with her and talk about their feelings and stuff? None of it made any sense.

And whatever it was they wanted from me, I couldn't face any more expectation tonight, so I let myself into the house as quietly as I could. Sometimes, if they were really engrossed in doing the bonding thing, they wouldn't notice I was back. No such luck today, though.

"Grace? Where have you been?" Mum appeared in the hallway, her hair coming loose and an apron tied around her waist. "Faith is here. We've been waiting for you to eat dinner."

I blinked. Mum had cooked an actual meal? And one that didn't involve popping holes in plastic and putting it in the microwave, judging by the smear of sauce on her apron. Was that weirder than her baking, or less weird? I couldn't decide.

"I had Drama Club, Mum." I dumped my bag at the bottom of the stairs, as usual, and kicked off my shoes. "Same as every other Friday. And I had to go – I've missed too many this term already." I didn't point out that I hadn't even known Faith was coming round. Given that she practically seemed to live at our house these days, I should have guessed.

"Family is more important than having fun with your friends, Grace." Dad sounded utterly serious when he spoke, and I barely managed to hold in a laugh. A bitter, harsh, painful laugh, but a laugh all

82

the same. There was no way to win with my dad. He wanted me to steal back the lead role, but didn't want me missing a family dinner in order to do it. Besides, he thought I'd been having fun? Wrong. And my parents thought they could just erase the last ten or so years of dysfunctional family life and replace it with a perfect, complete family now they had Faith back? Wrong again.

"Since when? Family wasn't ever more important than work for you two, until this summer." Throwing my coat at a peg, I grabbed my bag again. After years of coming second to whatever else the two of them had on their calendars, I wasn't going to be lectured now about making time for family.

"I don't know what you're talking about, and I don't appreciate your tone," Dad replied, his face red.

"You are part of this family, young lady, and that comes with responsibilities," Mum said, stepping in front of Dad. "Like not throwing parties without our permission, and showing up for family dinners on time."

I bit down on the inside of my cheek, trying to keep all the hateful words I was thinking inside. What did they know?

"You need to—" Dad started, but the words came spilling out of me before he had the chance to say more.

"What about your responsibilities to me?" I asked. "Like not lying to me my whole life. Or not always putting work first until your new, improved daughter shows up and suddenly you decide it's time to be a family? To be honest, I'm surprised any of you even noticed I wasn't here. You all seem perfectly happy without me."

And with that, I stormed off upstairs to my room. There was no way I was eating any dinner Mum had cooked for her perfect family and perfect daughter.

They didn't follow me, which I was glad about. I thought about messaging Yasmin or Skyping Jasper, or even calling Lottie. But I didn't want to talk to any of them right now. They'd have listened, I knew, and tried to be understanding. But who can understand suddenly having a big sister after years of being an only child?

I needed a distraction. Something to make me forget all about my dysfunctional family.

I reached under my bed for the sewing basket, pulling out Gran's half-finished quilt, but I didn't even know where to start with it. So instead I found my script of *Much Ado About Nothing*, grabbed a new notepad and pen and started to make notes. I wanted to be prepared for my meeting with Connor, whenever he decided to have it. Which meant knowing who I needed costumes for, at the very least.

Watching the rehearsal, it had finally dawned on me what Mr Hughes's vision for the play meant. Every single person on that stage needed at least one period costume, but most needed several. I didn't even know what people *wore* back then. Where on earth did you get 1920s costumes? Much as I hated to have to ask him, I hoped Connor had some idea, or we were completely stuffed.

Still, I could make a start. And by the time I heard a soft knock on my door, I had a list of every character, and a few notes on how many times I thought they'd need to change costume. I also had "wedding dresses?!" scrawled next to Hero, Beatrice, Margaret and Ursula for the last scene, when Mr Hughes wanted them all to come in for Hero and Claudio's wedding with veils over their faces, so Claudio didn't know who was who.

"Come in." Shoving Gran's quilt back under the bed, I scrabbled to sit up, rather than lounging on my front with my feet kicked up. There was always a chance that someone was coming to apologize, and it was good to look poised for that sort of situation.

The door creaked open and a plate of sandwiches appeared, followed by a blonde fringe. Faith.

"I thought you might be hungry," she said, holding the plate out like an olive branch.

"Thanks," I said, not moving to take it from her. "You can put it on the desk. If you like."

Faith looked around her, finally spotting the desk behind the door and putting the plate down. She waved a hand at the desk chair. "Can I...?"

"Sure." Although I couldn't imagine why she'd want to, and I really wished she wouldn't, but I couldn't think of a way to say "no" that wasn't supremely brattish. She must have heard everything that I'd said downstairs, and she had to know that her being here had made my life a thousand times more difficult. So what did she want to talk about?

Faith picked up the small cushion sitting on the chair – one Gran had made for me out of my favourite T-shirt once I outgrew it. Holding it to her chest, she sat down.

"What are you working on?" she asked, and I instinctively covered my notepad before deciding that was stupid. What did I care if she knew about the play?

"A costume list. For the school play."

"You're in charge of costumes? That's cool." She frowned. "I thought Nick ... your ... Dad said that you were understudying for one of the leads, though?"

86

I shook my head as she stumbled over what she was supposed to call the parents she'd only just met. Nice to know I wasn't the only one baffled by how to deal with the situation, even if Mum and Dad were trying to pretend it was all totally normal.

"That, too. But I … wanted a new challenge. That's why I'm only understudying. Couldn't be the lead actress *and* the wardrobe and props mistress." The whole situation sounded way better if I put it that way.

"That's good, then." Faith bit her lip, chewing it the way Mum often did when she was thinking too hard.

"I'm sorry, did you want something in particular? Only…" I pointed at the script with my pen, and Faith jumped to her feet, placing my cushion back where it belonged.

"Sure, yeah, you're busy. It was just … I wanted to ask you…"

I raised my eyebrows and waited for her to finish.

Faith took a deep breath and said, "I was hoping you might agree to be my bridesmaid next summer?"

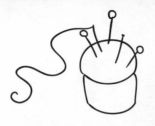

INFINITY SCARF

What you need:

A piece of lightweight fabric, 175 x 60cm

What to do:

1. Fold and iron your fabric in half lengthways, with the right sides together, and pin in place.
2. Sew along the long side of your rectangle, to give you one long tube of fabric.
3. Press open your seam, using an iron.
4. Turn the fabric the right way out and fold in half the other way, so the two open ends of your tube are together. Make sure the seams line up exactly.
5. Now to join both ends of the scarf. Take the two inner layers of fabric, pin them together then sew in place, removing the pins as you go.
6. Keep going around the circle until the two ends are joined.
7. If you're using a sewing machine, leave a gap of about 5cm, fold under the edges of the unstitched section to match the rest, then hand sew the gap closed.

"She asked you to be her bridesmaid?" Jasper said, as we walked down the corridors from the sixth-form common room towards the textiles classroom. "Maybe I'm missing something here, but isn't that a good thing? You know, one of those moments all little girls dream about, along with getting their first horse and turning into a fairy?"

I glared at him. "Not all little girls dream of being a fairy, Jasper." Although, to be honest, I totally had, from around the age of five until I was nearly eight. Horses freaked me out, though. "Besides, it's not like I have any objection to being a bridesmaid. It's just…"

"Being *her* bridesmaid," Jasper finished. He shrugged. "Yeah, I can see that. But I still think it's nice of her to ask. Do you think your mum put her up to it?"

I thought about it, about how nervous Faith had seemed, how desperate for me to say yes. "Actually,

I don't think she had. I think this was all Faith."

"So, what did you say?"

"I said yes, of course. It's not exactly easy to say no to someone when they ask you to be their bridesmaid. Especially since she started going on and on about colour schemes and shopping trips and everything." Up until the night before, I'd been pretty sure that Mum was more excited about it than Faith. In fact, I'd kind of assumed that she was using it as a way to try and make things up to her, in a "I might have missed most of your life, but let me give you a perfect wedding" sort of way.

It was always one extreme or the other with my parents. Either total disinterest in my life, or constant vigilance and grounding. I guess Faith had had it even worse. Nothing for twenty-two years, then everything all at once.

But Faith had been honestly excited about all the wedding plans, and me being a part of it. So how could I say no?

"Gonna be weird, I guess," Jasper said, and I nodded.

"At least she says I can pick my own dress."

"Maybe you could make it." Jasper nodded at the textiles classroom up ahead, and smirked at me.

"Funny man." As if I didn't have enough on my

plate with finding costumes for the entire Drama Club. "Come on. We're going to be late."

In some ways, walking into Sewing Club wasn't half as weird as turning up at Drama Club without an acting role. In other ways, it was loads weirder. *This* was not my place at *all*.

"Grace. You made it." Miss Cotterill sounded surprised to see me. Someone else who didn't think I was going to follow through. I wondered if she'd been talking to Connor. "And you brought a friend."

"This is Jasper," I explained. "He's keen to help out with the costumes."

"Actually—" Jasper started, but I spoke over him, before he could explain the Christmas-stocking plan to the whole room.

"So, where do we start?" I asked brightly.

Miss Cotterill didn't look nearly as enthusiastic as I was trying to be. "Well, I suppose we should find out how much you both know already, before I let you loose on the costume cupboard."

"I know nothing at all," Jasper said, cheerfully. "Starting totally from scratch, here."

"I have some experience," I said, trying to find a way to describe my talent level that a) didn't make me sound like an idiot and b) wouldn't end up with me in charge of a sewing machine without a clue how to use it. "But it's been a while. It will be really good to brush up."

Miss Cotterill looked resigned to having two complete novices in her group. With a sigh, she turned to face the room, and I took in the other people in the club for the first time.

Over in one corner, as I'd predicted, were a few Year Sevens sitting with one of the teaching assistants, trying to thread needles. Well, *that* looked like fun. At another table were a group of girls I thought were in Years Eight and Nine, who appeared to be making some sort of blanket out of old clothes. Then there were a few older girls, each taking up a table of their own for their projects.

And at the very back of the classroom was Izzy Maguire, shiny silver bangles running up both her arms, her black hair scraped back into a messy ponytail.

Izzy was one of those girls in school that everyone knew of, but no one really knew. She was in our year, but in different classes, so I'd never had much direct contact with her. But you could always pick Izzy out of a crowd. Even back in Year Eight she'd been the girl whose uniform somehow looked different to everyone else's, even though on the surface it conformed to the uniform code. She just had a way of customizing, or accessorizing, of adding a certain *something* that made her look unique. And whatever that trick was, she hadn't learned it from any of the magazines I read every month.

Yasmin said that Izzy just had natural style, the way some women do. Lottie thought that maybe her mother was French.

I just figured that Izzy Maguire didn't give a damn what anyone thought of her, so she wore whatever she liked and somehow it always looked great. Izzy wouldn't ever waste time figuring out how to spin a story, or make herself look good. In a strange way it reminded me of Connor, who didn't care what people thought, either. Except Izzy was less irritating.

"Izzy?" Miss Cotterill called, and she looked up. "We've got a couple of new members today. Beginners. They're going to be working on the costumes for the school play with you."

Izzy rolled her eyes. "And I'm sure they'll be a lot of help. Come on, then. I'll introduce you to the costume cupboard. We've got every possible colour of wimple and breeches you can imagine. What is it with this school and Shakespeare, anyway? The drama department knows that other people wrote plays, too, right?"

I shrugged. "Shakespeare's a classic, I guess. And besides, there aren't any wimples or breeches required this year."

"No? Hughes gone modern?" Izzy grinned as she grabbed a set of keys from Miss Cotterill's desk and headed out of the classroom. "Makes my life easier. You can all just wear jeans."

"No jeans, either. We're setting it in the 1920s jazz scene," I explained, following her past the drama room, to the edge of the backstage area.

Izzy paused outside a cupboard door. "Really? Well, that does make things more interesting. Don't know how much you'll find in here. We'll have to source – or make – almost everything." She sounded excited at the challenge.

Far more excited than I was, anyway.

Turning the key in the lock, Izzy yanked the door open. The cupboard went far further back than I'd imagined and was lined on each side with hanging rails stuffed full of outfits. Above them were shelves loaded with boxes of all sorts of shapes and sizes, and the floor was covered with more bags and boxes, too.

"It's going to take forever to sort through this lot," I said.

Jasper pushed past me and grabbed what looked like a musketeer's hat from a top shelf, shoving it on his head and striking a fencing pose with an imaginary sword. *"En garde!* Prepare to do battle with the ghosts of school plays past!"

"Don't joke yet, you promised to help me," I reminded him.

"No, I didn't." Tugging the hat off his head and shoving it back on the shelf, he gave me a too-innocent grin. "I promised to join Sewing Club to learn how to make a Christmas stocking."

"You actually want to learn to sew?" Izzy asked, sounding surprised. "I thought you were just here to get off with your girlfriend in the costume cupboard."

Jasper laughed harder than I thought was strictly necessary, although I was with him on the sentiment. "Not a chance. Grace blackmailed me into joining. And trust me, very much not my girlfriend."

I nodded my agreement. Still, I didn't think the idea of someone wanting to kiss me was *quite* that hilarious.

"In fact," Jasper went on, "that's who the stocking's for. My girlfriend Ella moved away and I'm going to visit her at Christmas. I want to make a Christmas stocking to fill with presents for her."

"Well, come on, then," Izzy said. "Let's leave Grace to her costumes, and you and I can go through some basic stitches. We'll have you knocking up

Christmas ornaments and accessories in no time."

"Brilliant." Jasper grinned at Izzy, and I had a horrible moment of foreboding. This was going to be Lottie all over again. Jasper was going to be the sewing champion, and I was going to be lost forever in the costume cupboard, trapped beneath somebody else's wimple.

What even was a wimple, anyway?

"I want to learn to sew, too," I called after them, as they headed back towards the textiles classroom.

"Good," Miss Cotterill said, appearing in the doorway. "Because I've got your first lesson set up in here. Come on."

Damn it.

I followed her back inside the class to one of the spare tables at the front of the room, where she'd set up some fabric with holes in it, like the sort I remembered using to make bookmarks and place mats for Mum in junior school.

"Don't you think I'm a little bit old for this?" I asked, as I took my seat.

"If you want to learn, you need to learn properly. Starting with the basics. So, today I want you to practise your basic stitches. The aida material will help guide you." She pulled out a large piece of paper with stitch diagrams printed in black and white.

"One row of each of these, please. Then we'll see."

I sighed but, since it didn't seem like I had a lot of choice, I picked up my needle and a couple of strands of the embroidery thread she'd left out for me to use.

"Good." Miss Cotterill nodded her head, then disappeared off to help one of the Year Eights who was struggling to thread the sewing machine.

Pulling the stitch guide closer, I read the first instructions. Running stitch. In out, in out. Easy.

Threading my needle, I tied a knot in the end of the thread and pulled it through, one square of fabric at a time. It felt weirdly familiar, given how long it had been since I'd done it. Maybe it would all come back to me faster than I thought.

After a row of running stitch, I tackled back stitch, cross stitch, and even some blanket stitch, making a neat run of thread along the edge of the aida. I turned towards the back of the classroom and was just about to go and show Miss Cotterill that I wasn't quite as incapable as she thought I was, when I heard the door open.

"You're here again, too, are you?" Miss Cotterill said, and a sudden, sinking feeling took up residence in my chest. "Let me guess, you want to learn to sew as well?"

"Not exactly," Connor said, and the sinking

feeling sunk altogether. "I'm here to get the key for the costume cupboard. And to see Grace."

Plastering on a smile, I turned to face him. "Here I am." Was he checking up on me? Making sure I really *had* joined Sewing Club? His pale eyes gave nothing away — neither surprise to see me there or disappointment in being proved wrong. Nothing.

"How are you getting on with those stitch samples, Grace?" Miss Cotterill came over to check my fabric. "Hmm, running stitch is good, and the back stitch. But your cross stitch is too tight, and your blanket stitch is a little loose in places. You need to be sure to pull the thread tight, remember. But not so tight that the fabric pulls, like in your cross stitch." She dropped it back on to the table, apparently oblivious to my burning cheeks. This was junior-school stuff, and I still couldn't do it well enough to satisfy her. And she had to tell me that in front of Connor, who didn't think I could do *anything*.

"Still, not bad for a first try," Miss Cotterill finished. "Perhaps you'd like to show Mr O'Neil the costume cupboard, while I put together some homework for you."

Homework. Brilliant.

"Come on, then," I said to Connor, not actually looking at him.

We'd left the cupboard door unlocked so we didn't need Izzy's key to open it this time. Just as well, really. Looking over at her table, she and Jasper were totally engrossed in some pattern book or another, and Izzy had a stack of different materials in red and green piled up in front of them. At least it looked like Jasper would get the chance to do something more than stitch samples.

"So you're planning on taking the theatre world by storm with your sloppy blanket stitch, are you?" Connor murmured, as we reached the cupboard.

"Shut up." OK, not the most eloquent of comebacks, but it served my purposes. I opened the door. "I thought the deal was that you'd call me to set up a time for us to meet." Not ambush me at the worst possible moment.

"I figured this was easier. I mean, it's not like I didn't know where to find you." He pulled his timetable from his pocket and waved it at me, pink ink shining.

I turned to face him, hands on my hips. "You mean, you were checking up on me. You didn't think I'd really join Sewing Club, did you?"

"Do you blame me?" Connor leaned against the doorframe, irritating smirk firmly in place. "I mean, it's not exactly the natural habitat of a diva extraordinaire, now, is it?"

Diva? "I am *not* a—"

"Really?" He raised his eyebrows. "Are you honestly telling me that you're not going to try and find a way to get that lead role? I saw you let loose on Mr Hughes at the auditions, remember?"

"That was different." I tried to ignore the heat rising up to my cheeks at the memory. So what if that *was* my plan? It didn't mean I wasn't still the best person for the part.

"Because you thought you were owed something." Connor dipped his head, as if I'd disappointed him somehow. I wanted to grab him by his scruffy hair and make him see the truth of the situation.

"I was!" I couldn't help it. I knew the words just confirmed everything he thought about me, but it was *true*. "I worked my way up from the chorus line in Year Seven to a major role last year. I did everything right. I was *good* – you saw my audition. I deserved to play Beatrice. And more than that, I was the right choice for it, whatever you think." I couldn't look at him any more, couldn't bear his assumptions and his superiority. Instead, I turned to the first costume rail, blindly pushing hangers to the side as if I were actually paying any attention to what was hanging on them. When in fact, all I could think about was

Connor Bloody O'Neil, and how he just wouldn't *listen* or understand.

"Mr Hughes didn't think so." His words made me stop, fingers digging into the red velvet of a long cloak, my jaw clenched so hard it hurt.

"Mr Hughes was making a point. But he didn't have all the information," I replied. Still didn't, in fact. Nobody in Drama Club did, except for Yasmin, and I was more than happy to keep it that way.

"Is this the part where you tell me how hard your life is so that I feel sorry for you? Because, honestly? Not interested. I've had enough of that this year." I perked up at his words. He said it like it was old news, but it sounded to me like there was a bigger story there. And I really, really wanted to know what it was.

I turned back to face him, but my hands were still clenched in the cloak so it sort of came with me, wrapping around my middle like a layer of armour. "Sounds to me as if you've got your own little sob story there. What happened? Tragedy, death and disaster?"

"No." No elaboration, just one, sharp word. "Look, I'm here to work, even if you're not. We need to meet, so let's meet. Now."

"Now?" If he was trying to catch me unprepared,

he'd be disappointed. "Fine. Where do you want to start?"

Connor looked around him. "What's the deal with this cupboard? Does it have the costumes we need, or not? Because I don't think they wore red velvet cloaks in the 1920s."

I dropped the cloak, my cheeks warming, and stared back into the cupboard at the rails and racks of costumes and accessories. "No, but there must be some stuff we can use."

"Guess we'd better start sorting through, then."

"*I'd* better sort through," I corrected him. "I'm the wardrobe mistress, remember? I don't need your help." Last thing I needed was him getting the idea that I was some needy girl who couldn't do anything herself. That would just totally round off the list of reasons he disliked me, I was sure.

"And I'm the stage manager," he countered. "Which means, in case you've never paid any attention to what Drama Club people are doing *off* stage, that I'm in charge of making everything run smoothly for this play. Including ensuring that our actors actually *have* costumes to wear by opening night."

I gaped at him. "How incapable do you think I am?"

He shrugged. "I don't know. That's why I need

to keep an eye on what you're doing. Because all I know so far is that you think you deserve to be a star, that you're rubbish at sewing and you can't even manage to set an alarm clock. I'll be honest – I'm not filled with confidence."

My blood felt too hot in my veins. "Then let me tell you a few more things," I said, biting out the words. "First, I've been a member of this Drama Club for nearly six years. I know what a stage manager does. Secondly –" I ticked the points off on my fingers as I spoke – "I'm determined. Stubborn even. And I like to have a plan. When I want something, I get it." Unless Lottie Hansen gets there first, anyway.

"Like you want to play Beatrice?" Connor folded his arms across his chest.

"Like I want this play to be a success. And I will do whatever I need to in order to make that happen." Up to and including taking on the lead role.

Connor stared at me for a long moment, his pale blue eyes steady. Then, finally, he shook his head and sighed. "Fine. So we're on the same side. But, look, do you even know anything about what they wore in the 1920s? Or about sourcing and hiring costumes?" I didn't answer. "Well, I do. So if you really want this play to be a success, you're going to have to accept some help."

"From you?" I laughed. "Trust me, I know more about clothes than you do. I'll be fine."

"Certain about that?" Connor asked. "'Cause despite the fighting talk, it still seems to me like you don't have a clue what you're doing."

"Then I'll learn." I looked up at him, meeting his gaze head on. He stared back, studying me, like he was looking for evidence that I was lying.

"Fine. I'll leave you to it, then. You can fill me in on how things are going when we meet next week." He paused in the doorway. "But you better learn quickly, princess. We've got a lot of work to do."

Like I didn't know *that*. About as well as he knew I hated that nickname, although that didn't seem to stop him using it.

And then he was gone. Somehow, despite the rails and boxes and racks crammed into the cupboard, it felt strangely empty without him. Like he'd crept in and filled up this area of my life that had been *perfectly fine* without him, thank you very much. But now, when he wasn't there, things felt … flatter.

And a lot less irritating.

Alone in the costume cupboard, I began to look through the hanging rails, my fingers slipping through silk, cotton, satin, linen, lace – a hundred styles of dress from a hundred past productions. Picking up a pale cotton scarf dotted with tiny printed cherries, I ran it through my hands. It was an infinity scarf, a big loop with no beginning or end. Wrapping it around my throat, I studied myself in the mirror behind the door. Cute. And accessorising was a great distraction from the way Connor's smirk made me clench my teeth. I really didn't want to think about Connor at all.

"Grace?" I spun round to find Miss Cotterill standing in the doorway, a small stack of books and magazines in her arms. "Your homework."

My heart sunk a little more. What on earth did she expect me to do with all that? But I stretched out my arms to take it from her all the same, and shoved them straight into my school bag. "Thanks."

"Club's over," she said, tilting her head as she looked at me. "You should be getting home."

I nodded. "I will. But … can I come back tomorrow? I think it's going to take a while to find what I need in here." And I needed to do it before Izzy and Miss Cotterill started attending rehearsals, to begin costume fittings. At least that would give me something to do in Drama Club beside stand around and watch.

"I think that's a very good idea," Miss Cotterill said approvingly.

"And … do you think I might be able to learn to sew something like this?" I pulled the scarf back over my head to hold it out to her.

Miss Cotterill smile. "I think we can arrange that, yes. Why don't you take it with you and see if you can figure out how it's made?"

Faith's car was in the drive again when I got home. Mum appeared in the hallway when I opened the door, but didn't yell this time. There was something in her eyes, though. A wary, watching, tense something.

"Are you hungry?" she asked, instead. "Your dad's just gone out for Chinese. We ordered you your usual."

It was a temporary truce, rather than a peace offering. Nothing had really changed, after all. But I love Chinese. So that, at least, I could smile at. "Brilliant."

Of course, the only downside was that with dinner arriving imminently, it was harder to run off and hide in my room. I ditched my shoes and coat in the hallway and lugged my school bag, weighed down with Miss Cotterill's homework, through to the lounge.

Faith looked up from her seat on the sofa and

smiled at me. "Hi! I love your scarf."

I touched the cherry-print cotton at my throat. I'd forgotten I was even still wearing it. I pulled it off and stuffed it in my bag. I'd examine it properly later, when I was alone.

Faith's face fell a little, but she carried on talking. "You're just in time. We're looking at patterns for bridesmaids' dresses."

"Patterns?" I dropped my bag next to my favourite chair, at the other end of the coffee table from her. "I thought we were going to go shopping for them?" Together. Which, admittedly, I hadn't really been looking forward to, but still. I was supposed to get to choose my own dress. That was part of the deal.

"Yeah…" Faith's smile turned awkward. "Mum offered to make my bridesmaids' dresses. As a wedding present."

I blinked. "Mum?! Mum can't sew."

"Of course I can." Mum bustled past with another stack of patterns. "Your gran taught me."

I might have gaped. Just a little bit. Never mind baking, this was a whole new level of weird. "But … I've never seen you."

"I did have a life before you were born, you know." She said it like a joke, with a smile on her face, but I couldn't help but glance over at Faith as evidence

107

of that very fact, and suddenly the atmosphere in the room grew heavier.

I looked away, curling up in my armchair with my feet under me. Reaching down, I tugged my bag into my lap and found the books and papers from Miss Cotterill.

Then I stopped, a thought pressing in on my brain. "Why didn't you carry on teaching me, then? After Gran died?" I hadn't wanted to carry on sewing on my own, not without Gran. But if Mum had done it with me, maybe the idea wouldn't have hurt so much.

Mum looked up from the bridesmaids' dress patterns and shrugged. "There didn't seem much point. People don't make their own clothes any more. We don't need to – we just buy them."

"But you want to make these dresses." And I wanted to make my own scarf.

"It's Faith's wedding. It's special, so it's nice to make the effort."

"Right," I said, as if I understood. But all I heard was that I hadn't been worth the effort. She'd never made me a skirt when I was a little girl, or taught me any of the skills her mother had taught her. It was easier to pay someone else to do it, I supposed, just like everything else – food, cleaning, even looking after me.

But now they had Faith, suddenly they were ready to do everything themselves, to be the perfect parents they'd never bothered trying to be for me.

As Mum and Faith pored over the patterns, and talked about silks versus satins, I looked down at my homework. *Styles and Fashions of the 1920s. Military Uniforms of the First World War. 1920s jewellery. Flapper Style and Accessories.*

Never mind bridesmaids' dresses. Miss Cotterill knew just what I needed to be interested in right now.

Settling down, I started to read and waited for my chow mein to arrive. Connor might know everything there was about stage managing, but I was going to be an expert in 1920s clothes by the time we met again to discuss the costumes. One way or another, I was going to convince him I took this play seriously.

Seriously enough to star in it, for definite.

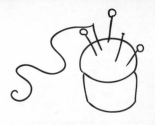

LAUNDRY BAG

What you need:

Rectangle of medium-weight fabric, 120 x 80cm
2m of satin rope cord to match

What to do:

1. Fold and press your fabric in half along the longest edge, right sides together, to give you your basic bag shape.
2. Pin in place along the bottom edge and side, leaving 4cm at the top of the side unpinned.
3. Sew along the bottom and side of the bag, stopping before your 4cm gap.
4. Continuing up the side of the bag, fold and iron the side edge of your fabric in the 4cm gap to make a very narrow hem, then sew in place individually (don't join the back and front pieces of fabric together).
5. Hem the top edge of your bag with a 0.5cm hem.
6. Fold over the top of your bag again so the top edge sits in line with the bottom of your 4cm gap, press and pin in place. This will be the channel for your drawstring cord.

7. *Sew in place, leaving the ends open.*

8. *Attach a safety pin to one end of your cord and use it to feed the cord through the channel until it comes out of the other end. Knot the ends of cord together at the length you want.*

9. *Turn the bag the right way out and it is ready to use.*

Over the course of that week, I spent more time in the textiles classroom than the food tech or drama room. Jasper actually stopped me in the corridor on the Wednesday to check I wasn't "pulling a Lottie" and secretly seeing the school counsellor without telling the rest of them.

I laughed, and didn't mention that my parents had suggested that I should. I'd talked them out of telling the school about Faith. My family wasn't anyone else's business – that's one thing Lottie and I could agree on. Besides, I didn't even know where to *begin* trying to explain all the things that felt wrong about this year.

By Thursday, I had a better idea of the costumes I needed, and I was very, very sick of the costume cupboard. So I dragged Yasmin along with me last period, which we both had free, to help me sort through the last few rails before we went to Bake Club.

Miss Cotterill had provided me with three laundry bags, as made by her Year Nines, to help with the sorting. One for costumes we wanted to use, ready to get them cleaned. One for anything we spotted that needed repairs, and the last for any costumes we felt were beyond saving. I guess she figured that if I was in there anyway, I might as well be useful to her, too.

"So, what else do we still need?" Yasmin asked, staring into the place where old costumes went to die.

Sighing, I scanned over my list again. "Quite a lot. We've got some basic dresses for most of the female cast. The cuts aren't too bad – low waistlines and the right kind of styles – and Miss Cotterill and Izzy say they'll help us tailor them. With a few 1920s-style accessories, they should do the job. But we're still short on military uniforms for the guys, and wedding dresses for the girls in the final scene."

"Plus some sort of knockout gown for you to wear to win Connor over?" Yasmin suggested.

I glared at her and didn't dignify her tease with a response. "I was thinking maybe just simple midi-length dropped-waist dresses in white with short veils? Oh, and I want Beatrice to have something special to wear for the masked ball, to make her stand out. Plus we need actual masks…"

"Right." Yasmin sighed. I didn't blame her one bit.

"So, no time for flirting with Connor, then?"

"No inclination," I said shortly. Even if I suddenly decided that Connor was the most attractive guy on the planet (unlikely), why on earth would I be interested in someone who so obviously disliked me? "Which leaves me totally free to help you out with Ash…"

Yasmin blushed and stared down at her hands. But when I bent down to try and meet her eyes, she was smiling.

"Unless you don't need my help?" I guessed. "Tell me! Are you two officially together, or what?"

"Not … officially. In fact, I have no idea." Yasmin sighed, then grinned again, as if she couldn't help herself. "But he did hold my hand."

"And you're only telling me now? When was this? Where? What happened? I want to know *everything*." After all, if I wasn't destined to have any sort of love life this year, I had to live through someone else. Hand holding wasn't much, but for Yasmin it was a start.

Yasmin laughed. "Come on. I'll tell you while we sort through these costumes."

The work went much quicker with two of us, and Yasmin's story definitely helped pass the time. Ash had walked her home and they'd talked about their families and school and the play, until they'd reached the corner of her road and he'd reached out to take her hand and…

"Then my nephew spotted me from the front garden and I had to run in," Yasmin finished.

I deflated. "That's it? I thought this was going to be some epic love story."

"It kind of is, for me." Yasmin smiled shyly. "I think he'd have kissed me, if we hadn't been interrupted."

"So, what happens next? What's your next move?"

"I don't know," Yasmin admitted. "Any ideas?"

I grinned. "Plenty. We can work on a plan together."

"Once we've finished up here," Yasmin said.

I looked around. "We're nearly there, I think. At least with the sorting. That's the last box."

I pointed at the box full of hats Yasmin was currently rooting through. A rose pink cloche hat caught my eye and I pulled it out, dropping it on to Yasmin's head.

"One moment," I said, adjusting it slightly before she could object. Rifling through a box of brooches I'd sorted earlier, I pulled out a sparkling flower pin and fixed it to the side. "Perfect."

I spun Yasmin around to look in the mirror and she laughed with surprise. "It actually doesn't look that bad!"

"You've got a face that suits hats." And I had an eye for accessories. "You should wear them more often. Say, on your first proper date with Ash…"

Yasmin reached up and took the hat off. "He has to ask me first."

"Oh, he will. Trust me."

She gave me a hopeful smile, then placed the hat back into the box. "Come on. We're supposed to be sorting out costumes, not my love life. What do we do next?" She sat on an ancient suitcase in the corner of the costume cupboard.

I glanced down at my costume list. Even with everything in the cupboard, we didn't have enough of the right sort of outfits and accessories. "Find the stuff we're still missing."

"OK, well, how about we take a trip to raid all the charity shops in town over half-term?" Yasmin suggested, leaning forward with her elbows on her knees. "We should find some stuff we can dress up to look the part. Plus they're great for beads and old costume jewellery and stuff."

"That's a good idea! And I'll talk to Mr Hughes tomorrow about some of the more complicated items. See if he has any ideas." This was why I needed Yasmin's help with the play. The budget Mr Hughes had given me to buy extra costumes and props wasn't huge, which was why I was hoping we could find most things we needed in the costume cupboard. But charity shops would be a great way to pick up some extras without spending too much. "Plus we can go do some actual shopping. It's been ages since I've had a proper shopping spree."

Yasmin beamed. "See! Now we have a plan."

"Yes, we do." And life was always better with a plan, just like Dad said. I glanced down at my watch. "But first we'd better get to Bake Club, before the new kids steal our places."

I shoved my costume list back in my school bag and grabbed my Bake Club basket. Time to switch focus for a couple of hours. I'd thought about nothing but the play for days. It would be good to think about something else for a while.

Bake Club was already in full swing when we arrived, late. Mac wasn't there this week, so Lottie and Jasper had teamed up and he was already putting her carefully laid-out ingredients out of order. He claimed he was trying to help her break her OCD tendencies, but I knew he just did it to mess with her.

Yasmin and I grabbed the last workstation, at the back of the class, and pulled out our recipe. We'd decided earlier in the week that we wanted to make something vaguely authentic to the 1920s to take to Drama Club the next day – even though I'd warned her that if we did it once, we'd be expected to bring cake every week. She thought it would be good for morale. I thought it would annoy Connor, proving that I was actually working for the good of the group. We'd settled on an apple-sauce cake Yasmin had found from some vintage site.

We were halfway through making up the mixture when Jasper appeared at our counter, clearly bored of Lottie taking over already.

"What are you guys doing next week?" he asked, bouncing up to sit on one of the counter stools. "For half-term, I mean."

He was grinning a little too manically for me to feel comfortable answering that question without asking, "Why?"

"Ella's visiting!" Another little bounce at his girlfriend's name. God, he had it bad. To be honest, I'd assumed that the moment she left town it would all be over between them, but no. Despite the distance, Ella's mum's obvious determination to keep them apart, and Jasper's reliance on Christmas stockings to symbolize romance, they still seemed to be going strong.

"Brilliant!" Yasmin beamed as she tipped the apple sauce into the mixture. "Are we all going to get together? Like a big Bake Club reunion thing?"

"That's what I was thinking," Jasper said. "I thought we could all meet at the White Hill Bakery, so that Mac and Lottie can be there, even if they're working. We can try and do it around their breaks or something."

"Sounds like a plan," I said. Anything to get me out of the house, away from more hideous bridesmaids' dress designs. "Yasmin and I were just planning a shopping trip anyway, so we may as well make a day of it."

"Perfect. Tuesday OK?" Jasper asked. "Ella is busy with her dad and visiting her gran and stuff most of the other days."

"Tuesday's fine." I frowned. "If she's going to be so busy, are you actually going to get a chance to see her much?"

Jasper's grin slipped a little. "I'm sure we'll manage. I mean, it's got to be easier than when she's hundreds of miles away, right?"

"Of course it will," Yasmin said, soothingly. I didn't say anything, because it's not nice to lie to friends. I'd learned that from Lottie.

As Jasper wandered back off towards Lottie and her perfectly even scones, I turned to Yasmin. "You should ask Ash along."

Her cheeks did the pink glowy thing they always did at the mention of his name. "To the Bake Club meet-up?"

"Yes, definitely. Why wait for him to ask you, anyway?"

"You think? It wouldn't be weird?"

"Do you want to see him over half-term?" I asked. "Because this could be your best chance."

"Yes," Yasmin admitted. "Actually, he kind of suggested it when we were walking home the other night, in, like, a casual way. I just wasn't sure what we could do. I mean, it's a bit weird being alone for the first time with someone you don't know very well. Walking home was OK, because there was a definite end in sight. But going out? Where would we go? What would we talk about?"

"And this way, the rest of us would be there to ease you into it. To get used to being around him, find out what he likes, that sort of thing?" This wasn't a problem I'd had with any of my exes. Mostly I'd dated within my old group of friends, until last year. After the party and the grounding debacle, let's just say I'd learned who my real friends were.

Yasmin nodded. "That sounds much better than 'I'm scared I'll have absolutely nothing to say to him the moment we're alone'. Let's go with your reasons." She smiled.

"In that case, you can admit that I was right and ask him along when you see him tomorrow night."

"You don't think anyone will mind?"

"No! It'll give us all a chance to scope him out, see if he's good enough for you." I grinned, just a little bit evilly. "And set Mac on him if it turns out he's not."

"Your dream has come true," Connor announced, as I walked into the hall for Drama Club the next day. He'd taken off his blazer and tie and rolled up his shirtsleeves, and his smirk had been replaced with a look of intense irritation. I suspected that had something to do with me, even though I hadn't done anything.

"Really?" I asked, looking at Yasmin and Ash across the room, as she opened her cake tin to let him smell the gloriousness of our apple-sauce cake. "You're moving back to your old school after all?"

He laughed at that. "Even better. Violet's off sick today, so you're playing Beatrice."

My gaze flew to his face – to his raised eyebrows

and expectant eyes. A warm feeling started in my chest. This was it. This was my chance to prove – not just to Mr Hughes but to everyone in the cast and crew – that I was the best choice for the role. Even if they didn't just give me the part then and there, from now on everyone in this room would know that they should. The moment Violet screwed up or lost her nerve or missed rehearsal again … people would start calling for me to take on Beatrice.

This was exactly what I'd been planning for all along. And I could tell from Connor's expression that he knew it. *That* was why his expression was so full of disdain.

Except things hadn't gone entirely to plan, although Connor didn't know it. I'd intended to spend my evenings learning the lines, so I could be word perfect the moment this chance arose. Instead I'd spent my time learning about 1920s fashion and sorting out the costume cupboard.

Still, it was early enough in the rehearsal schedule so the rest of the cast were using their scripts, too. It shouldn't matter too much. Except…

"I really needed to talk with you and Mr Hughes about the costumes this afternoon, actually."

Connor blinked, and I knew I'd surprised him. Good. It served him right for making assumptions about me, even if he had been right. I pressed home the advantage. "Now I've finished sorting through all the school costumes, I have a much better idea of what we're still missing."

"Right. Well, I'm sure we can do that in the break or something." He frowned, just a small crease between his eyebrows, but it was enough for me to know he was reconsidering things, just a little bit.

I nodded, trying not to smile. "Of course. I just don't want to lose focus on the most important role I have here – making sure the costumes are perfect."

And with that, I headed off for the stage, ditching my bag on a chair and pulling out my script, leaving Connor staring after me. Once I was sure he couldn't see my face, I grinned. I had a feeling that this was going to be a *great* rehearsal.

"OK, let's take Act Two from the top," Mr Hughes called, from his seat in the hall. "Leonato, Antonio, Hero, Beatrice, Ursula and Margaret – that's you."

My blood hummed with the excitement of being back on stage. I felt as if everything inside me was vibrating, ready to burst out in the lines of the play. This was a great scene for Beatrice. Full of jokes and clever words, and just a touch of insight into her real feelings about love. Perfect for displaying my understanding of the character.

But from the moment I stepped on to the stage, I knew there was something wrong. There, at the back of the hall, stood Connor – not backstage where he should have been. He was talking with the lighting guys and fiddling with something on the sound desk. My eyes narrowed as I stared out at him, until a dazzling flash of light forced me to close them.

"OK, let's go," Mr Hughes said, apparently unconcerned by his stepson's attempts to blind his cast.

"Was not Count John here at supper?" Leonato said, and I tried to focus on the script, to concentrate on the scene I was in. This was my chance, and I wasn't going to let anything ruin it for me.

"How tartly that gentleman looks." I moved across the stage as I spoke, just as Violet had been asked to in previous rehearsals. "I never can—"

A blast of music, and the rest of my sentence was drowned out.

"Sorry!" Connor called cheerfully, turning the volume down to leave a low crackle coming from the speakers. "We just need to check a few technical things. Carry on!"

As if it were possible to act out a scene well with that kind of chaos going on. I scowled at him, but he wasn't even looking at me. Damn him.

"Grace? Can you start that line again, please?" Mr Hughes asked, and I hurriedly turned back to my script.

This time, we managed to make it almost a third of the way through the scene before the lights started flashing different colours, right in the middle of Beatrice's speech about beards and hell.

I bit the inside of my cheek then soldiered on, talking over the mutterings and giggles from the cast members who were watching.

I knew what Connor was doing. He was trying to provoke me. He wanted me to stomp my feet and complain in front of everyone – just so he didn't have to deal with the idea that I might not be the girl he'd assumed I was. Just to try and prove to himself that I was still the diva he'd taken me for when we first met.

He was *so* wrong … except, I really, really wanted to stomp my feet.

But I wouldn't. I wasn't going to give him that satisfaction, not for a second.

We stumbled and tripped through to the end of the scene with only a couple more interruptions, but I knew that none of us up on stage had impressed anybody. Least of all me.

As we reached the last line, the lights returned to normal, and the crackling that had been emanating from the speakers ceased. I glared across at Connor and he smiled at me, without even the pretence of innocence, as he headed backstage again.

"Great job, guys," Mr Hughes lied. "Right, let's take a ten-minute break, then I want to do some of the Don John scenes, since Violet isn't here."

And just like that, my chance to prove I deserved that role was over. Disappointment burned in my chest, followed by frustration. Followed by anger.

While everyone else descended on the apple-sauce cake, which Yasmin had laid out on a table at the side, I slipped through the black drapes at the side of the stage to round on Connor instead.

"What the hell was that?" I demanded, hands on my hips like I were acting a part.

"A pretty rubbish scene rehearsal?" he answered, shifting one of the boards we were using in lieu of actual scenery at this point.

"You were trying to put me off. You wanted me to make a fool of myself up there." I followed him around to the back of the stage, since he was still paying more attention to the scenery than me.

"Oh, come on. You did fine." He shoved another board into place, then started dragging another into the wings. I followed. "And it's not like you're actually playing the part, so what does it matter?

I needed to check some levels on the lights and sound, and it's difficult enough finding time for those things during rehearsals. A real professional wouldn't have been put off by it."

"A professional stage manager wouldn't be trying to sabotage rehearsals," I countered, but he turned to face me, still smiling that same irritating smile, and I realized suddenly that I was too close to him.

"What do you care, anyway?" He leaned lightly against the board, arms folded over his chest as I stepped back, the curtain at the side of the stage brushing against me. "I mean, your only concern is making sure the costumes are perfect, right? So what does it matter if you didn't have the optimum conditions for reading someone else's lines?"

Proof, if I'd needed it, of exactly what he was trying to do – make me admit that I still wanted Violet's part. That I still planned to try and steal it.

"Look. I'm the lead understudy in this play. I'm not going to get as many chances as Violet to practise these scenes, and if something happens that means I have to get up on that stage and perform on the night, I want to be ready for it." I kept my voice even, calm and just a little bit condescending. "What you did wasn't just unprofessional, it was unfair to the other people on the stage. If you have a problem with me, fine. Feel free to tell me about it. Just don't take it out on the cast, or the production, OK?" I was kind of proud of that last bit.

I stared at him until he gave a very slight nod.

"Look, Grace…" He stopped, running his hand through his already messy hair. But I wasn't interested. Instead, I spun on my heel and headed off to get some apple cake.

Grace 1, Connor 0.

For now, anyway.

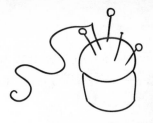

JEANS BAG

What you need:

An old pair of jeans

What to do:

1. Make sure the front and back of the waistband of your pair of jeans is level, then cut off the legs at the very top, so you have a very short denim skirt.
2. Turn inside out, and pin the bottom of the skirt together. Sew along it to make the bottom of your bag (you might need to even up the inside afterwards).
3. Use the legs of the jeans to create the strap for your bag – cut a rectangle of whatever length you want, and double the width you want (make it at least 6cm wide).
4. Fold the material for the strap in half lengthways, right side together. Pin and sew along the long edge.
5. Turn the strap right side out, then fold the short ends inside and sew in place for a neat finish.
6. Sew the straps in place and then sew a rectangle with a cross through it at each end of the strap for extra strength.

"OK," Yasmin said, "so I need to ask you something, and I need you not to get all … sarcastic about it." Yasmin looked at me earnestly from beneath the brim of her new dark red felt hat.

I paused from flicking through dresses on the charity-shop rail and considered her words. They sounded ominous. "Go on, then."

"You and Connor…"

"Yeah, we're totally planning on running off to Vegas together, you're right." Honestly. A few conversations with a guy and people automatically assumed it was love. Instead of, as was *actually* the case, mutual distrust.

"Not sarcastic, remember?"

I sighed and pushed another hanger to the "hideous and no good to me" side of the rail. Seriously, who had bought this stuff in the first place?

"OK. Sarcasm over." I picked up a pair of jeans with sweet, heart-shaped pockets on the back.

They weren't in my size, but I really liked those pockets... Suddenly I remembered something I'd seen on the internet when I was looking for infinity-scarf patterns. "Hey, don't you think these would make a cute bag?" I folded the legs out of the way to show Yasmin what I meant.

She blinked. "Uh, I guess so? Anyway ... Connor and Ash are pretty good friends, you know?"

"I noticed." Seemed Ash was the only person in Drama Club that Connor would deign to hang out with. "I was thinking he probably hasn't ever had a friend before, so Ash is kind of an experiment for him."

"Grace."

"Yeah, OK, OK. They're friends. What about it?"

"Well, I know you and Connor have to spend time together because of the play, and I know you moan about him a lot, but you're getting on OK really, right? You're just being ... Grace, with all the comments about him?"

Just being Grace? What did that mean? "Look, the guy took an instant dislike to me for reasons I don't fully understand and now seems determined to undermine every attempt I make at doing a good job for this play." And had some very valid suspicions about my intentions, not that I was admitting *that* to anyone. "Beyond that, we're totally best friends."

Yasmin sighed. "I'm sure that's not true."

"I'm pretty sure it is."

"And even if it is," Yasmin went on, as if I hadn't spoken, "why does it bother you so much? Why do you care what he thinks about you? I mean, it's not like he's the coolest kid in school, or that he's convincing your friends of your evilness. And if you're not interested in him ... what does it matter what he thinks?"

I stopped, staring at the neon pink waistcoat on the rack in front of me. Why *did* it bother me? It was annoying having to work with someone who so clearly despised me, but I knew I should just ignore him and carry on. So why couldn't I? Why did the very thought of him make me grind my teeth?

"I guess ... it just bugs me that he thinks he knows exactly who I am, what I'm like. And he keeps waiting for me to act that way."

"So? You won't." Something uncomfortable wriggled inside me at Yasmin's words. I *was* still planning to steal the lead. But if it was for the good of the show, didn't that make it OK? I'd seen Violet rehearse. Trust me, my taking over would be a relief for *everyone*.

"Yeah, but..." I thought about how to explain it.

Yasmin knew me well enough that she could probably guess, but I got the feeling she was waiting for me to say it anyway. "Maybe it's because I would have done, a year ago. I *was* that girl. But Connor didn't even know me then! And it's not like he's taken the time to find out what I'm really like."

"Do you want him to?"

"No," I lied. I mean, who made a snap judgement about a person like that, without ever actually talking to them properly? And then refused to change his mind, despite all the evidence?

"What about you and Faith?" Yasmin asked. "Are you getting on better with her at least?"

I shrugged. "Does it matter? It's not like we have anything in common ... apart from our parents."

"How do you know?" Yasmin asked, and I knew she was cross with me. "Have you spoken to her much, got to know her? Or are you treating her the exact same way that you complain Connor's treating you?"

A cold, sad feeling dripped down into my chest. She was right. I suppose one thing Yasmin did know about was family. After all, she had enough of it – siblings, aunts, cousins, nephews, everything – and they all seemed to enjoy spending time together.

"So, you and Ash, then," I said, changing the

subject. "The cake went down well?"

Yasmin rolled her eyes at me, showing me she knew exactly what I was doing, but didn't press the point any further, which I appreciated. Yasmin always knew when to step back and let you stew about her words on your own for a while. "Yeah, it did. He walked me home again that night."

"I saw."

"And I asked him to come and meet us at the bakery today, like you said."

"Great!"

"And he kissed me goodnight." The pink in Yasmin's cheeks was approaching fuchsia. It totally clashed with her hat.

"And was it good?"

"It really, really was."

I couldn't help the jealous little bit of me that wished I had someone to blush over, someone to walk me home and kiss me, before I had to go inside and face the weirdness of my new family.

"I'm really happy for you," I said, and I meant it, even if it wasn't the whole story. "Come on. Let's pay for this stuff and get on with the real shopping."

We headed over to the White Hill Bakery to meet the others a couple of hours later, laden down with high-street shopping bags and cheap plastic bags from our charity-shop rummage. I wasn't even sure what we'd do with some of the things I'd picked up – I just knew that the fabric felt right for the show, or that the pearly beads and sparkling clips would be perfect for something or other. The ribbons and scraps of lace just called out to me. I'd lay everything out in Sewing Club when we got back to school after half-term, and get Izzy and Miss Cotterill to help me figure it all out.

Ella and Jasper were already sitting at a table in the window when we arrived, but neither of them were looking particularly happy. They seemed awkward – like they'd forgotten how to be together.

"Ella!" Yasmin half shrieked as we walked in, and soon we were lost in the usual hugs and kisses and exclamations of how long it had been.

"How *are* you, Grace?" Ella asked, and I knew that meant that Jasper had told her about Faith.

"*Sooo* busy," I said, sitting down on a free chair. "The play this year is taking up pretty much all my time. Especially when you add in Sewing Club and everything."

"*Sewing* Club?" Ella asked, brow furrowed.

I glared at Jasper. "You managed to tell her about Faith but not Sewing Club?"

135

Jasper glared back, and I suddenly realized that his participation in Sewing Club was probably still top secret – partly through embarrassment, and partly to keep the great Christmas-stocking plan a secret until the big day. Rolling my eyes, I launched into a detailed and perhaps slightly exaggerated retelling of how I ended up in Sewing Club, leaving Jasper's part in it out entirely. Before long, Ella was laughing, Jasper was smiling again, and Yasmin had returned from the counter with coffee, cake, Lottie and Mac.

It was nice, having us all together again. Ella told us stories about her new school, and we pretended it didn't matter that we didn't know any of the people she was talking about. Mac and Lottie told her all about Paris, and the rest of us pretended we hadn't heard it a million times already. Yasmin and I talked about rehearsals, and I pretended I was fine with just being in charge of the costumes this year.

Then the bakery door opened and Ash walked in. With Connor.

As Yasmin got to her feet to welcome them, Ella leaned over towards me and whispered, "Who are they?"

"The dark-haired one who keeps staring at Yasmin is Ash. He's playing Benedick in the play. They have maths together, and a mutual crush that is edging towards dating."

"And the cute one who keeps staring at you?"

I checked again in case that gorgeous guy from Year Thirteen had wandered in when I wasn't looking. Nope, still just Connor.

"Seriously? You think he's cute?"

"Yes," Ella murmured. "And so do you, because you still have eyes in your head. So, who is he and why are you making out that you're not interested?"

"It's not like that. Trust me. He's the stage manager for the play. We have a mutual disgust thing going on."

"That's not what it looks like to me," Ella said, straightening up, but by then the boys had reached the table and pulled up chairs, so there was no time to argue back.

It was weird. I hadn't remembered Ella being so … confident, I guess. She'd always been the quiet one, the shy one. The one hiding behind Jasper, desperate for help but not quite sure how to ask for it.

I couldn't help but think that moving up North had been the best thing for her if it allowed her to become a little more herself. Even if it meant *we* lost her.

When I looked away from Ella, I discovered that Connor was indeed staring at me. He was also sitting right next to me.

"I'm going to get more cake," I announced, standing up quickly. "Anyone want anything?"

I took orders and cash, then darted over to the counter to make my own choice, glad for a moment alone.

Except I wasn't alone for very long.

"What?" I asked, when I realized that Connor had followed me.

"Just interested to see a princess in her natural environment," he answered.

I ignored him. Turning away, I eyed up the lemon drizzle cake. It looked like one of Lottie's, with the perfectly spaced candied lemon slices on the top. That could definitely be worth a go.

"OK, fine," Connor said after a moment. "I wanted to, I don't know, apologize. For the other day."

My gaze swung away from the cake to stare at him in astonishment. His cool blue eyes looked sincere. And somehow not as cold as they always had before.

"Seriously?" I asked. "You want to say sorry. To me." Unbelievable.

"Yeah, I do." Connor shifted his weight from one foot to the other, his hands deep in his pockets. "You were right. What you said the other day. I wasn't thinking about what was best for the play, and you were. So, I'm sorry."

"Well, OK, then." What else was there to say? "Are you having cake?"

Connor stared at the glass case as if he'd only just noticed it was there. "Yeah. What do you recommend?"

I shrugged. "They're all good. But that looks like one of Lottie's, so I'm going to give it a go."

As I leaned past him to point at the lemon drizzle cake, my body brushed against Connor's chest. Such a small thing, but it made my heart speed up all the same.

The girl behind the counter came to take our order and I paid. Connor carried the tray back to our table then sat down beside me again. I tried to ignore the way the air between us seemed to crackle, like it was filled with static electricity. Instead, I shifted my focus to the conversation the rest of the group was having, and the fact that Yasmin was holding Ash's hand under the table. At least somebody's romantic life was working out right this year.

"So, Connor," Lottie asked, wiping the table down with a napkin before leaning her elbows on it. "Which school did you move from?"

Connor shook his head. "You wouldn't have

heard of it. Just the local school in a little town over on the other side of London."

"How do you like St Mary's?" Mac asked. "Speaking as someone who got the hell out of that place as soon as possible."

"And not before you tried to burn it down," Jasper added, unhelpfully.

Lottie elbowed her boyfriend in the side. "You liked it more by the end."

"Parts of it." Mac leaned in to kiss her, just where her jaw met her neck. "I only liked some very specific parts of it."

Lottie smiled and turned to kiss him properly.

"Are they always like this?" Connor asked.

"Mostly, yeah." I sighed.

Connor cleared his throat. "So, St Mary's. Seems OK. Just another school, I guess."

Ash and Yasmin were not just holding hands, but also staring into each other's eyes now, and Jasper had his arm around Ella with her head on his shoulder.

No one was listening. No one except me. "Have you been to a lot of schools, then?"

"Some." He shrugged. "We moved when my parents divorced a few years ago, then again when my dad got remarried, and again now."

That sounded like a lot of moving around to me.

"Why this time?"

"Just the way things work out." Which wasn't an answer at all.

"Is it weird, having to call your stepdad Mr Hughes all the time?" I asked. It seemed as good a way as any to get him talking.

"The whole thing is weird," Connor replied. "The play, the school, everything."

I could kind of sympathize. It was enough having to deal with your family at home, but at school, too? Weird.

"But you like being stage manager?" I pressed.

"Yeah." He smiled, and I knew he meant it. "I like the feeling of pulling it all together, of everyone having their own part to play to make it all work," he said.

"What don't you like, then?" Because there was obviously something.

"The drama."

The drama. Did he mean the acting, or the actors? I had a feeling this was more about what went on with the cast backstage than on – the gossip, the romances. And, of course, the highly strung tendencies of some cast members. Violet, particularly, had been acting up to the starring role thing over the last few weeks.

I leaned back in my chair and picked at the cake

crumbs on my plate.

"So, how are the costumes coming along?" Connor asked.

"Slowly." I raised an eyebrow at him. "We missed our meeting last week. What with … everything."

"So let's have it now, then. It doesn't look like we'll be missed too much. And since I'm here, we might as well make the most of it."

Connor shifted in his chair so he was facing me and folded his arms across his chest.

"Why *are* you here, anyway?" I asked.

"Ash wanted me to come. I think he was a bit nervous about, you know, being—"

"Alone with Yasmin," I finished with a nod. "They really are a pair! So, costumes…"

"Yeah. What have you got so far?"

I pulled my list out of my bag, and Connor's eyebrows went up in surprise. "What?"

"You carry that with you everywhere?"

"Pretty much. Besides, Yasmin and I were shopping for some costume bits before we came here."

"Huh."

"What?" I asked again, irritation colouring my voice a little more this time.

"Maybe you are taking this seriously, after all."

142

What did I have to do? Endless hours in the costume cupboard, putting in extra time every single rehearsal … and it was a list that convinced him. "Of course I am. I've been telling you that from the start. If you'd just *listen* to me occasionally—"

Ella interrupted my flow. "Sorry, guys, but I've got to go. I promised Dad I wouldn't be back late."

There was the usual round of hugs and then, "See you soon" and "We'll email more, right?". But as I hugged Ella goodbye, I had a feeling that I might never see her again.

Everyone started to drift off after that. I looked down at my epic list, then at Connor. "We'll do this at rehearsal on Tuesday?"

"For sure." He smiled, and I felt my heart tighten up again the way it had when we'd touched. "I can't wait to see what you've come up with."

I watched him leave with Ash, staring at the door for a long moment after he'd gone.

"So, you and Connor," Yasmin said, exchanging a look with Lottie. "Still not friends?"

I swallowed. "Nope. Not at all." I didn't know what we were, but it didn't feel anything like friends.

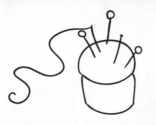

PHONE SLEEVE

What you need:

2 pieces of fabric – 1 patterned, 1 plain
Iron-on interfacing
Sheet wadding
Self-adhesive Velcro strip, 1cm wide

What to do:

1. Measure your phone, and add 3cm to the width and 4cm to the height

2. Cut out two pieces of each of the fabrics, the interfacing and the wadding to this size.

3. Start with the lining. Iron a piece of interfacing to the wrong side of both pieces of plain fabric. Place the two pieces of plain fabric together, interfacing on the outside, and pin.

4. Sew in place, about 1cm from the edge, along both long sides and the bottom short side – but leave a gap of 3cm on the short side for turning the right way later.

5. Place your two pieces of patterned fabric together, right sides facing, and add a piece of wadding to both sides.

6. Pin along the bottom edge and two sides, then sew in

place along those three sides, around 1cm from the edge again.

7. Trim the bottom corners, making sure not to cut through the stitching.

8. Turn the lining the right way out, then slide it inside the inside-out patterned layer, so the patterned fabric and the plain fabric are together.

9. Line up the tops of the patterned and plain layers and pin in place, then sew the top around 1cm in, keeping the layers closely aligned.

10. Pull the lining back out, then use the hole you left in the bottom edge to pull the outer layer through. Sew the hole closed once the case is the right way out, then push the lining back inside.

11. Slip your phone inside, then add a small strip of Velcro to the top of your case to hold it in place.

The first day back at school after half-term there was Sewing Club. I trudged out of my English lit lesson, waving goodbye to Lottie as she headed off to White Hill. Then I headed across school to the textiles classroom, a large bag full of material, clothes and odds and ends in my arms.

Jasper had beaten me there. When I pushed open the door, I saw him sitting with Izzy, measuring out a piece of bright red felt. It looked like they were going with the classics for the stocking.

Which hopefully meant that, once she had Jasper started off, Izzy would be free to help me with the costumes.

"Ah, Grace. I've set you up over here today, dear." Miss Cotterill pointed to a table in the corner of the room, and I sighed at the sight of it. There, neatly laid out on the table was a pattern, a sewing box filled with pins, needles and threads, and several rolls of fabric.

I held up my bag. "I brought some stuff we picked up for the costumes. I thought that maybe—"

"We'll take a look at those afterwards." Miss Cotterill pulled out the chair, and I sat. Clearly we were doing this *her* way. "First, I've got a new project for you, to help build your sewing skills. Since you did such a nice job on that scarf."

I touched the pale gold and cream scarf at my neck. It *had* turned out well.

"Is it one of the costumes?" I asked. "Because, really, I do need to get those sorted first."

"You said you wanted to learn to sew," Miss Cotterill said, firmly. "And if you want to make or fit any of those costumes that are so important to you, you need to have these basic skills. Besides, you have plenty of time to work on the costumes during rehearsals. That's how it's been done every other year. Just because you have a fancy title, doesn't mean you get to rewrite the rules around here." She picked up a few sheets of printed paper. "I chose something useful. So, take a look, and then you can select your fabrics." She ran a hand over the stack of patterned cotton beside me, like they were favourite toys she was letting me play with. "I'll ask Izzy to come over and see how you're getting on in a little while."

Left alone, I pushed my charity-shop finds to

one side and studied the instructions I'd been given. A phone sleeve. Well, that looked simple enough. Just two pieces of fabric sewn together with some wadding between them.

Easy. I could get this done in no time, then move on to what I was actually there for – the costumes.

Noting the type and amount of fabric the pattern called for, I turned my attention to the stack of material. There were stripes and spots, flowers and even flamingos. Eventually I settled on a thicker fabric with a red and green apple print. Quickly, I grabbed the tape measure and held it against my phone, cutting a piece of paper the right size to use as a pattern.

"Are you sure that will be big enough?" Izzy asked, suddenly beside me, and I dropped the pot of pins on to the fabric in surprise.

"What?" I began shoving the pins back into the pot, irritated by the interruption. "Ow!"

"You need to make sure you've left enough fabric for the seam allowances," Izzy explained. She started picking up the pins more carefully, while I sucked the tip of my pricked finger. "Otherwise the finished case will be too small."

I glanced down at the fabric. "I guess I was rushing," I admitted.

Izzy gave me a smile. "That's one thing Miss Cotterill will never let you get away with. She likes you to take your time and get everything perfect."

I groaned. "God, this is going to be like baking with Lottie all over again."

"Hey, it takes longer to get a decent finished product if you rush it and have to start all over again. Trust me, I speak from experience."

"Is that what you're teaching Jasper?" I asked, nodding over at the table where Jasper appeared to be failing to thread a needle with thick embroidery thread.

"Mostly I've been teaching him blanket stitch." She winced, watching him fail to thread the needle again, stabbing himself in the hand instead. "It's slow going."

"It looks it."

"He'll get there," Izzy said. "He just needs to take his time to get it right, and then practise. A lot. Whereas you seem fine. Well, once you stop rushing."

"Yeah, yeah." I shifted the paper and prepared to pin it. "Hey, could you give me a hand with some costume stuff after I do this, though? Also, I had this idea for a bag…"

"Sure." Izzy checked her watch. "Well, if there's time. Otherwise, next week, yeah?"

I glanced up at the clock. Only an hour left of Sewing Club, and I still had to pin and cut out my fabric. I'd have to finish it at home. How was I ever going to get the costumes sorted if I also had to follow Miss Cotterill's sewing lessons?

Izzy wandered back over towards Jasper, and I watched him look up and grin at her as he proudly held up two pieces of pattern paper shaped like stockings. At least one of us was getting what we needed from Sewing Club.

"You know, Connor, sometimes it feels like you're the only one who understands how I'm feeling."

Normally, I'd have rolled my eyes and kept walking when I heard Violet whining. But when I heard Connor's name ... I admit it, I was intrigued.

Backstage was a hive of darkened corners and secret spots, places you could hole up and learn lines, or have a private conversation when you needed to. And since Violet and Connor were tucked away just outside the costume cupboard, where I was heading with my bag of charity-shop finds, what was I supposed to do *except* hide behind a display board and eavesdrop?

"Violet, you're doing fine." Was that exasperation I heard in Connor's voice? I liked to think so. "Just keep going over your lines every day and they'll stick eventually. They always do."

Violet sighed. "I suppose. But honestly, I'm so nervous about the costumes being right, I'm finding it hard to concentrate. You know Grace has never worked backstage before, right?"

I bristled at that. *She* was worried? I was far more concerned about a Beatrice who couldn't learn her lines.

Of course, there was an obvious solution to *that*...

"You don't need to worry," Connor said. A warm feeling flooded my chest until he added, "It's my responsibility. I'll make sure Grace does her job properly."

I scowled. Like I wasn't already doing a perfectly good job without him, thank you very much.

Violet sighed again, louder and more pathetic this time. "It's just so ... intimidating having her here. You know what she's like. She's made it clear she's just waiting for me to screw up."

How dare she! I had done no such thing. Granted, I *was* waiting for it. But it's not like I'd told *her* that.

I risked a peek around the corner of the board I was hiding behind. Violet was sitting very close to Connor in a way that made me roll my eyes. But the frustrated expression on Connor's face made me feel a little better. Was this what he'd meant when he said he hated the drama of being involved in plays?

"Look, Violet. I think the best thing to do is rise above it. Act professional. Do the best job you can and ignore everything else."

Violet sat up straighter at that, and I ducked back behind the board in case she spotted me.

"Well, of course *I'm* being professional," she said. "But did you hear what Sara said about Robbie the other day? And I know people are saying that I've got it in for her because—"

"I'm sorry, Violet," Connor interrupted, not sounding very sorry at all, "I need to get these moved before rehearsals start."

I heard movement and realized that Connor was standing up. And that the things he needed to move probably included the board I was hiding behind.

"Maybe we can talk later?" Violet suggested, in what she probably thought was a flirty voice. It wasn't. "We could go and get a coffee or something..."

I held my breath waiting for Connor's response and my heart clenched at the idea of him on a date with my rival.

"I don't think that would be a good idea," Connor said, and my breath whooshed out. "You know, keeping things professional and all."

Which presumably meant "no way, you drama queen" in Connor language. And he thought *I* was a diva.

"I'll see you later," Connor added, obviously trying to get rid of her. Now what did I do? I could hear Violet walk off but I didn't want to move until I was sure which way she had gone, in case she spotted me. But if I didn't get out of there soon…

Suddenly the board in front of me shifted a metre to the right.

Connor blinked those pale blue eyes at me. "Hello, princess."

"Hi." I didn't even object to the nickname for once. "Sorry, I didn't want to interrupt, but I needed to take these to the costume cupboard." I held up my bag as proof.

He didn't look convinced of my innocence. "Not just fascinated by all Violet's issues?"

"No more than you seemed to be."

"Fair enough." He pushed the board another metre or so, and I put my bag down at the side to help him.

"So, is that what you meant by 'the drama'?" I asked, as we shifted the board towards the stage.

"Yeah, maybe. Although that was pretty mild, really." He sighed. "I guess I don't get it. We're here to put on a play. Why does it all have to be about these invented crises?"

"You know I haven't actually said anything at all to Violet, right? About her playing Beatrice, I mean." I didn't want to buy into the drama, but it felt important that he know that.

"I don't think you needed to." Connor gave me a rueful smile. "She knows you wanted the part, and that everybody expected you to get it. That's probably enough."

Guilt tugged at my middle. Was *I* the reason Violet was struggling with the role? No. I wasn't taking that on. It wasn't my fault she couldn't learn her lines. And if everyone expected me to get the part the first time round, maybe they'd support me when Violet still couldn't do it in a couple of weeks. This was a good thing for me.

So why did it still feel kind of bad?

"Well, I'm too busy with the costumes to worry about what anyone else thinks," I lied.

"Good." Connor looked approving. "Then you go and get on. I can handle this."

Leaving him to his boards, I went to retrieve my bag of accessories and costume bits.

It was funny. Last year, I'd have been right there in the middle of any "he said, she said", but this year

I wasn't bothered. I wasn't sure if I was showing some sort of new maturity, or if Violet's issues just weren't all that remarkable.

Definitely not as interesting as mine, anyway.

Like Faith. I'd thought that once she got used to the idea that we were part of her life, her visits might tail off a bit. You know, so she wouldn't need to visit as much. But Faith didn't seem to be visiting any less. In fact, if anything, she seemed to be visiting *more*. She and Mum had been on a wedding shopping expedition together, looking at fabric and patterns for the bridesmaids' dresses, as well as all sorts of other trinkets that weddings seemed to require.

Of course the main thing the wedding required was a groom.

To be honest, I'd started to get a bit suspicious about Faith's fiancé. As in, whether he actually existed. I mean, surely we'd have met him by now if he did, right? But Faith said Adam had been working away overseas on some secondment to another hospital or something (because *of course* he was a doctor. Who else would the perfect lost daughter marry?) for the last three months.

But now he was back. And coming to dinner tonight. Yay.

Unpacking my bag into the relevant boxes and

baskets, I took a moment to just enjoy the fabrics – the textures, the sparkle of sequins, the slip of the silk, the intricacies of lace. Even more surprising than my lack of interest in Violet's dramas was the fact that I was honestly enjoying researching the costumes. I liked finding out what people had worn – it was a lot more interesting than most of the stuff we learned in our history classes.

Picking out a diamante hairslide shaped like a bird, I slipped it into my hair, holding a few strands back from my face. Studying myself in the mirror, I decided it would be perfect for a family dinner.

But first, we had to get through this rehearsal. It was starting to sink in that we only had a couple of weeks left until the Christmas break, and after that it was all downhill to the opening night. Everyone still had their scripts in hand, I was still short of a few costumes, and I'd barely started looking at the props.

I really needed another meeting with Connor.

Stashing the last of my stuff in the costume cupboard, I headed back to the stage to see if he was done shifting temporary scenery.

"Look, can we meet now? I want to go through some stuff with you."

"Sure thing, princess," Connor said, and this time I scowled at him. I didn't want him thinking I was starting to like the name or anything.

He glanced up across the hall as the doors opened and Mr Hughes walked in. "But it might have to wait until the break."

He was right. Mr Hughes called out immediately for me to help run through lines with some of the cast. I'd thought that just doing the costumes meant I'd be sitting around until we had, you know, actual costumes, but Mr Hughes had clearly decided to take advantage of my willingness to help. At any given rehearsal I could be shifting scenery, running through lines, playing prompt, covering for missing actors, standing on stage to help get the lights positioned right … anything.

In some ways, being backstage was proving more exciting that being on it. And now I had Izzy and a few others from Sewing Club there, too, starting to measure and fit our actors for their costumes, it was busier than ever. I worked as much as I could on the costumes but, I had to admit, Izzy was much better at it than me.

"The break, then," I said, and Connor nodded.

"No break today!" Mr Hughes jogged up the stairs at the side of the stage and carried on straight past us. "No time!"

Connor sighed and ran a hand through his

dishevelled hair. I had to admit, with his hair going in all directions, he really was kind of cute.

I looked away. I'd spent weeks carefully not noticing that Connor O'Neil was, objectively speaking, kind of good-looking. But suddenly, it seemed to be all I could see.

"Aren't you supposed to have minions to do the heavy lifting?" I asked. No break meant non-stop work for Connor, I realized. At least the cast got a rest when they weren't on stage.

"Apparently not. Most of the tech crew won't show up for rehearsals now until next term. They say there's nothing more they can do until we get the blocking finalized."

"What about the guys doing the scenery?" I perched on the edge of a stack of chairs.

"They're working on it in the art department."

"So it's just you."

"It's just me. And you, for some reason."

I gave him a bright smile. "I like to be helpful."

"Sure you do, princess." The sarcasm in his voice lingered from the early days, but there was less bite to it now. Maybe he was starting to see me differently at last, too.

"Why else would I be here?" I tilted my head to look at him, honestly wanting to hear his answer.

"I'm not sure," Connor said, but he was smiling a little. "Maybe just sent to try me?"

I laughed and wondered if this actually counted as flirting. Was that what we were doing now? "No... I'm cooking up all sorts of schemes back here in the wardrobe department." Only half a joke, but I wasn't about to admit that.

"I knew it." He was grinning now, and I couldn't look away from his pale blue eyes. They locked on to mine and suddenly I forgot all about Violet and her dramas, or whatever it was Mr Hughes had asked me to do.

"Actually, while I have you both..." Mr Hughes's head popped back around to our little backstage area, and Connor stepped back. I let out a breath. "I meant to ask how the costume and prop meetings are going. Have you managed to get together yet this week? I know Grace has been very busy with Miss Cotterill."

Did he? How? God, was the whole staff room gossiping about me?

Connor answered for both of us, while I boggled at the idea of teachers discussing my mythical sewing skills.

"Not this week, no," he said, neatly avoiding having to admit that we were a couple of weeks behind.

Mr Hughes gave Connor a look I didn't quite understand. "Well, in that case, maybe Grace should join us for dinner after the rehearsal. You can catch up on everything. If that's all right by you, Grace?"

It was on the tip of my tongue to tell him I couldn't, maybe even explain that my sister was bringing her fiancé over to meet the family that night. But I didn't want these people to know about Faith, didn't want her to be part of this area of my life. Besides, I told myself, Mum and Dad would probably much prefer the chance to get to know Adam on their own, without me getting in the way. And a night off from the tension at home sounded like bliss.

Still, I knew I should be there. And I was absolutely going to tell Mr Hughes no. Right up until I saw Connor's face.

He was staring at the ceiling, like he was praying to heaven that I'd say no. But when I looked closer, I realized that wasn't quite it. He looked ... uncertain? Like he didn't know whether he wanted me there or not.

"Connor?" I asked. "What do you think?"

He looked down at me and I stared back. If he really didn't want me there, he was going to have to tell me – and his stepdad – why.

"We do need to meet," he said, like he was the one who'd been nagging about it. "So … you should come."

"OK, then. In that case, I'd love to," I told Mr Hughes with a smile. Faith and Adam could have quality time with Mum and Dad, and I'd get to meet Adam some other time. It would be fine.

"Great! That's all settled then. I'll let you both get back to work." He disappeared on to the stage, and I heard him call together the cast for Act One.

Connor headed off backstage again without another glance in my direction. I pulled my phone from its new case and texted Mum to let her know the change of plan. Then, before she could possibly read it and respond, I switched off my phone. I could always claim I ran out of battery later, or something.

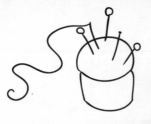

BOOK BAG

What you need:

2 rectangles of thick fabric, 45 x 35cm
2 strips of cotton webbing in a complementary
colour, 60cm long

What to do:

1. *Using a sewing machine, stitch a zigzag stitch around all the edges of your fabric. If you're sewing by hand, use pinking shears to stop the fabric fraying.*
2. *Hem the tops of both your rectangles.*
3. *Pin your webbing in place on the wrong side of your fabric, against the hem, to make handles, with 2.5cm of webbing overlapping the fabric.*
4. *Stitch the handles in place by sewing a rectangle over each end of the webbing and fabric, then stitching a cross in the middle of that rectangle.*
5. *Pin your two fabric rectangles together, right sides facing, and stitch around the three unhemmed sides.*
6. *Turn your bag the right way out and fill with books!*

Rehearsal ran late and it was pitch black and freezing cold by the time we reached Mr Hughes's front door.

The door opened, and light and warmth flooded out into the winter night. Mr Hughes paused, then turned to me with a finger on his lips. I frowned.

I glanced back at Connor, who just raised his eyebrows at me. Trying to tiptoe quietly, I followed Mr Hughes into the hallway, just as a woman with short, fair hair and tired eyes came down the stairs. She only trod on the outer parts of the steps, I noticed, like she was trying to avoid creaking floorboards.

There was definitely something I was missing here.

"Is she asleep?" Mr Hughes whispered, and the woman nodded. "Fantastic."

Together, we all crept through to the kitchen. Mr Hughes shut the door, while his wife switched on a baby monitor, and suddenly everything made sense.

"Sorry about that," Mrs Hughes said, talking at

a normal volume. She had a nice smile, I thought. "Lily is just impossible if she doesn't have quiet to get to sleep. Once she's down, she'll sleep through practically anything, though. It's just the first half hour that's a nightmare!"

"I didn't know you had a new baby," I said, smiling at Mr Hughes. "That's brilliant. Congratulations!" Even though Mrs Hughes had said that Lily slept through most things, I kept my voice a little lower than usual. I had already gatecrashed dinner; the last thing I wanted was to wake the baby.

"She's nearly six months," Mr Hughes said, with a proud new-father grin. "Connor didn't tell you?"

We all looked at Connor, who just shrugged. "It didn't come up."

"Oh, honestly." Mrs Hughes wrapped an arm around her son's shoulders. "Boys are hopeless, aren't they? He didn't even tell me he was bringing home a new girlfriend for dinner…"

Connor's face was a picture. Mr Hughes winced. "Ah, actually, sorry, that's my fault. Lizzie, this is Grace. She's organizing the costumes and props for the play, and she and Connor needed time to discuss the arrangements, so I suggested they do it here. Is that OK?"

Mrs Hughes shrugged. "Hey, it's your turn to

cook. If you want to feed one more, that's entirely up to you." She grinned at me. "I'm just pleased that Connor is making friends at his new school. Although I suppose a new girlfriend was a bit much to hope for." She gave her son a sad look, and I wondered what else I was missing here. New girlfriend implied an old girlfriend. What had happened to her?

I had so many questions about Connor. And I was in just the right place to get them answered.

Mr Hughes pulled on an apron from the back of the kitchen door. "Chilli OK, Grace?

"Sounds fantastic." Lunch was a long time ago, and I was starving. I turned to Connor. "Do you want to talk about the costumes now or after dinner?"

"Oh, do it after," Mrs Hughes said. "Dinner won't be long, and one of us will run you home later, Grace. You have told your parents where you are, though? I know you kids are nearly seventeen, but we do worry, you know. I'm just so pleased to have both my babies under one roof at last." She squeezed Connor's arm as she said that, and he pulled away.

"I've texted Mum and told her," I promised. And it was the complete truth. I just hadn't waited for her to object to it, that was all.

Dinner was delicious and afterwards, with the table clear and wiped down, Mr Hughes asked,

"Do you two want to work here or in the lounge?"

"Here's fine," I said. "I have a lot of papers to spread out."

"Plus easier access to coffee," Mrs Hughes said. "Connor always needs coffee when he's working on a show. I have to switch the whole house to decaf to make sure he ever sleeps."

She kissed him on the head and walked over to the baby monitor. She was about to unplug it when Connor said, "Leave that in here, Mum. I'll go up if she needs anything."

Mrs Hughes beamed. "Are you sure?"

Connor raised his eyebrows again. It seemed to be his default means of communication. "Sure. Go on, your programme is about to start."

"Lizzie and I are utterly addicted to this new police drama," Mr Hughes explained. "Come on, love. Let's leave these two to it."

They shut the door behind them and, suddenly, it was just me and Connor, staring at each other across the kitchen table.

Connor broke eye contact first and headed over to the sink to fill the kettle. Then, while it was boiling, he turned to me and said, "Well, come on, then. Let's see what you've got."

I pulled my files of notes, along with Miss

Cotterill's homework reading, from the book bag I'd made at home, using a cute Russian doll fabric I'd found, practising on Mum's sewing machine while she was still at work. "OK, well, going through the costume cupboard I've found quite a few things we can use as they are. Izzy and Miss Cotterill have agreed to help me alter and embellish a few other items to make them suit." I pushed the costume list across the table towards him and let him have a read before I carried on. "As you can see, the areas we're really struggling with are military uniforms for the guys, and wedding dresses for the last scene. I've been sourcing a few patterns for aprons for the maids and so on, in case we end up making the simpler costumes ourselves."

Connor's gaze flicked up to meet mine. "And you think you're good enough at sewing to do that?"

"No," I answered honestly. "Not yet. I'm still at bags and scarves level." I held up my bag as evidence. "But Izzy is. And I think with the right help we *can* do it. We don't have time to make costumes for the whole cast, so I think we need to focus on the items that will make the biggest impact. If they're really special, we might be able to get away with using what we've already got for the smaller parts."

"Sounds like you've got it all under control."

Connor dropped the list back on to the table. "So what do you need my help for?"

Standing, I followed him back across the kitchen as the kettle finished boiling. "I need you to help me check I haven't missed anything. And I'm worried about the military uniforms. And the props. And, well, most of it actually. And I'd love a coffee, thanks," I added, as he took only one mug down from the shelf.

With a sigh, he grabbed another mug. "You really are taking this seriously, aren't you?"

"Of course I am. It's important." Yeah, maybe it wasn't a starring role or anything, but that didn't mean it didn't *matter*.

"Well, yeah. *I* know that. I just didn't realize you did. Not until that day at the bakery."

"Then you weren't paying much attention." Too busy jumping to conclusions about me.

"Trust me, I was paying attention." He turned to look at me and suddenly he was incredibly close. And what did that mean anyway? I shuffled back a few steps along the kitchen counter.

"Sugar? Milk?"

It took me a moment to remember the coffee. "Um, just milk. Thanks."

Connor carried the two mugs over to the table

and I followed, sitting in the same seat as before. He, however, moved to sit next to me.

"Well, since we're doing this properly, we need to get on with it." He tugged my notes towards him and started reading through them. "First thing we need is a props list, right?"

"That would help," I agreed. "I know Mr Hughes has been talking about items as they've come up during rehearsals, but I've mostly been off helping with the costumes, so I haven't got a clear idea of what we need."

"Fortunately for us, I do," Connor said.

"You've done this a lot, haven't you? Worked backstage, I mean. You said you were in a youth theatre, where you used to live?"

Connor nodded. "Yeah. I was supposed to move up to be stage manager there for our summer show, before we left."

"Is that what you want to do?" I asked. "When you leave school. Work in the theatre?"

He opened his mouth to reply but, before he could speak, a small cry came from the baby monitor. We both froze, waiting in the silence that followed. Then Lily cried again, and Connor's shoulders dropped. "Hang on a min. She usually settles pretty quickly for me, and I need to fetch my script from my school bag anyway. I left it in the hall."

Alone in the kitchen, I tried to read through my notes again, but soon got distracted by Connor's voice through the baby monitor.

"Shh, Lils. Come on, now, go back to sleep for your big brother." The words were whispered, just a murmur, but they echoed through the empty kitchen. Then I heard him sigh and start to sing softly.

"*Hush little Lily, don't you cry. Connor's going to sing you a lullaby.*"

I smiled to myself, my cheek resting on my hand as I leaned closer to listen.

"*So you just close those little eyes, and dream of … uh … sheep and apple pies.*"

I bit the inside of my cheek to keep from laughing. Silly made-up lyrics or not, Connor was incredibly cute with his little sister.

"Did I hear Lily?" Mrs Hughes asked from the kitchen doorway, and I jerked round with a start.

"Um, yeah. But don't worry, Connor's gone upstairs."

Mrs Hughes smiled. "He's so good with her. And she absolutely adores him. I was worried, when she was born… I mean, the age gap is so huge. But it's all worked out incredibly well so far." Her gaze met mine. "And I really am very glad to see he's making friends at school. It was so hard for him, having to move again. I try to get him to talk to me about how he's feeling, but you know Connor. He keeps his emotions to himself and tries to deal with everything alone." She sighed, and I wondered if I was supposed to say something. But what? Actually, no, I don't really know Connor at all? We weren't really friends, although sometimes it felt like we might be inching towards something more. "Anyway. It means a lot to me that he's happy here."

"I'm sure."

I stared at the baby monitor, listening to Connor humming softer and softer, long after his mum had gone back to the other room. Then I heard a rustle and the click of a closing door, which snapped me out of my daze.

Connor came back down a few moments later, and I pretended that I hadn't heard him comforting Lily. Somehow I knew that would just make him more defensive. Like his mum had said, Connor kept his thoughts and feelings to himself. If I was going to be his friend, the last thing I needed was anything that made him build up more walls between us.

Instead, I made notes of props we needed as he flicked through the script, a page at a time, reading the scrawled notes in the margins that indicated movements, lighting, scenery and costume changes and, most importantly, the props required for each scene.

By the time we'd made it through the whole play, it was getting late. Soon, I'd have to turn my phone back on and face my mother's wrath.

Closing the script with a sigh, Connor pulled out his timetable, still covered in my pink pen. "OK. When do you want to do this again? I've got a few thoughts about the military uniforms, but I need to talk to Guy about them first." It was funny, hearing him call Mr Hughes Guy, but I supposed he must, all the time, at home.

"Let me go through the costume cupboard again on Monday, now I know what props we need. There might be some stuff hidden in the boxes at the back."

"Tuesday, then? We're both free first thing, by the look of it."

"Sounds good."

"I'll ask Guy if he'll run you home, if you like."

"That would be great." I paused, not sure how my next comment would go down. But I was leaving in a moment anyway, right? "You know, you have a really nice family, Connor." He huffed a sort of "if you say so" sound. "You have!"

"Yeah, maybe. Mum's OK. Still kind of

overwhelmed about having me living here, I think."

And there was my in. "Why did you move here, anyway?"

I didn't think he'd tell me. I'm not sure he thought he would, either. But after a moment, he said, "I stayed with my dad, after the divorce. He got remarried a year later, and my new stepmum had twin boys already, six years younger than me."

"Got a bit crowded then, huh?"

"Nah, it was OK. I got on well with them. We were a family."

"So, what happened, then?"

He looked away. "My dad got offered a great job in New York this summer. It was perfect timing for the twins – they were about to start secondary school."

"But you were about to start your A levels."

"Yeah. Luckily, it was easy enough for them to ship me back off to Mum and Guy. I moved in about two weeks before Lily was born."

I winced. There I was, miserable about having an extra sister in the house, when Connor had been practically kicked out of his own home.

"I don't know why I told you that."

"Because I pestered." I gave him a tentative smile. "If it helps at all… I understand about shifting families."

"Yeah? How? Your parents are still married, aren't they?"

I nodded. "They are. But … I kind of got a new sister this summer, too. Only mine's six years older than me."

Connor stared at me. "How the hell did that work?"

I grinned, but before I could answer, Mr Hughes opened the door. "Are you two nearly done? It's getting late. I better take Grace home."

"We're ready," I said, gathering my notes back together to shove into my homemade bag. "I'll fill you in on that last bit on Tuesday morning, Connor."

I liked the idea that he'd have a whole weekend to contemplate how, whatever he thought, he didn't know everything about me, after all.

Mr Hughes dropped me at the end of my drive and I hopped out, only slowing when I realized that Faith's car wasn't there. I must have missed them completely. Mum was not going to be happy.

I let myself into the house, turning to wave and let Mr Hughes know it was OK to leave now. By the time I turned back, Mum and Dad were both standing in front of me, glowering.

"Hi," I said, attempting a smile. "Sorry I'm

late, only there was this emergency Drama Club meeting... Did you get my text?"

Silence.

Without a word, Mum turned and walked away up the stairs, leaving me staring after her. Only after we heard the bedroom door click closed did Dad speak.

"In the lounge, please."

I did as I was told, my stomach feeling full of stones as I waited for him to follow me. I perched on the edge of the armchair and watched as Dad closed the door and sat on the sofa.

"Tonight meant a lot to your mother. And to me, and Faith and Adam, but particularly to Mum." His voice was perfectly calm, but I could hear the disappointment running through it. It felt worse than the anger I'd expected. "You know what we expect from you, Grace, as a member of this family. As our daughter. And you let us down."

"I know. I'm sorry." I stared down at my hands. "But the meeting really was important..."

"Your family are important. Faith is part of that family, and Adam will be soon. They're part of our lives now. And I know that's been hard for you to accept, Grace, but we've tried to make allowances, tried to let you adjust—"

"Really? How?" My gaze shot up to meet his. "By having her here, in my house, all the time? Were you just hoping that if she spent enough time here I'd simply forget it used to be just us?"

Dad sighed, and I knew he wasn't going to see my point of view. "This has been hard for all of us, you know."

"You think?" I asked. "Because it seems to me that everyone else is as happy as anything about the situation."

"Of course we're happy to have Faith back in our lives!" Dad yelled. Then he rubbed a hand across his forehead, a sure sign he was trying to keep a hold on his temper. "But that doesn't mean it's not hard. For Faith most of all. She's trying to adjust to a whole new family, remember? And your mum … she's still coming to terms with all the years we missed – that we gave up. So, yes, she wants to keep Faith close. She wants both her girls here with her."

"And what do you want?" I asked. Living up to what my dad wanted had been the most important thing in my life, once. These days, I barely even knew what he expected from me, other than to magically be OK with all the changes in our family.

"Honestly?" Dad sighed again. "I want you and Faith to be friends. Sisters even. I want you to make an effort to get to know her. Is that so much to ask?"

The sound of Connor singing a lullaby to Lily echoed inside my brain, and guilt swamped over me. "No, I suppose not." Except it felt like *everything.* It wasn't so easy to just suddenly pretend this stranger was my sister.

"Good." He got to his feet. "I'm going up to your mother. We won't mention this again. But Grace … next time—"

"I'll be here," I promised.

"Thank you." He paused at the door. "Oh, by the way, your mum and Faith left something for you to look at on the coffee table."

For me? As soon as he was gone, I dived forward to see what he was talking about. And there, just waiting for me, was the most hideous bridesmaid's dress pattern I'd ever seen.

Just when I thought I'd escaped without punishment, too. Perfect.

"Who are you waiting for?" Lottie asked, following my gaze as it flicked to the common-room door for the hundredth time.

"Connor. We were supposed to meet first thing to talk costumes. He's late."

"So… You and Connor. What's going on there?" Lottie turned in her chair towards me, tucking her feet up under her and putting on her best listening face. I groaned inwardly. "I mean, you were both chatting away when we met at the bakery at half-term. And Yasmin said you had dinner at his house on Friday…"

"A working dinner. For the play. Not a … whatever you think it is dinner."

"Are you sure? I mean, he's cute as hell, Grace. I know he's not your usual type…"

"Meaning?" Lottie thought I had a type?

"He's not, well, I don't know. One of the in-crowd, or whatever. But he seems nice."

"He's sarcastic and rude." But I was smiling as I said it.

"A match made in heaven, then," Lottie said, putting her hands up and laughing when I tried to bat her with my history textbook. "But really, Grace. Ash was telling Yasmin that you're the only girl Connor's really spoken to since he started here. And considering that Ash is pretty much the only other friend he's made… I think that makes you kind of special."

Maybe. But I couldn't let on that I cared about that until I was sure. The last thing I needed was everyone thinking I was crazy for a guy who wouldn't give me the time of day.

"You're wrong. He talks to me because of the play. That's it. Hell, he doesn't even show up to do that, most of the time."

Which was, of course, the exact moment the common-room door flew open and Connor O'Neil raced in.

"You're late," I said, getting to my feet as he reached us.

"Yeah, sorry. Lily was up a lot last night, keeping us all awake, and I pressed snooze a few too many times when my alarm went off."

I thought back to the first day I met Connor and missed the auditions and felt some sympathy. "Yeah, OK. It happens. Come on, let's grab that table over there."

Ignoring Lottie's smile, I dragged a chair over to the table and pulled my files out of my Russian-doll bag. They were starting to look a bit dog-eared, but I figured that just showed Connor I'd been working hard.

"So, about the military costumes," Connor said, pulling over his own chair and sitting a little bit closer than I'd expected him to. "I talked to Guy, and we might have an idea."

"Yeah? Great!" The uniforms had been my biggest headache for weeks. I'd looked at hiring them, but it would swallow up almost the entire costume budget, so I was keeping that as a last resort.

"Guy knows someone who runs a tiny theatre in London, and they have a few that we could borrow, for free. We won't be able to adjust them, and we'd need to go and pick them up nearer the time, but it might solve our problem."

"That would be perfect, thank you!" I scribbled a note to myself on my costume list. "Can you find out when I can go and get them?"

"Sure. So, in return, are you going to tell me the deal with your surprise sister?" He leaned back in his chair, hands behind his head.

"That's been bothering you this weekend, huh?" Which was, of course, exactly what I'd intended.

"Barely thought about it," Connor said, but I was pretty sure he was lying. "It's just that you're *such* an only child…"

"Why do people keep saying that? Besides, so were you until your dad got remarried."

"True. And now I have Lily, too. But we're not talking about me. I've already told you all my family dramas. I want to hear about yours."

I sighed and tucked my pen back inside my file.

"Fine. But it's not that dramatic, really. It just turned out that my parents had a baby back when they were, like, our age, and gave her up for adoption. This summer, she found us. That's all."

"That's a pretty big 'all'." Connor pointed out.

"Yeah, well. Life happens, right?" To my amazement, I actually sounded nonchalant about the whole thing. Maybe I was coming to terms with having my life turned upside down. "She's getting married next summer and she wants us to be part of the wedding. I get to wear the most hideous bridesmaid's dress in the history of the world."

Mum had showed me the pattern again over the weekend, along with the shiny lemon yellow fabric they'd chosen. It hadn't improved since I first saw it.

"Is she nice?" Connor asked. "Your sister, I mean?"

I bit my lip as I thought about it. The truth was, I had no idea. I'd avoided spending any more time with her than I had to, and even when we were in the same room it was always Mum and Faith on one side, me on the other. I had absolutely no idea what she was like, away from our parents.

"I guess so," I told Connor, not wanting to own up to my complete sisterly ignorance. "It's just still … weird."

"Yeah, I get that. Guy – Mr Hughes – he's great. He makes my mum happy, he's crazy about Lily, he's even trying to help me fit in here."

"By inviting me to dinner."

"Yeah. And the play and everything. He figured out pretty quickly how much I hated being dragged away from my old theatre. But the point is, I've still only known him for a year or so, and only properly since I moved in this summer. We're family, but we're still getting to know each other. And that's hard."

I gazed across the table at Connor and he met my eyes. This was the most he'd ever told me about himself.

He smiled and glanced away. I wondered if he was thinking the same thing that I was – that we had more in common than either of us could have first imagined.

Connor turned his attention back to the lists in front of us and our sharing moment was over. "How did you get on with sorting through the props yesterday?"

"OK. I found a few bits. Others we'll need to buy, borrow or steal as usual." A thought occurred to me. Now we were, well, bonding – or at least talking – Connor could totally help out more with this. "Actually, if you can be spared from rehearsals, we can go through them in the hall this afternoon.

Mr Hughes is just running small groups and chorus stuff anyway, to give us a chance to measure other cast members for their costumes. Miss Cotterill and Izzy are staying on after school especially. You can check out the props and costumes we already have then."

"OK," Connor said, fast enough to surprise me. "I'll see you there."

"Great." We stared at each other for another awkward moment, as if not entirely sure how to say goodbye. Then, with a nod, Connor gathered up his stuff and headed out, and Lottie slid into his empty chair.

"Seriously, you're telling me there's nothing going on between you two?" she asked.

I shook my head. "Just play stuff, like I said."

"Then you aren't paying attention." Lottie grinned. "I never thought I'd see the day when Grace Stewart didn't notice that a boy fancied her."

"You're delusional." I shoved my notes back into my file, while secretly wishing Lottie was right. "We just ... hate each other less these days. And we, well, found some common ground. That's all."

For now, at least. But it had taken us so long to move this far, I could be at uni before we got it together enough to take it any further.

"If you say so," Lottie said. But she was still grinning.

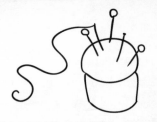

CHRISTMAS STOCKING

What you need:

Newspaper and a pen
Red felt
White or patterned felt
Red and white ribbon (optional)

What to do:

1. Draw a stocking shape of the size you want on the newspaper and cut out.

2. Fold your red felt in half and pin the stocking pattern to it.

3. Cut around the stocking shape to give you two identical felt pieces.

4. Draw a star shape on the newspaper, pin to the white or patterned felt and cut out.

5. Pin the star to the middle of the front stocking piece and, using an embroidery needle and three strands of embroidery thread, sew all the way around it using blanket stitch or whip stitch, removing the pins as you go.

6. Pin the stocking pieces together with the right sides facing outwards and tack around the sides and bottom with a

loose running stitch in white cotton thread, leaving the top
of the stocking open. Remove the pins.

7. Using an embroidery needle and three strands of
embroidery thread, sew all the way around the sides and
bottom of your stocking using blanket stitch. Remove the
tacking stitch and your stocking is finished.

8. If you like, you could sew a loop of ribbon to the top
corner of your stocking so you can hang it up.

"You know, I was so surprised when I got the part," Violet said, talking down at me from the chair she stood on, ignoring Miss Cotterill whipping the tape measure around her taking measurements.

It was our last rehearsal before the Christmas holidays, and we finally seemed to be getting somewhere with the costumes.

"I mean, everyone thought that you were a sure thing to play Beatrice," Violet went on. "I heard you even auditioned for the part after everyone else, as a special favour from Mr Hughes. I couldn't believe he still picked me! But he did!"

Across the hall, Connor was watching me. Well, he was pretending to be sorting through props, but I knew what he was really doing. He was waiting to see how I was going to react to Violet's total lack of empathy. And her inability to understand how things had actually happened.

I wanted to correct her. Wanted even to point

out how much more I was needed to take care of the costumes. But everything I thought of to say sounded too much like "I'm still bitter you got the role, and I think I should play Beatrice". And that wasn't the vibe I was going for at all, even if it was true. Not when Connor finally seemed to believe I wasn't all about the spotlight.

So instead I wrote down the measurements Miss Cotterill called out to me, and watched carefully while she explained to me how and why she was taking each one. I knew I'd be on my own doing this soon enough.

"Right, Violet, you go and slip this on and we'll see how it fits." Miss Cotterill handed her the dress we'd found for Beatrice to wear in the opening scenes. Violet hopped down from her stool and headed out to the toilets to change.

Maybe I could "accidentally" stab her with a pin while we were fitting the dress…

"You look like you're contemplating pain and torture," Izzy said as she wandered past, arms full of material.

"Only minor torture," I assured her. "And well deserved."

"Fair enough. Where do you want these?"

I squinted. "What are they?"

187

"Aprons for the maids," Izzy said. "Sewn by my own fair hands."

"Brilliant. Pop them over on that table. Ursula and Margaret are coming down next, I think."

Izzy laid the aprons out, then turned back to me. "So, what about the wedding dresses? I mean, I'm having fun altering and sewing sequins on the flapper dresses, but shouldn't I be sorting those, too?"

I sighed. "I know. I managed to get some netting to use to make the veils, attached to a headband or something. I'm just having a problem finding four white dresses than look more or less the same."

"I could just make them, too, you realize."

"Really?"

"Of course!" She waved a hand down over her body, showing off the dress she had changed into after school finished. It was a riot of colours, all sewn into one design. "Who do you think made this?"

I stared at the dress for another moment. "I guess we wouldn't be looking for something quite so—"

"Well, of course not!" Izzy interrupted. "They're wedding dresses. But we could find a simple pattern that suits the period and some white or ivory fabric – probably satin or silk – and a few sparkly embellishments, and I can make them up for you.

No problem."

"That would be fantastic!"

Izzy beamed at me. "Good. Then I'll raid the pattern filing cabinet in the textiles classroom after we finish here and see what we have that might suit. Otherwise I'll take to the internet and look at the sewing forums. There'll definitely be something there we can use."

"Thank you," I said. Finally, we seemed to be getting somewhere.

Violet emerged scowling, draped in a drop-waisted party dress that hung off her and trailed along the floor.

"Well, it might need some slight adjustments," Miss Cotterill said, squinting at her.

Izzy laughed. "Too right! I think the last person to wear that was the captain of the rugby team in some skit they did for a fundraiser a few years ago."

"It's the right style, though," I pointed out. "And colour and fabric."

Violet glared at me. "I'm not wearing this in front of a whole room full of people."

"Just wait and see," Miss Cotterill said breezily. "Grace and Izzy will fix it up right. It's amazing what you can do with a nice piece of fabric. Let me just grab my pins," she added, as she wandered off towards her sewing box.

Violet was still scowling. I smiled sweetly, just to annoy her.

"I know what you're doing." Violet leaned forward, her face close to mine and the words a harsh whisper.

"Oh?" I asked, refusing to back up an inch. "And what is that, exactly? In your opinion."

"You're trying to make me look ridiculous because you're jealous I got the part that you wanted." The look on her face as she folded her arms across her chest made it clear she thought it was obvious and impossible to deny.

Jealous or not, I wouldn't risk ruining the play over it. That was what Connor hadn't understood.

"You're wrong," I told her flatly. "I can understand how, in your position, you might feel that way, but quite honestly I'm more concerned with doing *my* job well than worrying about anyone else's."

Violet held out her oversized skirts. "And you call this doing your job well?"

"It's not finished yet." I just hoped the heat I could feel in my cheeks didn't show on my skin.

"Come on, Grace," Violet said. "Everyone knows you only got stuck with this job because Mr Hughes wouldn't give you the part you really wanted. No one thinks you can actually *sew* or anything. Besides, the way I heard it, your whole family is falling apart. Family crisis – wasn't that what you told Mr Hughes?"

"My family is none of your business."

"Yeah, I notice you didn't deny the rest of it, though." Violet's smug smile made me want to fight back, to slash her with a really cutting put-down. But Connor got in there first. I hadn't even noticed him coming over to join us.

"Come on, Violet. Grace is working very hard to ensure that all our costumes for the play are authentic," he said, and I stared at him in surprise. "She's the one who has done all the research and the legwork, deciding on the costumes for this production, so we need to trust her to make the best choices for everyone. You should be concentrating on making sure you know your lines, not worrying about what you'll be wearing." He smiled, which took the edge off his words. "Besides, I'm sure once Miss Cotterill, Grace and Izzy are done, you'll love it."

Violet didn't look convinced, not that I cared. Connor truly believed I was doing the job I'd volunteered for properly. He trusted me.

With a quick grin at me, Connor went back to sorting props. Miss Cotterill came back at last, so I stayed and helped her pin the dress on Violet, without stabbing her once, however tempting it was. And by the time we'd finished even Violet would have agreed it didn't look half bad – if she wasn't being a total diva. As it was, *I* knew it looked good, which was all that really mattered.

"We'll get it stitched up, then you can come and try it on again next week so we can make final adjustments," Miss Cotterill said, putting the lid back on the pin box. "Now go and get changed into the next costume, preferably without dislodging any of the pins, please."

Violet was bound to get a few pinpricks in the process, which only made me happier.

While Izzy and Miss Cotterill got to work on Hero's dress, I went to check on the props with Connor. But before I could get there, Mr Hughes bellowed out across the room.

"Grace? Connor? I need you two up here."

Connor and I shared a quick look, then dashed towards the stage.

"What's up?" I asked, as we got close. "I'm just doing fittings…"

"I know, but I need you to take on your other role for a minute, while Violet's busy. We're blocking the chorus dance for the masked-ball scene and Ash's understudy is off sick. I need you two to stand in for Ash and Violet while we do it, so I can see how it'll all look. Up you go."

I glanced back at Izzy and Miss Cotterill. I should be with them doing my real job but ... our director had given me an order. What else could I do?

Connor sat on the edge of the stage and boosted himself up, and I followed suit. I'd watched enough rehearsals of this scene to know where I needed to stand, so I moved into place, leaning against a table that would be replaced with a proper bar before the show itself.

"OK, and ... go!" Mr Hughes pressed play on the iPod and jazz music blared out. Behind us, the chorus started to dance the Charleston, almost in time, while Connor and I pretended to sip imaginary cocktails.

"And – Violet!" Mr Hughes said. "Sorry, Grace. Go."

That stung. Still, I stepped in with my first line, glad I'd memorized this scene at least. No one else was using scripts, and I'd hate to be the odd one out. "Will you not tell me who told you so?"

"No, you shall pardon me," Connor replied, speaking Ash's words.

"Nor will you not tell me who you are?" I leaned

closer, just like I'd always thought Violet should do in this scene. Despite the masks they'd wear for the ball, I'd always thought that Beatrice knew *exactly* who she was talking to, and enjoyed teasing him.

"Not now."

"That I was disdainful, and that I had my good wit out of the 'Hundred Merry Tales' – well, this was Signior Benedick that said so."

Beatrice wouldn't smile here, so I couldn't, even though I wanted to. Only a few weeks ago, if someone had said that I was disdainful I'd have known it had to be Connor. But now...

"OK, stop," Mr Hughes called. "That looks fine. Skip ahead to where Beatrice and Benedick join the dance."

Connor glared at his stepfather but he didn't argue. At least we didn't have to Charleston. At this point, the music turned smoother, and everyone took their partners for a slow dance, while at the side of the stage Don John told lies to Claudio.

Connor's hand came round to rest at my waist, as his other wrapped around my fingers. The steps they'd decided on for this bit were simple, and my feet followed Connor's lead without question. Which was just as well. All I could focus on was the warmth where he touched me, and how his eyes looked darker this close.

Licking my lips, I remembered what I'd wanted to say to him, before we were called to the stage.

"Thanks," I whispered, my eyes downcast. "For, you know, sticking up for me with Violet."

Connor shook his head a fraction. "Just telling the truth."

"You didn't have to, though." I glanced up again and caught him watching me, and suddenly I couldn't look away. What was it about his eyes that dragged me in? "Why did you?"

"I don't know," he answered, looking as baffled by all this as I was.

"It was almost like you, I don't know ... care."

"Maybe I do." He gave me a lopsided smile. "God knows why."

"Maybe we're becoming friends," I suggested, even though my heart was pounding.

"Maybe we are, princess," Connor said, and somehow it didn't sound like an insult this time. But as he spoke, I stumbled, pressing up against him for a moment until I could step back. My whole body tingled, and I saw Connor's throat bob as he swallowed. "Friends."

I smiled, slow and real. "Friends."

Friends would be good. But I knew there was

something much more between Connor O'Neil and me.

I couldn't wait to find out what it was.

Christmas was officially weird.

First off, it felt strange to have Christmas Day, just Mum, Dad and me, even though that was how we'd always had it before. Now there was an extra, unopened stack of presents under the tree, because Faith and Adam were spending the day with Adam's family.

Then, even weirder, we had a *second* Christmas on Boxing Day. Since it was my first time meeting Adam, and only Mum and Dad's second, it was a really big deal. More turkey, more presents, more everything. Dad even taped the Queen's speech to watch again at three o'clock, which took it beyond weird and into the realm of plain bizarre.

After the second watching of the speech, I escaped to my room for a little while to take an emergency phone call from Jasper.

"This is just weird," he said, the moment I answered.

"You should try being here. What's happened?"

"Nothing, really. I've only been here a couple of hours." I could hear his teeth chattering as he spoke.

"And you're, what, hiding out in the garden already?"

"Pretty much."

"Did Ella like her stocking?"

"She did," Jasper said, but I could hear a "but" coming.

"But?"

He sighed. "I don't know. I guess I just thought she'd be more excited about it."

"Things still feeling a bit distant?"

"Very. I don't know, Grace. I don't know what's going to happen."

"I'm sorry."

"Not your fault. Anyway. How was Christmas Take Two?"

"Also weird. But at least we now know that Adam officially exists. I finally got to meet him – he seems OK." I launched into a description of our bizarre Groundhog-Day Christmas that made Jasper laugh, at least, until he said he had to go back in for dinner. I hung up and headed back out to face the family, wondering if Jasper and Ella would still even be a couple by the time we got back to school. And also, despite myself, wondering what Connor was doing. It had been almost a week since I'd seen him, and I couldn't shake the irrational fear that if he went too long without me reminding him that I wasn't the girl he thought I was when we first met, he might forget. I didn't want to go back to the sniping and the sarcasm, just when we seemed to be getting somewhere.

I spent the rest of the holidays practising my sewing, using Mum's sewing machine while she was out at work or at some wedding fair or another with Faith. I finally finished the jeans bag I'd wanted to make, and I sewed a couple more scarves for belated Christmas gifts. I even took out Grandma's patchwork a couple of times, and tried to read up a bit on the internet about what to do next with it. I sewed a few patches together, but I barely made a dent in the pile. It was a huge project. It would have to wait until I had more time.

At New Year, I talked Mum and Dad into letting me have some friends round while they were out at some fancy dinner thing. After my Bake-Off celebration back before Easter, I was officially banned from ever having parties again, but I convinced them that this would be a much smaller get together. We could have all gone out into town, or found a party somewhere else, but Jasper said he was broke after Christmas, and Mac and Lottie were working from five that morning and, even with New Year's Day off, wanted something a bit quieter.

Since I was providing the venue, I let the others pick up food, entertainment and drinks. Now Mac had his own car and looked closer to twenty than his actual age of seventeen, I didn't imagine they'd have any problems.

I spent a whole day after I invited the others wondering if I should invite Connor, too. Eventually, on New Year's Eve during the day, I plucked up the courage, telling myself that he was new in town, Ash was his best friend, and it was a nice thing to do. Even if I wasn't completely sure, it would be wrong to leave him out. Right?

So I texted him.

Hey, we're doing New Year at my house. Ash is coming with Yasmin, obvs, plus Mac, Lottie, Jasper. You want to come? Starts at 7.

Three hours later, I got a response.

Sorry, got plans. But I'll try and stop by later if I can.

Which meant one of two things, I figured. One, he had gone back to thinking I was some diva he wouldn't spend New Year with if you paid him, even if it meant he had to spend it alone. Two, he actually had plans, which meant he had other friends who weren't us. And if it was the second option ... would he really run out on them to come and see me?

I was still arguing with myself about the likelihood when Lottie, Mac, Jasper, Yasmin and Ash all appeared on my doorstep with bags of food and DVDs. Mac's bag had the very distinctive clink of bottles in it, which was just as well as I'd also promised Mum and Dad I wouldn't raid the drinks cabinet this time.

As I grinned and let them in, I decided to forget all about Connor and the play for one night, and just enjoy being with my friends. If he showed up, great. If not, I wouldn't let it ruin my night.

Leaving Ash and Yasmin in the lounge, debating which film we should watch, I wandered through to the kitchen where Lottie and Mac were already kissing instead of making garlic bread like they'd *said* they were doing. I glanced around and found Jasper slumped on a kitchen stool watching them. From the look on his face, his Christmas visit to see Ella hadn't improved after he'd called me.

I yanked over another stool and boosted myself up to sit next to him. "So? What happened?"

"We did the present thing. I met her new friends, who all seem OK. Her mum tried to make sure we were never left alone. The usual." Jasper shrugged.

"We talked a *lot*."

He didn't make it sound like that was a good thing.

"And?"

"And we decided that the long-distance thing is too hard right now. We both have exams and new friendships and stuff going on … so we're going to try being friends instead. See how that goes."

"I'm sorry."

"Yeah. It is what it is, I guess." He jumped down from his stool. "Come on. I need a drink. Where did Mac put the beers?"

By eleven, I'd given up any hope of Connor joining us. But then, ten minutes before midnight, in the middle of the last chase scene of our second movie, the doorbell rang.

I bounced off the sofa before anyone else had the chance, earning myself a grumble from Jasper who'd spilled his drink when I jumped up. I didn't care. All of a sudden, my heart was pounding from more than too much sugar and movie car chases.

When I opened the door, Connor stood there, his face a little red. "Hey. You coming in?"

"Actually, princess," he said, out of breath, "you're coming out."

201

"Am I now?" I said, but I was already reaching for my scarf and coat from the rack behind the door.

Connor held out his hand and I took it, stepping on to the porch with him. I flicked the door on the latch behind me.

"It's nearly midnight," I said. His hand felt so warm in mine, and so right. Like it had when we were dancing.

"Exactly. I want to share my favourite part of New Year's Eve with you." I shivered, and Connor pulled me towards him, my back resting against his chest as he leaned against the brick pillar again, his arms wrapped around my waist. "Watch."

It felt a bit like a dream in that weird, slightly fuzzy, not quite making sense way. Why would Connor show up at midnight on New Year's Eve and make me stand outside in the cold? Maybe I'd actually fallen asleep on the sofa with Jasper. That made more sense.

But then I heard chanting from inside, my friends counting down to midnight, and people started spilling out from the house across the way.

"Five," Connor whispered in my ear. "Four. Three. Two. One…"

His words were swallowed up by a sudden explosion, followed by flashes of light, cracks and bangs and sparkles, as what seemed like every house in the neighbourhood but mine set off fireworks at exactly the same time.

"Happy New Year," I murmured, captivated by the display in the sky. So many colours, so many sounds. Each bang was followed by a cascade of silver lights, like sequins falling from the sky.

"I'm sorry I couldn't get here earlier," Connor said, as we watched. "I had to run from the station just to make it here in time for midnight."

I smiled at him over my shoulder. "You were here for the important bit. This is really your favourite part?"

"Yeah." He grinned back, and for a moment, I thought he might kiss me. But then his gaze darted away from mine to something over my shoulder. "Look."

He pointed up at the sky, and I followed his finger.

"What are they?" I stared at the flock of slow-moving lights, drifting through the sky. "Are they sky lanterns?"

Connor nodded. "Yeah. I've never seen so many of them at once before."

"Me, neither." Watching them float up to the heavens, I could only think about how beautiful it all looked, and what a perfect moment this was.

Finally they faded away into the night, and I turned to face Connor again, not sure what I wanted to say, but knowing I had to do something. His hands stayed loosely linked around my waist, holding me close, and I smiled up into his pale blue eyes.

"Connor..." I started, but before I could get any further, his lips were on mine, firm but soft and sweet, and it didn't matter that I couldn't find the words.

When the kiss ended and he pulled away, he murmured, "Happy New Year, Grace."

Behind us the front door flew open, and Mac's face appeared. "Are you guys done kissing? Lottie wants hot chocolate, and I can't find any."

I buried my head against Connor's chest to hide my blushing cheeks.

"We're coming in," Connor said. "I make the best hot chocolate ever."

He wasn't lying. He found the cocoa powder and marshmallows left over from one of our baking sessions, grabbed the milk and some spray cream from the fridge and pulled out a saucepan. Mac produced a bottle of whisky to give them a little extra kick.

"Where did you learn to make such good hot chocolate?" I asked, perched on a kitchen stool to watch him.

"At my old theatre." He stirred in the milk. "Whenever we had a late rehearsal, someone would end up making hot chocolate."

"It's a good talent to have." I watched as he poured out the chocolate into mugs, then topped them with cream and marshmallows. "Come and get it," I yelled to the others.

They did, thanking Connor then heading back through to the comfy sofas in the lounge.

"So," I said, once we were alone again. "Um…" I ran out of words.

"You OK?" Connor leaned against the counter beside me, too close for friends.

"Yeah. Just … surprised I guess."

"That I kissed you?"

"That you're here at all." I took a sip of my hot chocolate so I didn't have to look into his pale, watchful eyes. "It's not all that long ago, you hated me."

"I didn't hate you."

"You thought I was a drama queen who would wreck your play."

"Well … yeah. I did think that." He gave me an apologetic half smile.

205

"So what changed?"

"You did." With a sigh, Connor moved away and boosted himself up on to his own stool. "Here's the thing. This play matters to me. A lot."

"I got that." I picked a marshmallow off the top of his mug. "Why?"

"Because … this is what I want to do with my life. I want a career in the theatre. And back when I was living with Dad, I was working towards that. I had the school Drama Club and the youth theatre, but I'd also lined up some part-time work at the main theatre where we rehearsed, too. Learning the ropes, shadowing the ASMs – all while doing the boring admin work no one else wanted to do."

"And then you had to move." No wonder he'd been so grumpy at the start of term.

"Yeah." He grabbed a spoon and used it to stir the cream into his hot chocolate. "When I moved here, Guy tried to make it up to me. He set me up as stage manager for this show and … you know the theatre that's lending us the uniforms? Well, his mate there is interested in hiring me for the summer to stage manage their youth theatre summer production. He's coming to watch our show before he makes a decision."

"Which is why it needs to be good." Suddenly a lot of things were starting to make sense.

"It needs to be great," he corrected me. "Seamless. If I get that job, it's a real leg up on my application for drama school, after A levels."

"And you were worried that I would ruin it for you?" I gave him a half smile to show him that I wasn't really cross. Much.

"I was worried that you cared more about being a star than what was best for the show." Reaching out, he took my hand. "I think I know better now."

"I hope so." But that uncomfortable feeling was back, worming its way up through my stomach. I did want what was best for the play. I just wanted the lead role, too. But it wasn't like I was actively sabotaging the show to get it or anything. I had nothing to feel guilty about.

"So, what now?" I asked.

"I guess … I'd just like to get to know you better. Start over, maybe. What do you think?"

Start over. Without him assuming I was a diva, and with me understanding why this play mattered to him so much. That could work.

"I think that sounds like just the way to start the New Year," I said, and he kissed me.

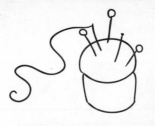

SIMPLE SKIRT

What you need:

Fabric of your choice
2cm-wide elastic

What to do:

1. Measure around your waist and the length from your waist to your knee.

2. Measure out your ironed fabric so you have a rectangle twice as long as your waist measurement, and as wide as your waist to knee measurement plus 7cm.

3. Using a sewing machine, sew a zigzag stitch all around the edges of your fabric. Or if you're sewing by hand, use pinking shears to prevent fraying.

4. Lay your fabric out in a landscape orientation and hem the bottom of your fabric.

5. Fold in half, right sides together, and sew a 1cm seam along the short side, to give you a tube of fabric with the hem at the bottom.

6. Measure your elastic and cut a piece the length of your

waist measurement plus 3cm.

7. *With your skirt still inside out, fold the top over by 3cm, to give you a fold just wider than your elastic.*

8. *Iron in place, pin and sew around the bottom of the fold, removing the pins as you go. Leave a 5cm gap at the side seam, to give you a fabric channel for your elastic.*

9. *Attach a large safety pin to one end of your elastic, and pin the other end to the fabric by the gap at the seam.*

10. *Use the safety pin to feed the elastic through the channel, making sure it doesn't twist.*

11. *Sew the two ends of the elastic together, then adjust the gathers that have formed at the top of your skirt until they are all even.*

12. *Sew closed the gap you left, so that the elastic is completely hidden.*

13. *Wear with pride!*

Back at school, everything felt grey and dark and depressing. Jasper still hadn't recovered his bounce and now his stocking was done and given, he said he had no reason to come to Sewing Club, which left me poring over dress patterns from the 1920s with Izzy.

"Jasper not coming?" she asked, the first week back at Sewing Club.

"Apparently not. He says now his stocking is done there's not a lot of point." I picked up one of the patterns. "What about this one?"

Izzy shook her head. "Too forties. So, did his girlfriend like it?"

"The stocking?" I winced. "They broke up. But not because of the stocking."

"Oh, that's a shame," Izzy said. But something about her tone didn't sound completely disappointed at the idea that Jasper was single again... "Now, this dress I could work with."

"Show me," I said, taking the pattern from her. We had bigger problems than Jasper's love life, after all.

By the time I showed up for the first play rehearsal after the break, we had the perfect design for Beatrice and Hero's party dresses. We'd decided to go for the same pattern, but made from different materials and colours. We were also going to embellish each one differently, to reflect the characters.

I skipped into the school hall with the pattern in hand, eager to show Connor ... and ask him how the rest of his Christmas holiday had been. We'd texted a few times since New Year, but that wasn't enough. I couldn't help it. I was smitten.

Except our almost-relationship seemed to have taken a backwards step over the last few days.

"Hey! Look what I've got!" I waved the pattern in his general direction the moment I spotted him.

Connor barely looked up. "I can't. In case you hadn't noticed, I need to get this stage cleared so we can start rehearsal."

I took in the stage for the first time. It was covered in chairs, boxes and tables. "What's been happening here?"

"Year Eight, apparently. They had drama last period and they ran over, so they didn't have time to clear the stage." He hefted one end of a table and started to drag it, so I dropped my bag and the pattern and dashed to help by picking up the other end. "I can do this myself."

I frowned. "Yeah. But why would you, when I'm here to help?"

"Because any minute now Guy is going to come out here and yell at me for distracting you when he needs you doing something else." Connor backed up through the curtains at the side of the stage, and I followed, still carrying the table.

"Why would he do that?"

"Because he's in a foul mood and he's taking it out on everybody else."

"Speak for yourself, Connor," Mr Hughes said, appearing in the doorway to the drama room. "Grace, I need you to help Violet with that scene in Act Two. She's having problems with some of the lines."

"Right." Of course she was. And of course I could help her. And of course she'd still end up playing the part. I was starting to think that Connor's bad mood was catching. "I'll just finish helping—"

"Now, please," Mr Hughes snapped, then disappeared back into the drama room.

I dropped my end of the table. "I see your point."

Connor gave me a tired half smile. "Yeah. Don't

212

worry, Ash will be along in a minute. He'll give me a hand."

"OK." I dashed back across the stage to grab my stuff, then headed into the drama room to face Violet and the severely bad mood of our drama teacher.

The rehearsal was a disaster from start to finish. No matter how we broke up the lines in the scene, Violet just could not get them. By the time we took it out on to the stage with the rest of the cast she'd improved, but still stumbled over a few. I stood at the side of the stage with a script to prompt, but rarely got the chance. The moment she slipped up, Mr Hughes would bellow the correct line from his chair on the hall floor. And, of course, Violet got more flustered with every mistake.

"I can't take this any more," Mr Hughes declared, after about half an hour of misery. "Take a break while I find some headache tablets. And while you're at it, try and find your ability to act again, please, people." He stalked off towards the drama room, leaving us all staring after him, speechless.

Then Violet burst into tears, and half the cast rushed to comfort her. I dropped my script on to the prompter's chair and went to find Connor.

He was propped up against the wall outside, coat huddled around him, staring out at the January rain from under the porch of the school hall. I leaned against the brickwork beside him and stared out, too, but it just looked dark, damp and miserable to me.

"So, are you going to tell me what's going on with you and Mr Hughes today?" Connor jumped at the sound of my voice and twisted towards me, blinking hard.

"Sorry?"

"Were you actually asleep with your eyes open just then?"

Connor brought his fist up to press against his eyes, first the left then the right. "Possibly. Lily's teething. I don't think any of us have slept since New Year."

Well. That explained a lot. "I'm guessing you and Mr Hughes don't do well with sleep deprivation."

"Not really, no."

I grinned. "Well, at least you're finding things you have in common."

Connor closed his eyes and laughed, far louder and longer than the joke deserved. "There is that."

"How's your mum?" I asked.

"Exhausted. We're all trying to do our share, but…"

"But that just means you're all tired and cross," I guessed.

"Yeah."

We stood together in silence, staring out at the rain. Then, a touch on my palm, that same tingle I remembered, and suddenly his fingers were wrapped around mine.

I bit my lip and listened to my heart race as I stared down at our interlinked fingers. Looking up again, I saw his serious eyes gazing down at me, and suddenly my fears were just spilling out of me. "Just then, inside… I thought that maybe you'd forgotten that you didn't hate me any more."

Connor swore softly and tugged me a little closer, wrapping his arms around my waist. "I'm sorry. Sorry that you ever thought that at all. Even from the start. I shouldn't have… It was just, when we met…"

"I didn't make a great first impression, I know." I almost laughed at the memory. For the first time, with Connor here beside me, it was just about funny.

"Yeah, well. I just … I've known a lot of drama girls."

"Known?" I raised my eyebrows at him.

"Oh, you know what I mean. There are always more girls than boys in these clubs and groups. And the girls … most of them were great. But some…"

"Were divas?"

"Were more interested in the drama than the play,

215

if you see what I mean." Connor sighed. "Everything was about whatever the latest crisis was. Who had kissed who, who'd broken up, who had what made-up issues. And they all wanted to be at the centre of it – for the glory or the popularity or whatever. They couldn't just let anyone sort out their own problems. They had to make it some big thing that involved *everyone*. On top of everything that was going on at home ... it was tiring. And it distracted them from what we were actually trying to do – put on a play."

"And you thought I was another girl like that." The thing was, a year or so ago, he'd have been completely right. But not any more. "And that having me in the play would ruin your chances of getting your summer job."

"I was wrong," Connor said, squeezing my fingers.

"Yeah. You were."

"And I'm sorry." I couldn't look away from his eyes, even as his lips nudged closer towards mine and I felt relief flooding through my veins. I hadn't kissed him in days, and I missed it.

"You two better get back in here," Ash said, sticking his head through the doors. "Mr Hughes wants to start again, and I don't think he's feeling patient."

"We're coming," Connor said. But as he turned to go through the door, I grabbed his hand to stop him.

He raised his eyebrows at me, and I realized I had to think of something to say. Probably something other than "can you just kiss me again already?"

I settled on, "You know, if it's really bad at home, if you need somewhere to do homework, or whatever, you can always come round to mine."

"You really did miss me since New Year, didn't you?" Connor joked, and I whacked his arm. Lightly.

"I'm just trying to help."

Connor squeezed my hand again. "And I appreciate it, really."

We were doing the staring into each others' eyes thing again now, and I thought for a moment that maybe we could just ignore Mr Hughes altogether and get back to the kissing again.

Then Mr Hughes bellowed, "Anyone who isn't back in this hall *right now* has to lay out all the chairs for assembly for the next *month!*"

We raced into the hall in record time.

The next day Faith stopped by the school, completely unannounced. As the lunch bell rang, I headed up to the gates with Yasmin and Ash, planning on nipping out to the corner shop to grab a sandwich

217

or something for lunch. Being allowed off the school grounds at lunchtime was one of the few perks of being in the sixth form so, even though there wasn't really anywhere to go, I liked to take advantage of it.

I'd hoped to catch up with Connor, to see if we might pick up where we'd left off at the rehearsal the day before. He'd been dragged straight home by Mr Hughes when we'd finished, and despite a text that evening saying he'd see me tomorrow, he hadn't. Yet.

We were only a few metres away from the gates when I looked up and saw Faith standing there, her hand on her handbag strap like she needed something to cling on to.

"I'll catch you up," I told Yasmin and Ash.

"Are you sure?" Yasmin asked. Then she followed my gaze. "Is that...?"

"Yeah." My chest felt tight at the sight of her. Like I was waiting for exam results. "It is."

"Right. Come on, Ash, let's go." Dragging her confused boyfriend along behind her, Yasmin marched through the school gates and towards the shop.

I took a deep breath and approached my sister. "Hi."

"Hey." She gave me an uncertain smile. "Um, sorry to just loiter like this. I was about to call you, actually. I wanted to see if you were free for lunch."

If she'd called, I might have been able to come up with an excuse – homework or rehearsals or costume stuff or something. But standing there right in front of her, my friends gone, I had nothing, except an odd feeling that every single student in the school was staring at me and this woman who looked just like me.

"Sure," I said, but I didn't move, not until she did.

She'd brought her car, so we drove a little further towards town to a cafe I'd been to a few times. Inside, we found a table and both stared at the menus for far longer than we really needed. After the waitress came and took our orders we were out of distractions.

"So…" I started.

Faith nodded, like she knew what I meant, even though I hadn't said it. "I just thought it might be nice for us to, I don't know, catch up?"

"Right."

We sat there in silence for another long moment.

"So, how's the play going?" Faith asked eventually.

"OK, I guess. We're getting there."

"You're still understudying this year?" She twisted her engagement ring round and round her finger as she spoke, her gaze darting between my face, the table and her hands. "Only, your dad said…"

"My main role this year is backstage, doing the costumes." I leaned back against the bench seat, trying to act like I didn't care about that.

"Sounds like a big job."

"Yeah, it is, actually." Not that anyone else in the play actually seemed to notice that. Except Connor, of course.

"When's the show on?" Faith asked, suddenly looking up again.

"Beginning of March. Why?"

"I'd like to come and see it, if that's OK with you."

I stared at her, baffled. "Again, why?"

"Because you're my sister." Faith shrugged. "Isn't that reason enough?"

"I guess," I said. "Just to be clear, I'm really not in it. At all."

"I know. But you've been working hard on those costumes. I'd like to see how they turn out. And, you know, support you." She gave me a small, timid smile, like she wasn't quite sure she was permitted. Like I might leave a note at the door to stop her being allowed in. "I used to do some sewing myself, actually. I made all my friends skirts one year in school, from this really great pattern… I could email it to you, if you wanted?"

"That would be … nice. Thanks." I frowned.

"I've never actually done costumes for a play before. They might be a disaster."

Faith laughed. "I'm sure they'll be fantastic. Besides, they can't be any worse than the bridesmaids' dresses, right?"

Was she joking? Or was this some sort of trap to make me admit that I hated the dress she'd chosen? "I think the dresses are going to be lovely. A really ... sunny colour, too."

Faith leaned across the table towards me and whispered, "Grace, they're hideous. The pattern is hideous and the colour is hideous. And if you never forgive me for making you wear it, I will totally understand." She sat back again and spoke in a normal voice. "One of the other bridesmaids has already asked to be demoted to get out of wearing it, you know."

She was serious. She really did hate those dresses as much as I did. "So why did you pick them, then?"

She looked up as the waitress brought our paninis. "Thanks," she said, then added, "I didn't, really," taking a mouthful of sandwich. "Sorry, I'm starving. Anyway, it was just that Mel ... sorry, Mum, was so desperate to make the dresses, and she really wanted to show off a bit, I think. I kept looking at plain dresses – you know, simple, elegant styles. But I think she thought I was

221

saying that I didn't think she could do anything more complicated. So then one day she showed up with this hideous pattern for a frilly dress and she was so excited about it... I just couldn't bring myself to tell her no."

Maybe Mum was trying as hard to live up to Faith's expectations as I always had to Dad's. "But why are they *yellow*?"

Faith groaned. "That was the florist's fault. I mentioned that I liked sunflowers a bit, and Mum gasped and said that they were her favourite flowers, too, and suddenly the florist was pulling out all these photos of a sunflower-themed wedding. Complete with yellow bridesmaids' dresses."

"You know, this is *your* wedding. I think you're allowed to say no."

Faith looked glum. "Turns out that's not really how weddings work. Anyway, the point is, I'm really sorry about the dress. But the fact that Mum is willing to make them – wants to make them, even... That means far more to me than what they look like or what colour they are."

I sighed and picked up my sandwich. "I guess I can see that."

"It must be hard for you, though," Faith said, and I tensed up, waiting to hear what she had to say next. Was she going to call me out on avoiding her?

Or, worse, try and set up some sort of regular sisterly bonding sessions.

"I think I can cope with wearing yellow," I joked, hoping she'd let it go. But she didn't.

"The day I found out that I was adopted ... my whole world changed. Everything that had been real wasn't any more. And, for a long time, that meant I didn't know quite who I was or where I belonged." She sounded like Connor had, telling me how his family had moved away without him. All matter of fact, as if by not putting any real emotion into it, it wouldn't hurt so much.

"I can't imagine that," I said, although, in a way, I could.

"My adopted parents were great, though. They made me theirs, they made home, home. But they were quite a lot older ... and when they died, I felt kind of adrift again. Until I met Adam. He's the one who convinced me to come and find you all before the wedding."

"Are you glad that he did?" I asked. Maybe we weren't all she'd hoped we'd be.

But Faith smiled, a true and honest smile. "Very. It means a lot to me to have this second chance with my first family. But I know it can't be easy for you."

"I'm fine," I lied.

Faith sighed. "Mum is trying really hard to make

up for the last twenty-two years, even though I've told her she doesn't have to. This is the way life happened, there's not a lot of point looking back now."

"I think Mum's trying to pretend it didn't," I mumbled, and Faith's smile turned sympathetic.

"Maybe she is. And I'm really sorry if it's making you feel left out, Grace."

"I don't," I said, too quickly to really be believable.

"OK." Faith studied me until I squirmed a little in my seat and shifted all of my concentration to my panini.

"It's just … don't you think they're being kind of hypocritical? I mean…" I trailed off. She might have asked, but could I really talk to Faith about this? She wasn't really my sister in anything except blood.

"I think they're trying to make up for a lot," Faith said, looking down at her sandwich. "And maybe … maybe they're not always sure of the best way to go about it, and maybe they get it wrong sometimes, or try to overcompensate. But they *are* trying. That's the part I'm focusing on."

"With you, maybe," I answered. With me, they just seemed to expect me to accept everything without complaining.

Faith gave me a small smile. "You know, I think that maybe they're not quite sure how to act with you, either. You're growing up, things are changing all around you. That kind of thing is always hard with parents; I know it was with mine. My adopted parents, I mean."

I tilted my head as I looked at her, a question I'd never even thought of before popping into my head. "Do you have any other brothers and sisters? Adopted ones, I mean."

Faith shook her head. "It was always just me and my parents. A bit like you, until I came along. So I've never had a sister before. It's all new to me, too." For some reason, that made me feel a bit better. "Do you think…" Faith bit her lip. "Maybe we could work out how to be sisters, together?"

I looked up and met her gaze. I'd wanted to say no. I'd planned to say no. From the moment she picked me up at the school I'd known we were leading up to this, and I'd expected to turn her down and walk away. To tell her I didn't need a sister.

But when I looked into her face, and I thought about that hideous yellow dress, about her offering me skirt patterns, and how she wanted to come to my play but wasn't sure I wanted her there…

"I'd like that," I said.

And I wasn't even lying.

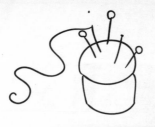

BUNTING

What you need:

2 pieces of fabric with complementary patterns
Ribbon

What to do:

1. On some paper, draw a triangle slightly larger than the size you want your bunting flags to be and cut out.

2. Fold your first piece of fabric in half, right sides together, making sure the edges match up and that it is well ironed.

3. Pin your template on and trace around your triangle using tailor's chalk.

4. Repeat until you have half the total number of triangles you need.

5. Repeat steps 2–4 with the second piece of fabric.

6. Cut out all the triangles, keeping the pairs together.

7. Pin each pair of triangles together, right sides facing, down the diagonal sides.

8. Sew down each side of your first pair of triangles, leaving the top unsewn and removing the pins as you go.

9. Trim away any excess fabric at the point, and turn your

triangle the right way out, using a pencil or chopstick to turn the points out properly.

10. Repeat for all the triangles, and iron them flat again, tucking in the fabric at the tops to give a neater edge.

11. Lay your triangles out along the back side of the ribbon, alternating the two patterns of fabric and making sure the spaces between the flags are even. Pin in place.

12. Machine or hand sew along the edge of the ribbon to hold the flags securely in place, removing the pins as you go.

13. Hang and enjoy!

"OK, we have a problem."

I'd known that Mr Hughes calling Connor and me into his office on a non-rehearsal day didn't bode well. His furrowed forehead had been a definite warning sign, and it worried me enough that I didn't even try to grab a moment with Connor on the way in. A proper hello would have to wait until we knew whatever the latest disaster was.

Connor and I looked at each other, then back at Mr Hughes. "Is this a costume problem?" I asked, hoping against hope the answer would be no.

"I'm afraid so." Mr Hughes sighed. "The friend who was going to loan us the uniforms for free now needs them for another play. He's very sorry but…"

"We're going to have to hire them," Connor said.

"Using the costume budget we've already spent on other things, because we thought we had the military stuff sorted." I dropped to sit on the nearest chair. "Great."

"We'll find a way around this," Mr Hughes said, with fake cheer. "Except ... the head's already told me we can't have any more money."

"Maybe we could make something that looks authentic?" Connor suggested, sitting beside me.

I shook my head. "Izzy is already making dresses and all sorts with Miss Cotterill. There just isn't enough time to make five First World War military costumes."

We all looked at each other in silence. "Any other suggestions?" Mr Hughes asked, looking about as hopeful as I felt.

"Maybe a fundraiser?" Connor asked.

"That could work," Mr Hughes agreed.

Just then, the door to the drama room opened, and Mr Hughes's Year Eight class started filing in.

"OK, why don't we all think about it over the next day or so, then we'll pool ideas at Friday's rehearsal. Sound good?" Mr Hughes said.

Connor and I nodded, but I don't think either of us held out much hope.

"Any thoughts?" he asked me, as we slipped out of the drama room and through the side door into the yard.

"Not yet," I admitted. "But I do have a few friends who might..."

"Bake Club?"

I nodded. "Yasmin's great at organizing stuff like fundraisers. And Lottie's obsessive enough to make it perfect. They'll help me come up with something."

"Great." Connor grinned. "Although between rehearsals, Sewing Club, Bake Club *and* a new fundraiser, I have no idea when you'll have time for me."

"I'll come up with something," I promised. And then, with my heart pounding in my chest, I stood up on tiptoes and pressed a quick, soft kiss against his lips. "I'll see you later." As I started to pull away, he grabbed my waist and kept me close, kissing me again, deeper this time.

Yeah, I was totally making time for Connor O'Neil.

On Thursday at Bake Club, I filled in the others on my fundraising issue. We all huddled around the back workstation, minus Mac, who was working, but with a surprise addition in the form of Izzy. I hadn't even really realized that she and Jasper were still friends, since he hadn't been back to Sewing Club after Christmas. But I was glad that he seemed to be coming out of his post-Christmas sulk. I made a mental note to talk to him about it, after I'd solved the more pressing problem of the costume budget.

"What about a bake sale?" Lottie asked. "We can all make stuff to sell. That could raise some money."

"But probably not enough." I sighed. "I was thinking the same thing, but I couldn't think of a way to make it enough of an event. You know, really get the whole school interested."

Yasmin had her thinking face on. She got this little line between her eyebrows, and her finger came up to tap at her jawline. I really hoped it was leading up to something good.

"Yasmin?" Lottie asked.

Yasmin held up the tapping finger in a "wait" gesture.

"Give her time," Jasper said, but we were all staring at her in anticipation.

Then Yasmin blinked and she was back with us.

"Got it," she said.

"And?" I sounded impatient. I didn't care.

"We make it a Valentine's Day Extravaganza."

"Extravaganza?" Jasper pulled a face. "It's going to be cupcakes, Yasmin, whatever day we do it. I'm not sure we can call it an extravaganza."

"Yes, we can," Yasmin said. "Because it isn't just

going to be cupcakes. It's going to be decorations and advertising and cake stalls in the halls. It's secret cake deliveries to the girl or boy of your choice, along with your card or flowers. It's going to take over the whole school for the entire day. And people are going to pay for it."

"Valentine's Day is still weeks away," I said, frowning. "Can we wait that long?"

"If you want the event, the spectacle, I think we have to," Yasmin said. "We need it to be something special, to raise the kind of money you need."

She was right, but it was still cutting it closer than I'd like.

"You think we'll be allowed?" Lottie asked.

"I think we just do it," Jasper said. "It's genius! It's a whole school takeover!"

"Are you lot plotting a revolution?" Miss Anderson's voice made us all jump.

"We're planning a bake sale, Miss." I gave her my best innocent smile. "To help raise money for the school-play costume fund."

Miss Anderson didn't look fully convinced. "And the whole school takeover?"

"We thought we'd decorate a bit. For Valentine's Day. Get people into the spirit of things so they buy more cake." Izzy sounded utterly convincing.

232

"I'm going to make the bunting."

"Well, in that case…" Miss Anderson disappeared to the shelf of cookbooks behind us. "You're going to want to make these." She left the book open for us, and we all stared at the red and white cupcakes in the photo.

"Red velvet cupcakes," Lottie read. "Perfect!"

"So, we're going to do this?" Yasmin asked.

I nodded. "Definitely. Thanks, guys." Romance, cake and fundraising. It would be perfect. I couldn't wait to tell Connor.

"No problem." Yasmin grinned. "Then we'd better get planning!"

Yasmin loved organizing things, and Lottie wanted to be in on all the details. So while they debated bunting colours with Izzy, and whether we'd provide the Valentine's Day cards, I tugged on Jasper's sleeve and led him over to the cookbook shelf, under the guise of looking for more recipes.

"How about these heart-shaped cookies?" he asked, flipping through the pages of *Sweet Treats*.

"How about you fill me in on what's going on with you and Izzy?" I folded my arms and stared him down. "Come on. She was asking about you when you didn't come back to Sewing Club, you know. So? Is this a rebound thing, or what?"

"It's a friends thing," Jasper said firmly. He let the book fall closed and shoved it back in its place. "She taught me how to sew. I thought it was only fair that I returned the favour by teaching her to bake."

"That's it?"

"That's it." Reaching up, he grabbed another book from the shelf. Since it was about cooking with mince, I didn't think it was going to help hugely. "Izzy knows all about Ella, and she knows that I'm kind of, well, you know…"

"Still hung up on her?"

"Something like that. Anyway. Izzy's cool, and I like hanging out with her. But we're just friends." He made it sound like he'd achieved some great milestone in male-female relations.

I was pretty sure he was just kidding himself.

"So … Izzy's completely all right with that, then? Just being friends?"

"Of course she is." Jasper looked at me with wide, clueless eyes. "Why wouldn't she be?"

"Somehow, I knew you'd be responsible for all the pink and red around the school today." Mr Hughes stood in the doorway to the school hall, arms folded. He was smiling, though, so I figured I wasn't in too much trouble.

234

"Actually, it was all Yasmin's idea." I straightened the plate of red velvet cupcakes so that Lottie couldn't complain. "The whole of Bake Club helped. Izzy and I did make the bunting, though," I admitted, looking up at the strings of pink and red flags that hung around the hall. They covered most of the school, actually. It turned out that making bunting was simple when you got the hang of it, and Izzy and I had gone a little overboard with our pretty triangles. Jasper had been hanging it up since the caretaker opened the school at seven, and I wasn't sure he had finished yet.

"So when you said bake sale..." Mr Hughes trailed off.

"I meant incredible Valentine's Day Extravaganza that is totally going to save my costume budget."

"Fair enough." Mr Hughes shrugged and turned to go. "Hey, if any of the teachers ask, tell them I gave you permission for everything, OK?" he called over his shoulder.

I beamed at his retreating back. "Thanks, Mr Hughes!"

Yasmin and Lottie arrived with another couple of plates of cakes and biscuits. Miss Anderson had let us in early to finish baking that morning, but we'd done most of it at Bake Club the night before.

Yasmin had spent the weeks since we came up with the idea meticulously planning everything down to the last detail. All we'd had to do was follow the recipes and the plan.

Now there was only half an hour until school started and, any moment, students were going to start arriving and walk into our Valentine's Day Extravaganza.

We'd started hinting that something was going to happen with some posters Jasper had designed, which we'd put up around the school at the beginning of last week. We hadn't wanted to give too much away too early, but we also needed to make sure that people remembered to bring money in on the day. Jasper had done a great job of suggesting that we could solve everyone's Valentine's Day anxiety, without actually saying how.

I just hoped the plan was going to work.

At least the manic preparation for the takeover meant I hadn't had time to obsess about whether I should be doing something for Connor on Valentine's Day. Were we there yet? I wasn't sure. What did "get to know each other better" really mean anyway? And did it involve gifts?

The Valentine's Day Extravaganza started with just a couple of confused-looking Year Eights, cash in hand, uncertain exactly what was going on. Yasmin, ever the saleswoman, stood up and explained.

"First off, we have a selection of cakes and biscuits for you, or your loved one. But that's not all." She leaned across the stall and dropped her voice. "I bet you two girls have a certain someone you'd like to send a romantic gift to, right?"

The girls exchanged a look, giggled and nodded.

"Well, in that case," Yasmin said, straightening up, "let me recommend our deluxe package. Choose any cake and card, write your message, give us a name and a class and we'll deliver it to the guy or girl of your choice in their next lesson, all for only three pounds."

Given that the cakes were selling for one pound, but cost pennies to make, and that Yasmin had picked up a stack of cards at the pound shop, three pounds sounded a little steep to me, but the girls handed over their money readily enough.

As they wrote their cards, Jasper checked the class schedule he'd swiped from somewhere, then passed me their sealed envelopes with an amused grin on his face. On the front of the first one were the words "Connor O'Neil".

"You know, Mr Hughes's stepson," the Year

Eight girl told me, earnestly. "He's soooo hot."

"Yeah. I know him," I said, handing the card back to Jasper and trying not to scowl. It wasn't Connor's fault that other people had noticed he was cute, too.

Then the door opened and in strolled Connor O'Neil himself, eyebrows raised as he took in the decorations. The Year Eight girls took one look, giggled and ran off again. Jasper just kept grinning.

"So this is your answer to our costume fund issues, huh?" Connor asked.

"Well, I had a little help," I admitted. "But yeah, hopefully. So, you got anyone you want to send a Valentine to?" I waved one of Yasmin's pound-shop cards at him.

"I like to think I could do a little better than that," Connor said.

I liked to think so, too, not that I'd seen any evidence of it just yet. "How about a cake, then?"

Connor shook his head. "I'll come back and get one later. Guy— Mr Hughes needs me in the art room to look at the scenery boards. I'll see you later, though?"

I nodded. "Sure. You know where I'll be."

He gave me a slow smile, and for a moment I thought he might kiss me there, in front of everybody. That would be enough of a Valentine for me.

But then Jasper popped up beside him. "Connor O'Neil," he announced loudly. "I have been charged with delivering this very special Valentine to you!" He handed over the bright pink envelope and a red velvet cupcake. Connor took it with a look of trepidation.

"This something to do with you?" he asked, raising an eyebrow at me.

"You should be so lucky," I told him, straightening up the cakes again. "But apparently you're very popular with Year Eight."

Connor slipped the card back into the envelope and shoved it in his bag. "Pity for them that there's only one girl I'm interested in, then, isn't it?"

I'm not going to deny it, I blushed at that. Maybe I didn't need cards, or cake, or presents after all. Knowing I was the only one Connor cared about … that felt a lot better than any of that other stuff.

Before I could think of a suitable reply, the next lot of customers came in – a gang of Year Sevens. Then a guy from Year Ten, and a few from Year Eleven – and Connor simply waved from behind the crowd as he left. I'd have tried to catch him up to say goodbye properly, but I was too busy because, from there on things didn't really stop.

Word got around quickly. Once the first few customers had told their friends what was happening, they all wanted to get involved. Some just bought cakes, others took up Yasmin's offer of the full Valentine's package. Soon we had to rope in a few Year Nine girls to help with the deliveries in return for a free cupcake and card for their own crushes.

We took shifts, depending on our classes, although most of the custom came during breaks and lunch, and in between periods. Just before lunch a tired-looking Mac turned up, and I handed him a red velvet cupcake straight off.

"You look like you need the sugar," I told him.

He unwrapped it with a grateful look. "Thanks. I've been at work since four thirty."

"Aw, and you still came here to see Lottie on Valentine's Day." I packaged up a couple of cookies for him, too. No way one cupcake was going to see him through.

Mac looked up at me with wide eyes. "Valentine's Day? Oh God, she's going to kill me."

"You forgot? Mac..."

"I know, I know. I need to fix this."

"And quick," I agreed. "We can give you a card and some cake, but..."

"That's not going to cut it," Mac finished. In a couple of bites, he demolished his cupcake. "Right. If she asks, you haven't seen me. I'll be back later."

Of course, that was the moment Lottie walked in from her food tech class. She took one look at Mac racing out of the door, and turned to me with her eyebrows raised.

"Have I mentioned recently that your boyfriend is an idiot?" I said.

Lottie rolled her eyes. "Let me guess. He forgot Valentine's Day?"

"Yep."

Lottie stared at the door Mac had run off through. "He'll make it up to me."

After an afternoon of more cake, more deliveries and almost running out of cards, we were all exhausted by the end of school. In fact, we were totally ready to pack up for the day when Connor walked back through the doors again.

"Heard you guys have had the whole school crazy in love all day," he said, helping himself to a cupcake. Yasmin held out a hand, eyebrow raised, and he dropped two pound coins into it before grabbing another cupcake. "How much did you make?"

"Including your two pounds ... £684.50."

Yasmin slammed the lid of the cash box closed and locked it. "Think that will do you for your costumes?"

"Wow. It definitely should do." Connor grinned and turned to me, his second cupcake balanced on his palm as he held it out. "For you."

I raised my eyebrows. "Me? You realize I actually made these cakes, right?"

"Yeah, well." He shrugged. "It's Valentine's Day. Also, I have a favour to ask you, and that kind of thing tends to go better with sugar."

"I should have known. Go on." I peeled the heart-covered paper case off the red velvet cupcake and took a bite. Perfect, if I did say so myself.

"Are you free next weekend?" he asked, and I raised an eyebrow. Maybe this was more of a line than I'd given him credit for.

"Depends. What have you got planned?"

"I thought we could go into London." He ducked his head. "Actually, I already made an appointment for us at the National Theatre costume-hire place. We can reserve our costumes now, then pick them up the week of the show. And we could look for the last few props we need, too."

"I can do that. It sounds like fun." Actually, what it sounded like was our first real date. I was already planning my outfit when another thought occurred to me. "Wait. You already made the appointment? How did you know we'd raise the money?"

Connor gave me a lopsided smile. "I've never yet seen you not get what you wanted, if you wanted it bad enough."

"What about the role of Beatrice?" I stopped and felt my face flush. What made me say that? After months spent convincing him that I wasn't scheming to steal the part, I'd pretty much just admitted that I was.

"Well, I figure there's still two and a half weeks until curtain up," Connor said, and I couldn't quite tell if he was joking. "Plenty of time yet."

The door opened, and a sheepish Mac stuck his head around it.

"Uh-oh," I murmured to Connor. "We might be in for a scene now."

"What happened?" Connor whispered back.

"Mac forgot Valentine's Day," I said, and Connor rolled his eyes – whether at Mac's forgetfulness or the importance placed on the day, I wasn't sure.

"Hey, Happy Valentine's Day," Mac said, as he reached Lottie.

Lottie looked up from the cakes she was packing up and smiled. "Happy Valentine's Day to you, too."

Connor glanced over at me, and I knew what he was thinking. So far, so good.

"I missed you earlier," Lottie went on, and I braced myself for yelling.

"Should we be watching this?" Connor muttered.

"Probably not." But I didn't move.

Mac winced. "Yeah, sorry. I just..." he sighed. "Truth is, I forgot Valentine's Day, and I wanted to get you something special. But I couldn't find anything."

"You're an utter idiot," Lottie said fondly and reached out to touch his arm. "Grace says so."

My eyes widened. "Hey. You really don't need to drag me into this!"

"Look, I'm sorry. It's just been really busy and—" Mac cut himself off as Lottie rolled her eyes and rose up on her tiptoes to kiss him. "You're not mad?" he asked, as the kiss ended.

"Think about it, Mac. What is the best present I've ever had?"

Mac blinked at her. "I don't know."

Honestly. Boys were so oblivious. "Here's a clue," I called out to him. "You gave it to her. Last year."

"But I've never given you a proper present.

244

That's the point. I wanted to… Oh."

"There you go," I muttered, as Mac pulled Lottie up to kiss her again.

"You are the best girlfriend ever," he said, as they broke the kiss.

"I know," Lottie replied and kissed him again. "I don't need presents. I just need you."

"So … what did he get her?" Connor asked, looking bemused beside me.

"He baked her a birthday cake." I explained. "It was a whole thing. Anyway, she liked it."

"So, would a cake be enough to win your heart?" Connor asked, a mocking smile on his lips.

I looked down at the empty cake case in my hand. "I'm more of a diamonds girl," I joked.

"I guessed as much." Tugging my arm, he pulled me to the side of the hall where we were almost in private. He reached into his bag and pulled out a small parcel, wrapped in shiny silver paper. "Well, maybe this will do for starters."

I blinked at it in confusion for a moment before taking it, excitement and nerves making my blood pump faster. What was it? Carefully unpeeling the paper, I slipped out the book inside. It was small and old, and the boards of the cover were a faded red. But there, in silver lettering on the front, were the words "Foods and Fashions of the 1920s".

"It's from the 1940s," Connor said, looking a little uncomfortable. "I found it in this second-hand bookshop before Christmas and thought you might like it... I just hadn't found the right time to give it to you."

I flipped through the yellowing pages. There were photos and sketches of the sort of clothes I was trying to recreate for the play, between recipes for cakes, bakes and dishes of the period. Yasmin and Lottie would definitely want to get a look at this.

And there, just inside the front cover, was an incongruous yellow post-it note.

To our Wardrobe and Props Mistress Extraordinaire. Something to remember our version of Much Ado by. Connor x

"I figured you probably already know all this stuff, but I thought it could be, like, a keepsake?"

Glancing up from the book, I saw uncertainty playing on Connor's face. I smiled at him to put him out his misery.

"I love it," I told him. "But ... I didn't get you anything. I wasn't sure if we were... Well, I guess we never talked about if we were ... at the gift stage, I suppose."

"Well, if it helps, I can think of something I

want from you for Valentine's Day," Connor said, wrapping an arm around my waist.

"Yeah?"

"Mmm-hmm." Dipping his head, he kissed me. The sort of kiss that made every inch of me tingle. The sort of kiss that promised a lot more to come.

"I think that makes us even. Don't you?"

"Maybe," I said, grinning.

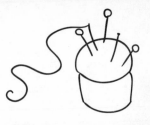

BABY BLANKET

What you need:

1 piece of soft cotton 75 x 100cm
1 piece of fleece or plush fabric 75 x 100cm

What to do:

1. Iron your cotton and place it right-side down against the right side of your fleece.
2. Align the two pieces of fabric so they match exactly, then pin in place.
3. Tack around the outside to hold them together, then remove the pins.
4. Using your sewing machine, or backstitch if you're hand sewing, sew all the way around the rectangle, about 1cm in from the edge. Start on one of the short sides, and stop 10cm before you reach the end, leaving an unsewn gap.
5. Cut through and remove the tacking stitch.
6. Turn the blanket the right way out through the gap, then fold over the loose edges of the fabric in the gap to match the rest, and pin in place.
7. Iron the blanket again on the cotton side to make sure the

edges are neat.

8. *If you're hand sewing, neatly sew the gap closed using slip stitch or whip stitch.*

9. *If you're using a sewing machine, sew another line of stitches all the way around the blanket, 7.5mm in from the edge, making sure you catch and sew up the gap.*

I met Connor at the station that Saturday, feeling strangely self-conscious out of school uniform and without any of the cast or my friends around. I'd purposefully not dressed up too much for the occasion – we were going to root through old costumes, after all. But still, I wanted to look nice. I'd used the tutorial Faith had emailed to make a skirt from some gorgeous pale green fabric I'd found in the costume-cupboard scraps bin that we had permission to use, so I wore that paired with a pretty cream top, tights, boots and my favourite jacket. A little make-up, but not too much, and my blonde hair loose with just a little added wave, and a vintage clip in the side.

I looked like I cared, but not like I'd tried too hard. Hopefully.

Connor was waiting for me at the ticket machine and held up two tickets as I approached. "Ready?"

"Absolutely." I took my ticket from him to get through the barrier, then stuffed it in my pocket.

We only lived twenty minutes out of London, so by the time we'd talked about what we were looking for at the theatre, we were practically there. We got off at Waterloo, then took the tube down to Oval and walked to our destination.

The costume-hire place was incredible. I'd spent so long searching through rails of clothing at school, I'd thought this would be one more day doing the same. But the costumes here were so much ... more. Costumes from every production the National Theatre had ever put on, costumes that had been worn by real actors, in real plays. Suddenly I wanted to try them all on, and see how they felt.

The costumes were organized by period, which made things easier. The costume-hire assistant led us to the right time zone, so to speak, and then left us to figure out what we needed.

"What about this?" Connor asked, holding up a green military jacket.

"Looks good," I agreed. "But let's see what else there is, too." I frowned, flicking through different uniforms from different armies. "We need slightly different ones for Don John and his guys." The bad guys couldn't look exactly the same as our heroes, after all. "And it would be good if we could find one with lots of medals or stripes for Don Pedro, to show that he's the prince, or leader. Do you think?"

"Absolutely," Connor said. Then he grinned. "You know, I can't believe I ever thought you weren't taking this seriously."

I ducked behind a rail to look through more costumes, without answering. Because, the truth was, I hadn't taken it seriously. Not to start with. Without Miss Cotterill and Izzy, we probably still wouldn't have any costumes at all.

It took us a while, but eventually we had a set of costumes we were both happy with, and that hinted at the order of power and which side people were on, without being too obvious. It all came in just under budget, too, which was a huge relief.

We filled in the paperwork to reserve them, and took the details down so Mr Hughes could confirm, pay and then pick them up, nearer to the show.

"Can you believe it's only two weeks away now?" I asked, as we stepped back out into the grey London day.

"Think we'll be ready?" Connor asked.

"Of course we will!" He raised his eyebrows at my certainty. "Well, I'm not saying the last couple of weeks might not be a bit fraught…"

He laughed and bumped his shoulder against mine. "We'll be fine."

"Yeah." There was a warmth in Connor's eyes that made me want to kiss him, just because. Smiling, I rose up on my toes, and Connor's hand came to rest at the small of my back, and…

And then my phone rang.

Connor looked away and, the moment gone, I fumbled in my bag to find the phone. It was Jasper, of course, and I knew he'd just keep calling if I didn't answer.

"Hey, what is it?" I asked, knowing I sounded impatient and not really caring.

"OK, so, it would really help me if you didn't take this as an opportunity to say 'Jasper, you're an idiot'," Jasper said, the words coming fast and frantic.

"I make no promises."

Connor was mooching along beside me, taking in the traffic, the buildings – and totally eavesdropping on my conversation.

"Fine. So, I was hanging out with Izzy at her house, right?"

"Right." I had a feeling I knew where this was going.

"And she, um, well…"

"She kissed you?" I guessed.

"Yes!" There was panic in Jasper's voice now. "I thought we were just friends!"

I sighed. "OK, so what did you do? Wait, if this happened at Izzy's house, where are you now?"

"I kind of ... left."

"Jasper..." *Such* a boy.

"I know! I know. But it was awful," he whined.

"Kissing Izzy?"

"Well, no. Not that part. But then I started thinking about Ella, and I kind of pushed Izzy away..."

"And you ran out on her!" That made sense. In a twisted, Jasper sort of way.

"Yeah."

"And called me."

"Yeah. Can I come hang out at yours for a bit? She won't find me there."

"Trust me, Jasper, she isn't going to be looking for you. Because you are an idiot."

He sighed down the phone. "I know. But... I could actually do with talking to you about it all. Figure out what I do next."

"Buy her flowers," I suggested. "All of the flowers." I rubbed my forehead and tried to think of something more helpful. Jasper was still my friend, even if he was a complete incompetent at romance. "Look, I'm in London today sorting out costume hire. Why don't you give Lottie or Yasmin a call?

I'm sure they'd love to do tea, cake and relationship analysis with you."

"Yeah, OK. I guess." He sounded more down than I'd thought he'd be. Normally, he was perfectly happy to go to Lottie or Yasmin with his girl issues. Probably because they tended to be a lot more sympathetic than me.

"I'll call you when I get home, though," I said.

"That would be good. Talk later." He hung up.

"Everything OK?" Connor asked from beside me.

I shrugged. "It will be, I'm sure. Just Jasper having girl issues. So, what do you want to do next?"

I wasn't sure what I expected him to say, or even what I wanted him to say. We'd sorted the costumes, we'd looked at props while we were there. This was now officially first date territory.

"How about we head up to the South Bank," Connor suggested. "We can grab some lunch."

I couldn't help the smile that spread across my face. "Sounds good."

The South Bank was packed as usual, despite it being a bitterly cold Saturday in February. We walked past the London Eye, turning slowly against the grey sky, and then up past the National Theatre.

"Kind of hard to believe that Ash and the others will be wearing costumes that were actually used on that stage," I said, as we looked up at it. The building itself was nothing special, but inside... "Have you ever been?"

Connor nodded. "My dad took me a couple of times. It wasn't really his thing, but he tried to make sure we did some stuff, just the two of us."

"You must miss him a lot." How hard must it have been for him, to be thrown out of his own home, to have his family move so far away. And then to have to start a new school, too... No wonder he'd been kind of moody with me last term.

"Yeah. He's asked me to go out and visit in the summer, though."

"To New York? Wow."

"Yeah. I said I'd think about it. If I don't get the job at the theatre..." He flashed me a smile that let me know he didn't want to dwell on it. "Come on. I'm starving."

We found a coffee shop further along the South Bank that served hot sandwiches, and sat in the window while we waited, watching the whole of London walk past us.

Including one very pretty blonde girl, about our age, who stopped just outside, and stared in.

"Damn." Connor ducked his head, letting his sandy hair fall in front of his eyes, and grabbed my hand to turn me away from the window.

"You OK?" I asked, staring back over my shoulder at the girl. Her eyes widened, then she waved in at us.

"Fine," Connor said, but since he was still staring at his feet it was clearly a lie. "Just don't look at her."

"Why?" I asked, but Connor didn't respond. After a moment, I glanced back again, just in time to see the girl walking off.

"She's gone," I told him. Connor's whole body relaxed at the news – I could actually see his shoulders drop as he let out a long breath.

"Good. Oh, look, here comes our lunch." He motioned towards the approaching waitress, then turned back to sit at the counter, staring out of the window again, as if nothing had happened. As if he expected me to ignore the incredible weirdness of the last few minutes.

Um, no.

I waited until the waitress had left, watching Connor as he focused in on his sandwich, before speaking.

"Are you planning on explaining to me what just happened?" I asked.

With a sigh, Connor put down his sandwich. "It's really not something I want to talk about."

"Fine, but you could at least tell me why I just had to hide from a girl I've never met."

"Or not." Connor took another bite of his sandwich, then wrapped the rest up in his napkin. "Come on. We can eat these on the way to the station."

I blinked. That was it? Our date was over without me even getting to finish my lunch? No way.

I followed him outside, sandwich in hand, but stopped by the door.

"Station's this way," Connor said, turning back when he realized I wasn't walking with him.

I shrugged. "It's a nice day. I'm going to spend it here in London, away from your bitterness and sulking."

Connor scowled. "I am not—" I raised my eyebrows and he sighed. "Yeah, OK. Sorry. Just thinking about Kirsty puts me in a bad mood these days."

Kirsty. At least I had a name, now. "But she didn't always?" I guessed.

"You're not going to let this go, are you?"

"What do you think?"

He sighed again. I figured that meant he'd got the point.

258

"Come on," I said, slipping my arm through his. "Let's find somewhere to eat these. And talk."

We found a bench looking over the Thames a little way along, and sat staring out over the water at the boats and people and birds, eating our sandwiches. Then, when we were finished, Connor took the wrappers and put them in the bin. And when he sat back down, he was just a little bit closer, his thigh pressed against mine. I shivered, more from his nearness than the cold, and he reached out and put an arm around my shoulders, holding me close.

It was almost a perfect date moment. Except...

"So, Kirsty?" I asked.

"You are relentless."

"It's part of my charm."

"Trust me, princess, you have far superior charms."

The nickname didn't sound like an insult any more. More like an endearment, maybe. Whatever it was, something about the way he said it made me feel warmer inside. And almost made me wish I hadn't asked about his probable ex-girlfriend.

But it was too late now.

"I knew Kirsty from the youth theatre," Connor said. "She was in my school, but a couple of years below me. But that kind of thing didn't matter so much at the theatre."

"You guys dated?" I guessed.

"For a while."

"Until…" It was like pulling teeth.

Connor sighed. "OK, fine. Here's the story. I had a ridiculous crush on Kirsty. Even though I knew she was always at the centre of everything, always at the side of whichever boy was getting into fights, or whichever girl was crying backstage. She lived for the drama, for people to be watching her, but it took me a while to realize that. I thought she was something more than just the popular girl with blonde hair. We talked. She told me about her family, her dreams. She listened to me when I told her the same. I thought she was…" He shook his head. "I thought she was something she wasn't. That she was special."

My sandwich felt very heavy in my stomach. Was this why he'd taken such an instant dislike to me last term? Not just because he thought I'd be bad for the play, but because he thought I was another blonde, popular girl, just like Kirsty?

And, even more worryingly, was I?

"What happened?" I asked, even though I wasn't completely sure I wanted to hear the answer.

"We dated. I thought it was the real thing. I … I guess I was in love, for the first time, and I thought it would be… Anyway. It turned out that she was more interested in getting to know my best friend, who was playing the lead in our play that season."

"Ah."

"Yeah. She used me to get what she wanted. She cheated on me and then, when I found out, she made it all about her trauma. She'd be in tears at rehearsals, with a gang of other cast members around her, all glaring at me for making things hard for her. She told some story about how we both knew we were better as friends, that I was more like a brother to her, that she hadn't done anything wrong, but it was still so hard… And everyone believed her. Even though it was me who'd had my heart ripped out and stomped on."

I squeezed his hand a little tighter. "I'm so sorry."

"So, all of this was going on and I was somehow at the centre of all this drama … and there was already so much of that at home, with my parents' divorce, then them both getting remarried, then dad deciding to move … it was drama all the time, and the only thing I wanted was to be left alone to figure it out." He stared down at his lap, and I reached up to take his hand where it lay against my shoulder. "I just wanted the theatre to be a place that I could be myself, without having to act."

I gave him a small smile. "You realize most people go there for the opposite reason?"

He laughed, short and sharp. "Yeah. I guess they do."

"So, what happened next? With Kirsty, I mean?"

"The usual. It was just one more Drama Club drama. And it made me feel so…"

"Manipulated?" I guessed. I knew exactly the sort of dramas he was talking about – I'd been in the middle of plenty of them before last year. But I knew about real problems now, and real friends – the ones who were there all the time, not just when things were going wrong.

"Stupid," Connor said. "I was an idiot for not seeing what she was like sooner."

I looked over at our interlaced fingers as I tried to think of a delicate way to ask this question. There wasn't one, so I just asked it anyway.

"Is that why you hated me so much when we first met? Not because you thought I was a diva but … because I reminded you of her?"

"Perhaps. I think…" Connor winced. "Well, that first day, I was in a bad mood to start with. And then I saw you throwing your strop, and I could just tell you were one of *those* girls. A girl who wanted the drama. And in my head that meant you were someone like Kirsty. Someone who'd use anything and anyone to get what they wanted."

"And that's what you thought I was doing when I offered to do the costumes."

He looked up and gave me a half smile. "Was I right?"

I glanced away again. "Maybe. To start with. I mean, it got me the opportunity to audition for the understudy role."

"And now?"

"Now I want these costumes to be the best I can possibly come up with." All true. I just hadn't completely given up on the idea of Violet dropping out at the last moment, either.

"Yeah, I know." The smile he gave me felt warmer, more real than any I'd seen before. And it felt like it was just for me. That no one else in the whole world had earned a smile like that from Connor.

"You're a lot more than I ever gave you credit for, princess."

"You should have been paying more attention, then," I said, remembering the conversation we'd had in his kitchen, before Christmas. The words came out soft, but it didn't matter, because he was only a matter of centimetres away anyway.

"Trust me. You're all I'm paying attention to now.

Everything else … it's just unnecessary drama." He rested his forehead against mine, so close now I could barely breathe. "All I want to think about is this."

I don't know if he kissed me or I kissed him, we were so in sync, my eyes fluttering closed as our lips touched.

It wasn't our first kiss, but somehow it felt like it was. It felt special. Maybe because it was the first time a boy had kissed me and I'd known, beyond any shadow of a doubt, that he was kissing me, Grace, and not just "the popular girl" or "the best looking girl in the year" or "the star of the show". Connor didn't care about any of that.

Which meant he cared about me. Just me.

And that felt incredible.

That evening, after dinner, I disappeared to my room again as normal. Only, this time, I came back to the kitchen a few minutes later. Mum looked up in surprise as I entered, my arms full of fabric and Gran's old sewing box. Faith just smiled, though, like she'd known it was only a matter of time.

"That skirt turned out great," she said, as I sat down at the table. "What's your next project?"

I took a breath before I answered. It was a simple enough question, but somehow the wait for my response seemed loaded with tension – as if I might yell or snipe or complain.

Listening to Connor talk about his issues over the last year had made one thing very clear to me. This was *my* family drama, yes. Which meant it was up to me how I dealt with it. True, I was still mad and confused about everything, but Connor was right – being at the centre of a drama was exhausting. And I had other things in my life I wanted to focus on.

Faith had made the effort to come to my school. So maybe now it was my turn. I'd try taking a page out of Connor's book for a change and just go with it. Just this once.

"A friend of mine has a new baby sister," I explained, showing Faith the pattern I'd printed out from the internet. I'd found the fabrics in my trawls through the charity shops and the remnants basket at the posh craft shop in town. "I thought I'd make her a little baby blanket."

Faith passed the pattern to Mum, who said, "I think that's a lovely idea."

"Thanks," I said. I just hoped that Connor would, too.

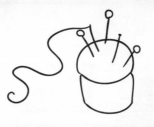

DROP-WAISTED T-SHIRT DRESS

What you need:

Patterned fabric
Plain jersey T-shirt

What to do:

1. *Measure your waist and the length from your waist to your knee.*
2. *Measure out your ironed fabric so you have a rectangle twice as long as your waist measurement, and as wide as your waist to knee measurement.*
3. *Using a sewing machine, sew a zigzag stitch all around the edges of your fabric to prevent fraying.*
4. *Fold in half, right sides together, and sew a 1cm seam along the short side, to give you a wide tube of fabric.*
5. *Sew a gathering stitch around the top of the skirt, around 1cm in. Pull the threads to gather the skirt together, until it has almost halved in size.*
6. *Slide your T-shirt inside your skirt upside-down, so that*

the right sides are together and the bottom of the T-shirt is lined up with the top of the skirt.

7. Pin in place, first at the seam, then opposite it, then splitting the skirt into quarters, then eighths. You may need to adjust the gathers to fit the T-shirt.

8. Stitch together, making sure that the skirt and top are lined up all the way around.

9. Trim any loose threads and turn the right way around.

10. Try on to check the fit, then hem to the desired length.

Monday came, eventually. I made it to school early, and found Connor already in the mostly empty sixth-form common room. I felt relieved not many people were there to watch as I pulled up my chair to sit beside him at one of the study tables.

"You're here early," I said, unable to keep the smile from my face.

"I'm here early every day," he replied, but he was grinning, too. "I get a lift in with Guy. So you're the one who's here unusually early today."

I shrugged and pulled my bag on to the table. "Maybe I had work to catch up on."

"Maybe you just wanted to see me again." Connor leaned in closer, his shoulder pressing against mine.

I pulled back, just a little. "Maybe I was worried you'd spent the whole of yesterday pining for me, despite the couple of dozen text messages we sent each other, and I wanted to put you out of your misery." Very different text messages to the short, impersonal one he'd sent me about New Year. That already seemed like a lifetime ago. He felt more like Connor with every text sent, even when we were just chatting about homework or whatever.

He laughed. "You're absolutely right, of course. I pined endlessly."

"Really?" I turned to face him and found him closer than I'd thought.

"Absolutely." He moved even closer and kissed me, soft and sweet, right on the lips. "Or I would have been if I hadn't had to spend the day helping Guy look after Lily while Mum had a day out with Aunty Bea."

"Ah. Sounds … tiring."

"Very. Her new favourite game is throwing her mushed-up food all over the kitchen. By the end of lunch it looked like we'd been hit with a carrot bomb." He kissed me again, a little longer this time. I could really get used to this. "But I was thinking of you the whole time," he added, as he pulled away.

"So glad that carrot mush reminds you of me," I murmured, and he laughed.

"What about you?" Connor asked. "What did you get up to yesterday?"

I shrugged. "Not much. Some sewing." I didn't

want to tell him about the blanket just yet. Not until it was finished, and I knew if it was good enough to actually give as a gift, or not. "Jasper came over and filled me in on all his latest relationship catastrophes."

"Do I want to know?" Connor asked.

I considered. "Probably not." Seemed to me that Jasper was still freaking out over not spotting something that absolutely everyone else had – that Izzy wanted more than just to be his friend. He'd talked it through with Yasmin, Skyped with Lottie, and then come round to go through it with me again. All without making any significant progress on the matter, since he was still stuck at "Oh my God, she kissed me!"

"Fair enough. Have you got Sewing Club after school?" Connor asked, and I nodded.

"Same as always. Why?"

"I thought that maybe we could get coffee or something."

"Sorry. But I really need to finish up a few bits of sewing with Izzy before we start rehearsing in costume at tomorrow's rehearsal." Never had I wanted to skive off so much. "Maybe tomorrow? After rehearsal?"

"It's a date," Connor said, then kissed me again.

I floated off to history in a happy cloud of memory-kisses, and managed to keep my good mood through an entire hour of Jasper rehashing the Izzy-kiss. As we entered hour two, however, I cut him short.

"OK, look. I have to spend an hour and a half with Izzy this afternoon, finishing off costumes. I can pretty much guarantee that the first question she's going to ask me when I walk in there will be how you're feeling about things. Even if it should be 'why is he such a complete idiot?'"

"Hey!" Jasper sat up straighter in his chair as he objected.

"Hey, yourself. You ran out on the girl after she kissed you."

He slumped down again. "Yeah, fair enough."

"The point is, if you want an easy way of letting her know what you want to happen next, I can help." Jasper looked up with hopeful eyes, so I quickly added, "Which doesn't mean you don't still have to talk to her – and apologize to her, for that matter. But I can lay the groundwork a bit, if you like."

Jasper was already nodding. "Please. I don't understand how I made such a mess of all this."

"Neither does anyone else, believe me." It had been so simple when he'd got together with Ella the year before. Well, simple apart from her trying to hide her grandma's dementia, and then moving two hundred miles away, anyway. So not really that simple.

"You really didn't know she had feelings for you?" I asked.

Jasper shook his head miserably. "Not a clue. Why? Did you?"

"Kind of." In the sense that she asked an awful lot of questions about him for someone who was just a friend. "Maybe it's one of those things that's always easier to see from the outside."

"Like you and Connor?" Jasper asked.

I couldn't help myself. A smile spread across my face at just the thought of it. But we weren't talking about me and Connor. "So, what do you want me to tell Izzy?"

Jasper stared at me, as if he could convey the inner workings of his poor, confused mind through his eyes.

"Yeah, you're gonna need to work on your telepathy powers." I grabbed a clean sheet of paper and a pen, then handed them to him. "Will it help to write it down? I could just deliver a letter, if that's easier."

Jasper shook his head. "I wouldn't know what to say, or even where to start." He sighed, dropping his head to rest on his arms for a moment. I glanced over to make sure Mr Edwards wasn't watching, but he was far too busy helping someone on the other side of the room with the primary-source exercise we were *supposed* to be doing.

"I've really screwed things up with Izzy, haven't I?" The words were muffled through the fabric of his school jumper.

"Yeah, you have. But that doesn't mean we can't fix it. I mean, you'd been completely oblivious to her as a girl up until Saturday, too, and she still wanted to kiss you then."

Jasper looked up long enough to glare at me. "I thought you were supposed to be helping me."

"I am," I promised. "If I can tell her that you are honestly sorry and that you're embarrassed by how thoughtless you've been, that could go a long way towards getting Izzy to forgive you."

Jasper sat up. "Really? OK, well, start there. Tell her I'm sorry. And that I know I'm an idiot. Tell her … tell her I really, really didn't want to hurt her. That's the last thing I'd ever want. I just … I got confused, and I wasn't sure what I should want, or what to do…"

"And now?"

"Now?" Jasper blinked at me.

"Do you know what you want now?" I pressed.

A small line formed across his forehead, and I could see his chest expand as he took a deep breath. "Yeah. Yeah, I think I do. But I need to tell her that myself."

I wanted to hug him. Maybe boys weren't always stupid after all.

"I think that's a brilliant idea."

"Could you ask her to meet me, though? Tomorrow – no, not tomorrow. I've got that stupid French thing all day. Wednesday, then. Second period – we're both free. In the textiles classroom." Jasper looked lighter, somehow, now he'd decided what to do. Like he could see the path ahead of him clearly at last.

"I can do that," I agreed. Suddenly, I wasn't dreading Sewing Club nearly so much.

"He wants to see me?" Izzy asked, sounding dubious. "Are you sure? And … why? I thought running out on me was a pretty clear answer to the whole thing."

I shrugged. "I'm just the messenger. All I know is that he's sorry, he knows he was an idiot, and he wants to meet you here second period Wednesday to talk."

"What do you think he's going to say?" she asked.

"I really don't know." I tried to be sympathetic. I mean, if it was me, waiting for some big conversation with Connor, I know I'd have quizzed anyone who knew him to find out what it was about. I'm not all that good at being patient.

"But, do you think it's... Well, do you think it's going to be a good conversation?"

I looked at Izzy. Her black hair was caught up in a brightly coloured scarf, and she'd changed into one of her home-sewn patchwork dresses after school again. She was the absolute opposite of Ella in almost every way – confident where Ella had been shy, dark instead of blonde, and fiercely individual, while Ella had been happy to go along with the crowd, most of the time.

And yet, I was pretty sure that Izzy was at least *as* perfect a match for Jasper, in very different ways to Ella. And I had a suspicion that he'd just figured that out, too.

Isn't it funny how you never know what you need in a boyfriend or girlfriend until you tumble headlong into it, completely unexpectedly? I smiled to myself, wondering if Connor had finally figured that out about me, too.

"Yeah, I think it will be a good conversation," I reassured Izzy, and she smiled.

"OK. Then I guess I'll just have to try and distract myself until Wednesday."

"Good luck with *that*."

She laughed. "Yeah. Not easy. Ooh, but I can start by showing you what I came up with for the last of the girls' costumes."

She held up a dress, the top part made of jersey T-shirt material, and the skirt a silky, shimmery material. The low waist and sleeveless top gave it a 1920s flavour.

"This is great!" I took it from her and examined it. "Will you have time to make enough of them?"

"Oh, they're easy," Izzy said, which I'd learned to translate as easy for *her*. "I just took a long vest top from an old production and sewed a skirt on to it. There's loads more of the tops, too, and enough to match sizes to actresses. Think they'll do?"

"I think they'll be perfect."

Finally everything was coming together.

Tuesday's rehearsal, on the other hand, was absolute chaos. First, we took up half the time getting everyone into their costumes. We'd have to get faster at that before the opening night. But when everything was still new and different it took a while, and even Connor standing at the door glancing at his watch couldn't hurry things along.

"You want these to be right, don't you?" I asked, and Connor rolled his eyes at me. I took it as a sign of affection.

Of course, things would be going considerably quicker if I had any help. "Have you seen Yasmin?" I asked him, and Connor shook his head. Come to think of it, I hadn't seen Ash, either, since I gave him his costume and he disappeared to put it on. He'd been in a foul mood, too, barely speaking two words to me. Hopefully Yasmin was cheering him up at that very moment.

"Want me to look for her?"

"Nah. I'll find her when I'm finished here." Yasmin had already done me a favour by agreeing to come in on Tuesdays and Fridays from now until the opening night. I didn't want to push it by interrupting her private time with Ash.

Mr Hughes stuck his head round the door. "Are we ready in here?"

"Almost," I told him brightly. "In fact, we're good to go for the opening scenes." I'd have a little while until the next scene break when I had to change some people's costumes again.

"Then let's get on it!" Mr Hughes clapped his hands, and our actors started to drift onstage.

"The costumes look great," Connor said, when we were the only two left.

"They'll look even better when we have the military uniforms from the National Theatre next week."

"They will." He grinned at me. "I better get out there."

I nodded. "And I need to find Yasmin."

But suddenly the question of where Yasmin had got to was answered when the door flew open and she and Ash stormed in. Behind them, I heard Mr Hughes yell, "I don't care what your problem is, but I want you both to sort it out quickly and privately so I can get on with my rehearsal!"

"Everything OK, guys?" I asked, as Connor and I stared at each other in confusion.

"Ask her," Ash said, his face dark and stormy. "She won't tell me the truth."

Yasmin rolled her eyes. "You're being ridiculous."

"Ridiculous! *You're* cheating on me and *I'm* being ridiculous?" Ash yelled.

"Hey, keep it down," I said. The last thing we needed was to interrupt the rehearsal again or we'd have the entire cast weighing in on the situation. "Now, what happened?" Because I didn't believe, not for one second, that Yasmin had cheated on Ash.

There just wasn't a chance that was true.

And really, Ash should know that, too.

"It's just some stupid rumour," Yasmin said, sounding exasperated. "I don't know why you even listened to it!"

"Because it's not just a rumour," Ash replied. I heard a slight wobble in his voice and realized that, for all his attempt at a big, angry-man impression, he was actually truly upset. "It's an eyewitness account from someone I trust. They *saw* you, Yasmin. You and him, together."

"Well, of course we were together! We're friends!"

"Hang on. Is this about Yasmin and *Jasper?*" Because, if so, this was getting less believable all the time. "OK, someone start from the beginning. Please."

"Last night," Ash said, the words coming out tight. "I had a visit from a friend. They said they'd been trying to figure out whether they should tell me or not, but if it was them, they'd want to know. So they told me what they'd seen."

"Which was me and Jasper having coffee at the White Hill Bakery," Yasmin interrupted. "That's all."

"If that was all, why would they need to tell Ash?" Connor asked.

"Because they weren't just having coffee," Ash

said. "They were kissing."

"No, we weren't! I told you, Jasper is my friend. We were talking about *his* ridiculous relationship stuff." Yasmin's frustration leaked out from her in waves.

"It's true," I added, wanting to help. "Jasper called me first, but I was in London, so I told him to call Yasmin. Connor was right beside me. You heard me, right?"

I looked up at Connor, but his face, so open and friendly since Saturday, had started to close down again.

"If he was just your friend, why didn't you tell me you were meeting him?" Ash asked, and Yasmin stared at him in disbelief.

"Because I thought you were my boyfriend, not my probation officer." She shook her head. "Look, if you don't want to believe me, fine. I don't want to date someone who doesn't trust me, either, so that works out just great for both of us, doesn't it?"

This was a disaster. I mean, I applauded everything Yasmin was saying, and I was proud of the way she stood up to Ash's accusations. But she was crazy about him. And as strong as she was being right then, I knew that this was going to break her heart.

Ash stared at her for a long moment, then snapped

his gaze away. "I thought I knew you," he said. And then he walked out.

My eyes widened, and I turned to the one person I hoped might be able to talk some sense into Ash. "Connor! You have to go after him. Convince him that this is stupid, that Yasmin would never cheat on him."

Connor's pale eyes were steady. "I'll go after him because he's my friend, and because someone needs to convince him that the show is more important than whatever drama you guys have going on."

Drama. He thought this was drama? This was *Yasmin*. And she mattered a lot more than whatever issues he had.

As the door shut behind him, Yasmin let out the sob she'd been holding in for who knew how long. I hurried to her side and wrapped my arms around her, but my gaze still focused on that closed door.

Connor would get over himself and help me fix this. He had to.

Within a couple of days, the whole school was talking about Yasmin and Ash. St Mary's was notorious for gossip, and a story as good as this wasn't going to be missed. Yasmin might not be hugely well known outside of our year, but she was a member of Bake Club and helping with Drama Club, so that was enough to get people talking anyway. Jasper, meanwhile, appeared to be missing the worst of it – probably because he was single. I'd called and filled him in from the rehearsal that Tuesday night, and his main concern had been what Izzy would think, of course. But no one else seemed to care – they were too busy talking about Yasmin.

It might not have been so bad if Ash wasn't so popular. He was that unusual mix of sporty, good looking, academic and also nice – at least, normally. Yasmin told me that he'd only joined Drama Club last year because Mr Hughes had needed the help backstage. Getting up on stage this year was a big thing for him.

"I don't understand how you can still be defending him," I said, taking another spoon of chocolate chip cookie dough from the bowl and eating it raw. As soon as the bell had rung for lunch, Yasmin and I had dashed for the food tech classroom and started mixing. A day like today required cookie dough.

"I'm not." Yasmin dug in with her own spoon. We were sitting on the floor behind the back workstation, because we figured that at least no one passing the room would spot us there. Yasmin had had enough pointing and whispers for one day. "Trust me, I'm far angrier with him than you are. He should know me better."

"Yes, he should." Just like Connor should know and trust me. Except I hadn't seen Connor or spoken to him since he'd left to find Ash. Just a few brief, terse texts that didn't sound much like Connor any more.

"But the thing is—"

"No. No thing," I interrupted. "He's wrong. We're right."

"Yes. But I can kind of understand why he's reacting this way. A bit."

I raised my eyebrows at her over the mixing bowl. "Because he's a ridiculous male?"

"Because of his parents," Yasmin corrected me.

"God, parents. Is it me, or are they to blame for everything?"

Yasmin smiled, which was nice to see. "Pretty much."

"So, what did Ash's do?" I wondered if it was as bad as mine, or Connor's. Or even Lottie's or Mac's. Or whether every family had its own special way of screwing people up.

"His dad cheated on his mum," Yasmin said,

simply. "Ash saw him out for dinner one day, kissing another woman. He told his mum and she didn't believe him, not at first. And then by the time she did, it turned out that almost all their friends had known for ages."

Ouch. That had to hurt. "Did they split up?"

Yasmin nodded. "Eventually. Apparently they tried to make it work for a while longer and it was just awful. I guess that's why…" She sniffed, and I handed her the bowl of cookie dough. Her need was greater.

"Still. Just because his dad was an absolute idiot, doesn't mean Ash can assume that you're equally untrustworthy."

"I know." Yasmin scooped up a huge spoonful of dough. "I just keep thinking … who would have told him that? I mean, it had to be someone he trusted. And yeah, maybe he'd be predisposed to believe them because of what happened when he tried to tell his mum, but still…"

"He had to trust them. And they had to know that this was the best possible way to break you two up." The more I thought about it, the more certain I was. Whoever had started this rumour had to have known the effect it would have on Ash. They had to have planned on it.

Which meant they had to know all about Ash's family history. Which meant a friend … or an ex-girlfriend.

"I just don't understand why anyone would care if we're dating or not," Yasmin said, sighing into the cookie dough. "I mean, what does it matter?"

"It doesn't," I agreed. "Unless the person doing it had a reason to want you or Ash single again…"

"You think it's someone who wants to date Ash themselves?"

"Makes sense."

Yasmin looked thoughtful. "It does… I'm just not sure it narrows down the field of suspects."

I slumped back down against the counter. She was right. Ash *was* a popular guy.

"What about Connor?" Yasmin asked.

I blinked at her. "How do you mean? He was with me, so he couldn't have claimed to have seen you and Jasper. And anyway, he wouldn't."

"I didn't mean that," Yasmin said. "I just thought … you asked him to speak to Ash, right? So, what happened?"

Ah. That. I looked away. "Um, actually, I haven't really spoken to Connor much since then."

"Oh."

"Yeah."

"Because of me?" Yasmin asked, sounding miserable.

"No," I said, firmly. "It's probably because he's Ash's best friend, and he's trying to help him. Like I'm helping you. As soon as we straighten all this out…"

What? What *did* happen then?

"Anyway. Don't worry about Connor and me. Let's focus on the most important part first," I suggested.

"Which part?" Jasper's face suddenly appeared over the counter, peering down at us, followed by Lottie's a moment later.

"What are you two doing down there?" Lottie asked.

"Hiding from the mob," Yasmin said.

Lottie came round to sit with us. "It's not that bad. No one really cares that much."

"Maybe not, but right now it feels like it's all anyone is talking about." Yasmin handed over the mixing bowl, and Lottie grabbed a fresh spoon from the drawer.

"Well, then, just remember that the people talking about it are mindless gossips with nothing better to do," Lottie said. "We all know you wouldn't do anything like this."

"Neither would I!" Jasper protested, joining us on the floor. "Not with Yasmin! No offence."

Yasmin sighed. "None taken. I wouldn't kiss you, either." She grinned. "Izzy would kill me."

Jasper groaned. "God, Izzy. *Just* when I was starting to make sense of things with her."

"Surely she doesn't believe this nonsense?" I said.

"Of course not. But it doesn't help."

"Did you talk to her today like you planned?"

Jasper shook his head. "Not really. We sort of stammered through the first bit of me saying I was sorry, but by then she'd heard about the thing with Yasmin, so I explained what had really happened ... except I don't know what really happened. Who the hell started this rumour?"

I shrugged. "We don't know. Yet. Actually, maybe you can help."

Jasper stopped with a spoonful of cookie dough halfway to his mouth. "Me? How?"

"Well, you and Yasmin were the only people we know were there. But someone must have seen you together to be able to start this rumour in the first place. Otherwise, Yasmin would have been able to say – no, I was with my mum, ask her, or whatever. So, who else was in the bakery that day?"

Yasmin shook her head. "Sorry, I really don't

know. I had my back to the window, so I wouldn't have seen anyone walking past. And the bakery was really quiet that afternoon – we didn't get there until quite late. I don't remember anyone else coming in."

"Must have been someone walking past, then," I muttered. "So, it's all on you, Jasper."

He winced. "Sorry, Yasmin. I was kind of caught up in my own stuff that day. I wasn't looking."

We all slumped down a bit at that, and Lottie handed the bowl over to me.

"So, what do we do now?" Yasmin asked. She sounded defeated, like she'd given up on her own relationship already. And I just couldn't let that happen.

"I'll talk to Connor," I said decisively. If anyone had a better insight into Ash's state of mind, it would be him. They were friends. And the few glimpses of Connor I'd had over the last day and a half, he'd always been with Ash.

Besides, it would give me a chance to find out what was going on with Connor and me. I mean, it couldn't just be him avoiding the drama again, could it? That was stupid. This wasn't drama for the sake of drama – it was our friends.

"And if all he can tell us is that Ash hates me?"

Yasmin said, staring into the bowl.

"Then I'll figure something else out." I put an arm around her and squeezed, feeling her lean into my shoulder. "I'm going to fix this," I promised.

I just hoped I could.

APRON

What you need:

A rectangle of thick fabric, 80 x 65cm for the apron
A rectangle of fabric in a complementary colour or pattern,
35 x 20cm for the pocket
2m of 30mm cotton tape, cut into 4 lengths of 50cm
for the apron ties

What to do:

1. Fold and iron your fabric in half lengthways and sideways so you have a cross in the middle. Open back up and lay out in a portrait orientation.

2. On what will be the top end of your apron, measure 15cm to the left and right of the fold and mark.

3. Draw a diagonal line from these points outwards to each side crease, halfway down the edge of the apron, to give your apron shape. Once you're happy with the shape, cut along these lines.

4. Hem the apron all the way around.

5. Pin two of your ties at the outer edges of the top of the apron, and the other two at the waist (where your diagonal

line ended). Sew firmly in place.

6. Hem all four sides of your pocket.

7. Pin the pocket piece into place on your apron, using the cross in the middle as your guide.

8. Sew around the sides and bottom of your pocket to hold it in place, then sew another line up the middle to split it into two sections.

9. Wear and bake!

I found Connor in the sixth-form common room the following morning, sitting in the same chair he'd been in on Monday. He looked considerably more uncomfortable to see me this time, though.

"Hey," he said, as I sat next to him. "I haven't seen you around this week."

Because he'd been avoiding me – avoiding this conversation. And if there was one thing I hated more than anything it was being pushed aside and ignored. "I kind of had other priorities. Like my best friend's reputation being trashed by the whole school and her boyfriend being a complete and utter—"

"Hey," Connor interrupted me. "Whatever happened, it's their business. Not ours."

"You really believe that? Then why are you taking Ash's side?" I leaned forward in my chair, hands resting on my knees, waiting for his answer. The muscles in my arms and shoulders ached they were so tense – and from the way he was tapping his thigh with his fingers, so was Connor.

He thought I was going to cause I scene, I realized. Make more drama for him.

Maybe I would. Maybe he deserved it after this week.

"I'm not taking anybody's side," Connor said, which was just a blatant lie. "Ash is my friend – he was my friend before, he's still my friend now. I'm trying to keep him ... stable, for the show as much as for him. I'm just not getting involved in any of the—"

"Drama," I finished for him. "You know, Connor, for someone who wants to work in the theatre, you have a real issue with that word."

"You know what I mean," he said, scowling. Other people were starting to notice us now. Some were obviously listening in, others outright staring. I bet Connor hated that.

Part of me wanted to let rip – to really put on a show for everyone watching. But I knew Connor now, I knew how that would hurt him. So instead, I lowered my voice and tried reason.

"Look, this isn't like that. Someone is trying to hurt my friend – by lying about her, by ruining her relationship. And I'm not going to let that happen." One thing I'd learned about friends in the last year

– their opinion was far more important than what other people thought about you. Even someone as important to me as Connor.

He reached across to try and take my hand, but I snatched it back. I needed to know he understood before I figured out if we could even carry on being together.

His eyebrows lowered into a frown. "Look, I know you're upset for your friend, and I get that you want to help her. But I don't appreciate being put in the middle of that. It's their drama, not mine, and I don't want anything to do with it."

"Or with me," I guessed. "Not while this is going on." Hadn't he already made that clear with his utter lack of communication?

With a sigh, he reached for my hand again and, this time, I let him hold it. "Look, I don't care about Yasmin and Ash," Connor said. "I mean, they're my friends, sure, but I care a hell of a lot more about you and me. So … be there for your friend, I get that. And I'll do the same for Ash, because he needs someone right now. But I'm not getting involved with the gossip and the 'he said, she said'. And if that's where you're going to be while this is going on, right in the middle of it all … I guess I might need to step back a bit until it's over."

"You're asking me to choose between my friends and you?" Because that was what it sounded like. And I didn't do well with ultimatums. "You want us to break up?"

"No." He spoke the word firmly, gripping my hand even tighter, but I still wasn't sure I believed him. "I want you to choose not to be part of the drama."

I shook my head. "You don't get it."

"Yes, I think I do." Whether he knew it or not, his voice was louder now. And sharper. And people were watching again. "You can't leave it behind, can you? Even though you knew how I felt about all that, you had to throw me into the middle of it, sending me after Ash. As if nothing I said to you in London counted for anything."

"I thought our friendship – our relationship! – counted for more." I yanked my hand out of his and stood up. "Obviously I was wrong."

Connor leaned back in his chair, staring down at his knees. "I'm not doing this."

"Of course you're not." I almost laughed. "Look, if you want to end all this, tell me something. Do you know who told Ash? About Yasmin and Jasper, I mean?"

He groaned. "No. No, I don't. Does it really matter?"

"Yes. It really does." If I could figure out who it was, I could find a way to make them tell the truth.

I hesitated, wishing things were better between us, but knowing they couldn't be until this was all sorted. Were we ultimately incompatible when we felt so differently about things? "I guess I'll see you at rehearsal tomorrow?" I said, and he nodded.

"Yeah. Wait – Grace." He grabbed for my hand again and held it, looking up at me with those pale blue eyes I'd once thought were cold. Now I could see nothing but feeling in them.

"I get why you think you have to do this, I do," he said, finally, which was more of an admission than I'd hoped for. "And … I guess the most important thing to me is that it doesn't come between us."

"You're the one putting it there," I pointed out.

"I know." He looked down at our joined hands, his thumb rubbing across the back of mine. "I know you now. I trust you. If you say you're not doing this for the drama, I believe you. I know you won't let any of this affect the show—"

"Is that all you're worried about? The show?"

"No!" Connor blurted out. Everyone was watching us now. "No," he said again, softer this time. Standing up, he pulled me closer. "What I care about is us. All I want is for everything to just go back to normal. Yes, I want the show to be a success, you know I do. But mostly I want for us to be good again. Because I care about you, more than any show."

I sighed. "I can't promise not to support Yasmin in this, so I can't stay out of the drama completely. But I can promise I won't let it affect us – or the show. OK?" It was the best I could do. I wanted the show to be a success, too – for Connor, as much as anything. He deserved that summer job, and I wanted to make it happen, however I could. But for it to work, Ash needed to be on form. And I knew he'd act better if he wasn't angry and confused about Yasmin.

Which led me straight back to finding out who had been telling Ash lies and setting him straight. Just as long as whoever it was wasn't involved in the play, it should be fine.

Except I had a sinking feeling that everything these days had to do with the play. Even this.

Connor nodded, relief in his eyes. "OK."

"Then I'll see you tomorrow," I said. Once I'd figured out how I was going to fix everything.

I had a free period last thing that afternoon, but I didn't want to risk the common room or the library so instead I hid out in the empty textiles classroom and finished off a project I'd started the week before – a striped apron. Holding it up, it was too long for me, and more of a manly design anyway, but it was an actual working apron with straps and everything and I'd made it all by myself, with no help from Izzy or Miss Cotterill or Faith.

I felt unbearably proud of it.

Maybe I could tackle Gran's last patchwork quilt after all. I'd learned so much over the past few months, and I felt more like an actual seamstress. Gran would be so pleased, I thought.

Packing up the apron, I gathered my things and headed out to the food tech classroom. I was early for Bake Club but, as it turned out, I wasn't the first one there.

"Hey. What are you doing here?" I asked, as I tossed my bag down by my workstation.

Mac looked up from the pastry he was rolling out. "I was helping Miss Anderson with a couple of classes this afternoon, and she said I could use the room to bake something special for Lottie. I've been working a lot of extra hours lately, so we haven't seen much of each other."

"That's nice. Glad you learned something from Valentine's Day." I perched on the stool opposite where he was working and watched him line the pie tin with the pastry. It was weird. Mac wasn't any less attractive than he'd been last year – if anything, he was looking hotter than ever. Before last year, the fact that he had his own flat and car would have been more than enough to interest me. But I wasn't the slightest bit interested any more. The attraction had gone completely, and I knew who was to blame.

"So, what's been going on around here?" Mac asked, placing a circle of baking parchment in the middle of the pie and loading it with baking beads. "Lottie called earlier, she said things were kind of tense."

I laughed. "That's one way of putting it."

Mac picked up his pie and carried it to the ovens, then came back and washed his hands. "So, tell me."

"You really want to hear?"

Mac nodded, and I launched into a retelling of the whole miserable business. He listened far better than Jasper ever would have, with hardly any interruptions. He winced when I got to today's conversation with Connor.

"What if he doesn't really believe I've changed?" I finished.

Mac shook his head. "Give the guy a break. He didn't say that."

"He thinks I want the drama."

"He wants you to think about you and him, not other people. That's different."

I pulled a face. I hated it when people talked sense in the face of how I felt. "And the show. Either way, I feel like I'll always be one mistake away from being that Grace again. The one you all thought was a complete bitch at the start of last year."

Mac didn't lie, didn't say, "We didn't think that." Which I appreciated. Instead he said, "You're not that person any more. You've changed. Any fool can see that."

"But what if the fool I want can't?" I sighed. "How did you do it, Mac?"

"Do what?"

"Convince people that you'd changed. That you were worth taking a chance on?"

He shrugged. "I don't know. Maybe I didn't. All I really cared about was that Lottie believed it. No one else mattered."

"So, how did you convince her?"

"I'm not sure. I guess ... we talked about a lot of things. I told her things I'd never told anyone."

"Like?" Because that sounded interesting.

"Like about my past, and stuff. You know, my mum. My record. Why I set fire to that car when I was twelve, that kind of thing. But … I don't know. Maybe it was just spending time together, doing things together, being the same person she hoped I was, day after day. Just showing up and being myself."

Just showing up. Well, that I could do. Had been doing. Showing up every day and doing the job I'd been assigned, even if I was still hoping for the one I deserved. Until Yasmin needed me more.

"Of course, it could have been the chocolate brownies," Mac added, and I laughed. "Hey, don't mock. My double chocolate chip brownies are legendary."

"They are." I watched him as he started to mix the filling for his pie, rolling my eyes when I realized what it was. Lemon pie. Of course. "Mac?"

He glanced up. "Yeah?"

"Why *did* you set fire to that car?" I couldn't help it.

He stopped mixing and put his bowl to one side. "If I tell you … you can't tell anyone. OK?"

I nodded. "Of course. Lips sealed and all that."

"And I'm only telling you because you've had a lousy day."

"OK. So?"

"You know my brother, Jamie? He had this girlfriend, when I was about eleven or twelve, Beth.

She was … gorgeous. Not just beautiful, but nice, too. She'd hang out with me sometimes when Jamie was working. And she was just one of those people you couldn't help but like, you know?"

"Like Lottie."

"Yeah, maybe." He smiled at the idea, but then his face turned serious again. "Anyway, she had this ex who was a real piece of work and he wanted her back. One day Beth showed up with a black eye, and she wouldn't tell Jamie what had happened. But she told me. And I went and set fire to his car."

He sounded so matter-of-fact, like this kind of thing happened every day. Maybe it had, before he met Lottie. But he'd changed now. He'd still defend his friends, I knew, just without the violence or arson he'd resorted to before. Just like I was doing with Yasmin. And, I supposed, Connor thought he was doing with Ash.

Mac pushed himself up off the counter as the timer beeped and went to rescue his pie crust. "Happier now?" he called back over his shoulder.

I nodded. "A little." Then, as a last minute thought, I reached into my bag. "Hey, Mac? I made something I thought you might like."

His brows drew together in confusion as I handed him the apron. "I'm going to make them for everyone in Bake Club," I explained, in case he thought it was weird for me to give him a gift. "But I'd like you to have this one." Not that I thought he'd ever wear it or anything – he still grumbled about the plain white one he had to wear at work. But he'd given me something – a secret, and just maybe a little faith – and I wanted him to have something in return.

"Thanks." Mac unfolded it and smiled. Then, to my amazement, he tied the straps behind his head and fastened the ones around his waist. "How do I look?"

"Like a changed man," I joked.

Saturday was the technical rehearsal – something none of us were looking forward to. We'd all agreed to come in for the full day, though, even though it was the weekend, to get through the gruelling job of making sure everything worked right. Mr Hughes had picked up the costumes Connor and I had chosen from the National Theatre, so this was also my first opportunity to make sure everything fitted right. We'd tried to choose uniforms as close as possible to the actors' sizes, since we knew this was one set of costumes we couldn't alter to suit us. I'd find out in the break how well we'd done.

Most of the rehearsal would be done out of

costume. Tech rehearsals are theoretically just a full run through of the whole play, with lights, sound effects and scene changes and so on. So you'd think it would only take as long as the play takes to perform. But no. I'd been to tech rehearsals that lasted two whole days. And I wasn't very optimistic about this one.

"Grace, can you prompt for today?" Mr Hughes asked, and I nodded my agreement. It would be a nightmare, because with all the stopping and starting to check the lights and stuff it was pretty much guaranteed that everyone would forget half their lines. But at least it meant that nobody would bother me.

I took my seat in the prompter's chair as Mr Hughes called the cast to the stage.

"OK, everyone. I know this might be a long and tedious day for us all, but it's vital to making sure this show runs without a hitch next week. So, I'm going to ask you all to be patient with us. Hopefully we'll manage a good run-through of the play, too, to keep it all fresh in your minds before next week. Now, let's get going!"

The cast members who weren't in the opening scene headed into the wings, and the four starters got into position. Lights started to change and focus.

If I leaned forward just a little, I could see Connor at the lighting desk at the back of the hall, working with the tech guys to get everything perfect.

My heart still bumped a little against my insides when I saw him, even after everything. I wanted to run out there and kiss him … but I was also a little scared. How could we be together when we were so different?

We stumbled on through the first couple of scenes with only one prompt, until Mr Hughes called a pause to fix something or other to do with the lighting plan, and we all sat around waiting to start up again.

Ash was on stage, his face still glum. It was hard to tell in a tech rehearsal, but he didn't seem to be giving the character of Benedick much feeling today, either. I wondered if he was as broken-hearted as Yasmin was. Was he just too proud to admit that he was wrong?

On stage, Violet came and sat beside him. They weren't in costume, but she was wearing the 1920s-style headband I'd made for her anyway, the sparkly beads and sequins flashing in the changing lights. She'd hugged me when I gave it to her the week before and had barely taken it off since. I was starting to regret making the damn thing.

I watched as she smiled a sickly, sympathetic

smile, resting a hand lightly against Ash's arm as she spoke to him.

Suddenly, I had a very clear idea exactly who might have wanted to split up Ash and Yasmin, and why. And I also knew that no one would believe me if I told them. They'd just think I was trying to discredit Violet out of bitterness that I couldn't win back the role that should have been mine. And Connor... I was most afraid of what Connor would think. At best, that I was seeking drama. At worst, that this was some sort of last-ditch attempt to win the part of Beatrice. I knew that he said he'd been wrong about me when we'd first met, but he hadn't been, not entirely. What if he realized that and decided he definitely was better off without me?

Because if Violet was behind things and I tried to prove it ... that was pretty much the opposite of keeping things drama free for the good of the show, like I'd promised. But if it would clear Yasmin's name, how could I not?

I couldn't stop staring at them, my mind whirring with possibilities and plans. Violet lived three doors down from Ash, I remembered. Their families were probably friends, which meant she'd almost certainly know all about the circumstances around Ash's parents' divorce. It had to be her.

But there was no way I could prove it. And without proof … Connor might just think the worst.

I was so engrossed in my thoughts, I didn't hear the footsteps behind me, and jumped at the sound of Jasper's voice coming from just behind my left ear.

"Hey. Your phone was off, but your dad said you were here." He crouched down beside me. "What's going on?"

"Deathly boring tech rehearsal. What are you doing here?"

"I needed to talk to you."

"About?" I kept my gaze firmly on the stage, in case we started up rehearsals again, but that didn't seem likely for a while anyway.

"Izzy." Of course. What else did Jasper have on his mind these days? "I really want to make things up to her. For being, well, you know…"

"Kind of rubbish for the last six months?"

"For things not going as well as I'd have liked," Jasper said. "I want to do something really special for her. To show that I want to start something with her, despite everything that's happened."

"Like you going on about Ella for months, being totally oblivious to the fact that Izzy liked you, then pushing her away when she tried to kiss you?" I only said it to make Jasper blush, which he did.

"Yeah, that," he said. "So, will you help me?"

"Of course I will. Just let me know what you need me to do."

"I will. As soon as I've figured it out myself. I was hoping you'd have some ideas."

All of my ideas seemed to focus on finding a way to prove that Violet was the one who'd started the rumour about Yasmin. "I'll think about it," I promised Jasper. "And, in the meantime, you can do something for me."

Jasper groaned. "I should have known you agreed far too easily."

Ignoring him, I pointed my script out on to the stage. "Look at those two. Do you think that Violet looks like someone with a motive to want Ash single again?"

"Definitely. Wait, that's Violet?"

"Of course it is. She's the year below us."

"Yeah, I know. I've heard you talk about her a lot, but I hadn't really put it together who she was." He frowned and shuffled closer to the stage.

"What? What is it?"

"That headband … does she wear it a lot?" Jasper asked.

"Pretty much constantly since I gave it to her," I said, rolling my eyes. "Why?"

"The way it flashes in the lights... I remember, when I was at the bakery with Yasmin, I saw someone through the window and the street lights were doing the same to something on their head."

"You think it was Violet?" Did that count as proof? I was pretty sure no jury would convict on the testimony of the sparkly headband. But we didn't have juries at school. All we had were rumours.

"It definitely could have been." Jasper turned back to face me. "So, what do we do about it?"

I chewed on my lip while I considered. I needed to get Violet to confess. But how?

"I'll talk to her after the rehearsal," I decided. No point in making this endless day any worse by upsetting the lead early on. Besides, it gave me time to figure out what on earth to say to her. "Maybe I can hint that you saw more than just her hairband."

"Yeah. Good luck." Jasper got to his feet. "Will you let me know how it goes?"

"Of course. Don't suppose you want to stay around and help, do you?"

Jasper grinned. "Sorry," he said, not at all apologetically. "I've got a fair maiden to woo."

I rolled my eyes. "Go on, then. I'm sure you'll come up with some spectacular plan guaranteed to make her fall at your feet."

"That's the idea!" Jasper waved as he walked off and, finally, Mr Hughes called for us to start up rehearsals again. I turned my attention back to the script – but my mind was already planning my conversation with Violet.

I just needed to find a way to make her confess the truth to Ash without Connor ever realizing I'd been involved. How hard could that be?

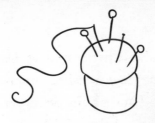

1920s HEADBAND

What you need:

Velvet fabric
Thick elastic in a matching colour to your fabric
Feathers, sequins and sparkly buttons to decorate

What to do:

1. *Measure from the bottom of your left ear, over your head (where the headband will sit) to the bottom of your right ear.*

2. *Cut your velvet into a rectangle to fit this length, and twice as wide as you want your headband to be, plus 2cm.*

3. *Fold your rectangle in half lengthways, with the right sides together, and pin then sew in place with a 1cm seam allowance. Turn the right way out.*

4. *Figure out where the middle of your headband is, and sew decorations to one side for an authentic 1920s look.*

5. *Measure around the back of your head, from ear to ear, and cut your elastic to that length.*

6. *Tuck the ends of your velvet inside for a neat finish, then slip one end of the elastic into each to complete your headband circle. Pin and sew in place.*

The tech rehearsal went on through the afternoon and into the evening. We took breaks for meals, and Connor took orders for a fish and chip shop run when it became obvious none of us would be home in time for dinner. I was beginning to despair of ever getting to talk to Violet alone. She'd clung to Ash's side all day, even when I was quite sure he didn't want her there. Connor was starting to look a little askance at her – not that I was watching Connor or anything.

Oh, OK, I totally was. And, I had to admit, I was impressed. I definitely had no doubts about why Mr Hughes had chosen to appoint his stepson as stage manager. He kept the tech rehearsal entirely calm and as stress free as possible – something I'd never seen done so well before. He'd be a great asset to any professional theatre.

"Just the curtain call to rehearse!" Mr Hughes called out, far too cheerfully. Everyone on stage and backstage groaned in unison, and he laughed. "OK,

OK. We'll save that for Tuesday afternoon, after the dress rehearsal. Then we open that night, and I want everyone on top form for all five performances. Rest up tomorrow – next week is going to be a long one."

He didn't know the half of it, I thought. And neither he nor Connor knew that my day wasn't even over yet. I had one more very important thing to do first.

I waited until most people had started to drift off down to the hall to gather their things, then I struck, just as Violet looked like she was about to swan off with Ash.

"Violet?" I called, and she turned to face me, annoyance plastered across her face. "Can I borrow you for a moment?"

"Can't it wait?" she whined. "I've had a really long day."

We all had, but I didn't mention it. Instead, I said the one thing I could guarantee would get her back to the drama room with me. "I'm sorry. But there's a slight problem with your costume for the last scene. Could you just come and try it on for me one more time so I can get it fixed? I'd hate for you to have to go on stage next week in something that made you look bad."

It worked.

I'd stashed her costume in the drama room during the dinner break, in anticipation of this. I handed it to her and let her change behind one of the screens we'd set up, ignoring her grumbling about incompetent stage hands.

I wasn't a stage hand, I reminded myself. I was the wardrobe mistress. And I was far better at my job than she was at hers. In fact, I was better at hers, too.

"It looks fine," Violet said, stepping out from behind the screen in her simple white wedding dress. "What's the problem with it?"

I squinted as I looked her up and down, pretending to find a fault. "Let me just check that back hem," I said, moving behind her with a tin of pins in hand. "So, how's Ash doing? I saw you were trying to cheer him up today."

"He's coping really well," Violet said. "I mean, obviously he was hurt by that…" She seemed to remember who she was talking to and changed her tack. "Hurt by everything that happened. But he's not the sort of guy to sit around and mope."

"No, I suppose not." I stuck a few pins in the hem of her dress to make it look like I was doing something. "What I don't understand is who would want to spread such a vicious rumour in the first place. I mean, it would have to be someone who

314

really hated Yasmin. Or really wanted Ash."

Violet flinched, and I narrowly avoided stabbing her with a pin. As satisfying as it might have been, it probably wouldn't have helped win me a confession.

"I imagine whoever saw them just thought that Ash had a right to know," she said airily.

"But that's the thing, isn't it? There wasn't anything *to* see. Whoever told Ash made it up. But for some reason, he's reluctant to say who told him. I suppose they must have asked him not to, in case Yasmin – or her friends – came after them to make them tell the truth." I paused, carefully planning my next words. "But I figured that whoever had started the rumour must have seen Yasmin and Jasper at the bakery that day, at the least. Yasmin was too upset to remember anyone who was there. But Jasper... Jasper remembered a few things." Another pause. Nothing like a bit of dramatic tension to build up to a confession. "Like a very unique 1920s headband sparkling in the street lights outside."

Violet's hand flew up to her head, as if to check the headband was still there. "I don't like what you're insinuating."

"I'm not insinuating anything." I straightened up, all pretence of pinning over now. "I'm telling you that Jasper saw you outside the bakery that night.

315

I'm telling you that I know it was you who lied to Ash. So the only question is, am I going to tell him the truth – that you made it up so you could try it on with him yourself – or are you going to call him and tell him that you made a mistake? That you didn't see what you thought you saw."

It needed to be her. It *really* needed to be her.

She turned, slowly, to face me, and I could see in her eyes she was calculating her options, weighing up her choices. Wondering how to beat me.

"I'm not telling anyone anything," she said finally. "And there's no point in you doing it. No one's going to believe *you*."

I couldn't let her know that I thought she was right. "Connor will believe me."

"Really?" She arched a brow at me. "Are you sure? I heard you two arguing, you know, last term. He thought you were after my role. This would be all the proof he needs, right?"

"I'm not going to explain mine and Connor's relationship to you. Things are different now."

Violet's smile was cruel. "How much are you willing to bet on that?" She leaned in closer, as if to whisper a secret. "You might not have noticed, Grace, but you're not the be all and end all at this school any more. In fact, you barely matter. You're not going to tell anyone because they'll think you're just a bitter, twisted, mean girl trying to get back at me for being a better actress than you."

"A better actress?" I shouldn't have laughed but it came out before I had a chance to think.

Violet wasn't smiling any more. Her expression cold and stony, she grabbed the neckline of her costume and pulled. The ripping sound echoed through the empty room, as she casually stepped out of the tattered dress. She tossed it across the room, where it landed on a window jamb, its delicate silk caught on the metal.

My heart sank down towards my toes, but I wouldn't let myself wince, wouldn't let her know that she'd just potentially destroyed hours upon hours of Izzy's work, and I had no idea how, or even if, I could fix it in time.

Striding across the room in her underwear, Violet stepped behind the screen to get dressed again. I just kept staring at the torn fabric hanging from the window. At least, until the door opened and I darted forward to grab it before anyone else saw.

"You two finished in here?" Connor asked, just as Violet emerged from behind the screen. "Mr Hughes is waiting to lock up."

"Oh, I think we're done. Aren't we, Grace?"

Violet said, an innocent smile on her face. I knew this was it. This was the moment to tell Connor what I'd discovered, to prove that I trusted him to believe me, whatever Violet said.

But I couldn't. I just wasn't sure enough. And I'd promised him I wouldn't do anything to jeopardize the show – like wreck one of the most important costumes just days before opening night.

So instead, I nodded. "For now, anyway."

Connor looked between us, a small frown on his face. "Well, OK, then. Let's go. Big week next week, as Mr Hughes keeps reminding us."

Yes, it was. There was no way I was going to let Violet ruin it.

I spent Sunday panicking about the dress.

I called Izzy, but she was away on some textiles course until Monday night and so she was absolutely no help at all.

"How bad is it?" she asked over the phone.

"Bad."

Silence.

"I'll be back late tomorrow night. We can meet and look at it on Tuesday morning?" But even she didn't sound too hopeful of us getting it fixed before the dress rehearsal that afternoon.

Connor texted around lunchtime, and my heart jumped when I saw his name on my screen.

Hey, want to do something today? I could come over?

Did that mean everything was fine and normal? Or did he suspect something? Or, worse, had Violet told him – or Ash – about my accusations?

Either way, he couldn't come round. He'd see the dress, and then he'd know something had happened. Or I could hide it, but then it definitely wouldn't be mended in time for the dress rehearsal.

In the end, I lied.

Sorry, got family stuff on today. See you at school, though x

I felt bad about it all afternoon.

At teatime, Mum knocked on my bedroom door to see if I was ever planning on coming out. And then, because she believes parents can just do these things, she walked in without waiting for me to say it was OK.

"You can't sit in here sulking all day," she said, leaving the door wide open behind her.

"Want to bet?" I replied. I didn't even really mean it; I was just so fed up of everything.

A look of frustration crossed Mum's face. "Honestly, Grace. I don't know what else you want us to do. I thought things were getting better, but this weekend…

Look. Maybe we did make a mistake, when we were younger. Our circumstances were very different back then. When we made the decision to give Faith away ... it seemed like the only option at the time, but maybe it wasn't. Either way, none of it was Faith's fault, and now we're trying to make it up to her. I don't understand why you can't support us in that."

"You made another mistake." The bile and the bitterness rose up in me all over again. Maybe Connor was wrong. Maybe some situations needed a little drama, or nothing ever got resolved. "You should have told me about Faith before she showed up on our doorstep."

Mum's face froze at that and when it unfroze, she suddenly looked much older than I'd ever seen her before. Stepping further into the room, she leaned against my desk, as if she needed the support.

"You're right," she said, and I almost fainted in surprise. I don't think I'd *ever* heard either of my parents say that before. "We should have. But ... there was a chance we'd never see her again, and that was hard for me to accept. I didn't want to burden you with the knowledge that you had a sister out there who didn't want to know you."

I sat up a little, so I was perched on the edge of the bed. I'd never thought about it like that before. About what it would be like to know that Faith existed but not have her in our lives. I wasn't sure if that would be better or worse, quite honestly.

"I'm sorry, Grace. Sorry that everything has been so ... unexpected and difficult for you this year. But we're trying, really we are. I *know* this is hard for you, but you have to understand that it's hard for us, too. For all of us. We're all adjusting, and we're doing the best we can to find our own way through."

"There should be a handbook for this sort of thing," I said, and Mum laughed.

"There should."

I watched her, still looking tired and worn, but trying. Maybe my parents weren't the only ones who had expectations. I'd been so busy trying to live up to theirs, I hadn't even realized how much I expected from them. I expected them to get it right, every time, and to know all the answers. But nobody could live up to that, could they? Not even me.

We're doing the best we can, Mum had said. Wasn't that just what I was doing? With the costumes, with Connor, with Yasmin. And maybe that best would be enough, and maybe it wouldn't. One way or another, we'd all come out the other side of this.

"Everything OK in here?" Dad asked, his head appearing around the edge of the door.

Mum looked at me. "I think so. Grace?"

"Yeah." I nodded for good measure. "I think everything will be." Not yet, perhaps. Faith was still a stranger, really, and the new dynamic between us all would take some getting used to. But eventually, we *would* get used to it. And until then, we'd keep on doing the best we could.

"Good," Dad said. "Then who wants some coffee and cake? I picked up a coffee and walnut sponge from the bakery. It has perfectly symmetrical coffee beans on the top."

One of Lottie's. I hopped up off the bed. "Great!"

But before I could follow him, Mum spotted something.

"What's that?" she asked, staring at the ruined silk lying in state across my bed.

"One of the costumes from the play," I said, my miserable cloud descending again. Not only had I totally failed to fix Yasmin's relationship, or my own – in the process, I'd ruined the best costume in the whole damn play.

"What happened to it?" Mum picked the dress up carefully, like it was some sort of injured animal.

"It met with an accident," I said flatly. Violet, as far as I was concerned, was an accident waiting to happen.

"How are you going to fix it?"

"I have absolutely no idea," I admitted.

Mum stared at the dress. Then she turned to me. "Come on. I know what we need to do. Nick, put the kettle on."

Dad and I looked at each other, then at Mum's retreating back as she darted out of the room.

Maybe this weekend could be saved after all.

"OK, see this tear here?" Mum peered over the glasses perched on the end of her nose and pointed at the one she meant. I leaned closer around the sewing machine to get a look.

"Yeah?" It was a long one, all down the left side of the dress.

"This one is easy. It's just along the seam, and the fabric is still intact, so we can just re-sew it. This one, however…" She pointed to another rip on the opposite armhole. "This one has torn the fabric. We're going to need to reinforce it before we can re-sew it."

"Can we do that?" I asked, worried. "It needs to still match the other three dresses that are the same."

"We can do it," Mum said, and her confident tone gave me hope. "And since it's under the arm, no one will see any repair job we do anyway."

"Great!" It was all going to be fine. I felt like I could breathe for the first time since the confrontation with Violet.

"But this one…" Mum tapped next to a tear in the fabric I'd almost forgotten about in my excitement. This one was more of a hole, and I figured it must have happened when I grabbed the dress off the window jamb.

"It's right on the front of the dress," Mum said, running her fingers over the silk around the hole. "Any mending we do is going to show, even from a distance under the stage lights. Especially when it's next to the other dresses. And on fabric this fragile… I'll have to think about this one."

"Do you think we can fix it, though?" Otherwise, what was the point in mending the other tears? "If I need to find a new dress…" I didn't have a clue what I was going to do, to be honest.

Mum shook her head. "We'll fix it." She flashed me a smile. "Just trust me."

"OK." I took a deep breath as Dad placed the coffee cups on the table. "And, um … thanks. For helping me."

Mum's smile became deeper at that, almost a little sad, and she sniffed, before pushing her glasses back up her nose. "I'm glad to have the chance. You've always been so good at doing everything on your own."

"Have I?" It didn't feel like it.

"Grace," Dad said. "You're a marvel. Always have been."

I grinned and reached for a piece of cake. "Then let's get started."

The first tear took Mum moments to fix. I watched her carefully, and listened as she explained what she was doing and why. The silk was slippery under her hands and took careful handling with the sewing machine.

Then, while she was looking for something to reinforce the second tear, muttering something about seam tape, there was a knock on the front door. Feeling fairly superfluous to the proceedings anyway, I ran to answer it – only to find Jasper on my doorstep, his arms full of brightly coloured fabric.

"I figured out how to make things up to Izzy!" He beamed.

"By smothering her in fabric?"

Jasper shook his head. "Let me in and I'll explain."

Since I had a feeling I was going to be expected to do something or other with the mass of material Jasper had brought, I led him straight through to the kitchen, where the sewing machine was set up on the table.

Dumping his bundle of cloth on a chair, Jasper peered down at the dress Mum was working on.

"Violet's costume for the final scene," I explained, in response to his curious look. "It met with an … accident, yesterday."

Jasper raised his eyebrows. "Was that accident called Violet?" he murmured, his words inaudible to Mum over the sound of the machine.

I nodded. "But Mum knows how to fix it. Mostly."

The machine stopped clacking and whirring, and Mum pulled the dress out and held it up. Apart from the hole in the front, it looked as good as new.

"It looks great, Mum. Thank you."

Mum beamed. "Well. We're getting there, anyway." She spotted the stack of fabric on the chair. "Do we have another project on our hands?"

"Jasper is trying to impress a girl," I explained, and he glared at me.

"These are the offcuts from the dresses she makes. I thought maybe there might be something I could do with them? I need something … impressive."

"A grand gesture with fabric…" Mum stared off into the distance. Jasper and I exchanged looks, and I shrugged when he mouthed, "What's going on?" at me.

Then Mum clicked her fingers. "I've got just the thing! But you'd better phone your sister, Grace. We're going to need all hands on deck for this one."

Phone Faith. I'd never done that before. And, nice as she'd turned out to be, I wasn't entirely sure I wanted to set that kind of precedent just yet.

"What about Violet's costume?" I asked, stalling. "We've got to get that last hole fixed first."

Mum gave me a mysterious grin. "I think Jasper's grand gesture might just be the answer to your dress issues, too. Call Faith and I guarantee that by the end of the night I'll have solved both of your problems."

Well. That decided it. Leaving Jasper and Mum sorting through fabric, I darted out into the hall to call Faith and ask her to come over.

School on Monday was unbearable. Everywhere I turned Violet seemed to be smirking at me. Yasmin looked sadder than ever and was refusing to come anywhere near the drama room, or the play.

"I'll help bake the refreshments like I promised," she said, when I asked if she could help backstage for the dress and first performance. "But Lottie will come and set them all up. I don't want to... I think it'll be better if I just run things from the food tech classroom this time."

I didn't like it, but I couldn't blame her, either. "Don't worry. I'll ask Izzy if she'll help. She's back tonight." The high from fixing Violet's costume – and inadvertently sorting out Jasper's love life – was fading. I still needed Violet to own up. That way, everything would be fixed and Connor would never have to know I was involved.

Mr Hughes was running some last-minute scene rehearsals after school, but I wasn't needed for them. Instead, I was with Izzy in the textiles classroom, ironing and spot cleaning the costumes to make sure they were in perfect condition for the dress rehearsal.

At least it meant I didn't have to see Connor for one more day. The temptation to just tell him what Violet had done would be too great. And, as much as I hated it, she was right. There was a real chance he wouldn't believe me – that he'd think this was just another scheme to get Violet into trouble and take over the lead role.

I couldn't risk that. Especially when things were already so fraught. He'd asked me to stay out of Yasmin and Ash's dramas, to focus on our relationship and the play instead, and I hadn't. Instead, I'd gone after Violet and almost ruined everything.

Tuesday came quickly enough, though, and there

was no way to avoid him at the dress rehearsal, so I didn't even try.

"Everything ready for tonight?" I leaned against the edge of the wall beside the stage, my arms full of costumes.

Connor looked up, his eyes dark and unreadable. "Think so. How about you? Costumes all sorted?"

"All ready to go. Even Violet's." I cursed mentally the moment the words slipped out.

He frowned. "What was wrong with Violet's?"

"Doesn't matter," I said, as breezily as I could. Hoping I'd got away with it, I turned to head into the drama room, which had been turned into a dressing room, with the addition of plenty of screens to keep the male and female cast members apart.

"Grace…"

I paused, turning to look back over my shoulder. "Yeah?"

"When this is over … can we, I don't know … catch up? I feel like it hasn't been just us in weeks." He sighed. "I just want to go back to how we were on New Year's Eve."

I smiled softly. "Me, too. And yeah, once this play is over, maybe everything can go back to normal." And once I'd forced Violet to tell Ash the truth.

"I'd like that," Connor said, probably imagining

a drama-free future for the two of us.

Even though the chances were, I was about to make things a million times worse. But I had to. For Yasmin and for Ash.

Leaning over, my armful of costumes still between us, I pressed a light kiss to Connor's lips. I'd have everything sorted soon, however much drama it took. I just hoped that things could go back to how they were supposed to be when I was done.

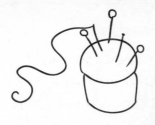

FLOWER CORSAGE

What you need:

Long piece of fabric (scrap pieces work well)
Felt in a matching colour
Button
Badge-back pin

What to do:

1. Cut your fabric into a long rectangle, 8 x 50cm.
2. Fold in half, with the wrong sides together, and tuck the ends under. Sew a long, gathering stitch 1cm in from where the edges meet.
3. Gather your fabric into tight ruffles then coil it up into a spiral, sewing it in place by hand as you go. Keep wrapping the strip around your centre and sewing in place, until you reach the end.
4. Sew your button in place at the centre of the flower.
5. Cut a circle of felt to cover the back of your flower.
6. Sew your badge-back pin to the centre of the felt, then glue the felt circle securely in place on the back of your flower.
7. Wear your corsage as a brooch to brighten up your outfit!

The first half of the dress rehearsal didn't go too badly. A few stumbles and a couple of skipped lines, but by the time we broke for the interval the cast were starting to get into the swing of things.

While they took a short break and got changed, I hung the next set of costumes out ready for quick changes backstage after the interval, one eye on Connor, shifting the scenery ready for the second half.

"Where's my dress for the last scene?" Violet asked, suddenly appearing in the middle of the stage, calling back to me.

Rolling my eyes, I hung the other costumes I was carrying on the quick-change rail and carried Violet's mended dress on to the stage. Connor looked up and smiled at me.

"It's right here," I said, holding it up for inspection. "Good as new."

Violet's gaze scanned over the dress, obviously

looking for flaws. Eventually she said, "What's that flower on the front? That wasn't there before."

"It's going to look great on stage," Connor said, coming round to look at it.

"It's a flower corsage. I made it from complementary fabrics so it shouldn't look too out of place, and I've added corsages to the other three dresses, too, so they still match." I could tell from her expression that Violet was desperate to be able to call me on not being able to fix that last hole, and having to resort to hiding it instead. But if she did that, she'd have to explain how it got ripped. In front of Connor, and anyone else who was listening.

A flash of curtain on the other side of the stage, and I saw Ash off in the wings, checking through his props. My eyes widened. This was my chance. If I could get Violet to confess while Ash listened, everything would be fixed. Yasmin would be happy again. But Connor would know exactly what I'd done.

I took a deep breath. I couldn't wait until after the show. I had to chance it now.

"The other rips we mended cleanly," I said, my heart racing as Violet's face turned stony. "The one on the left needed reinforcing, so you might want to be a little careful with it. The hole in the front should

333

be completely covered by the flower, though."

Violet had frozen, staring at me. Connor just looked puzzled until, as predicted, he asked, "What happened to the dress? It was fine on Friday."

I raised my eyebrows just a fraction and waited for Violet to answer him.

"Uh, Grace asked me to try it on again after the tech rehearsal," she said at last, her cheeks turning pink. "It must have got damaged."

"Yes... And how was that again?" I asked.

Connor's gaze flew to my face, but I didn't dare take my eyes off Violet for a second.

"I can't imagine," Violet said after a moment, her smile nasty. "What did you do to it?"

Suddenly, the answer came to me, and I smiled apologetically as I spoke. "Actually, I'm really sorry. That tear on the front happened when I tried to get it down from the window jamb in the drama room. After you ripped it off, destroyed two of the seams, and threw it across the room."

Her face turned white, then bright red.

"What?" Connor yelped. "Why would you do that?" he asked Violet.

"Why? Because *she* was making all sorts of horrible accusations about me."

"All I said was that Jasper saw you that night at

the bakery," I said, as mildly as possible. "So we knew that it must be you who lied to Ash about what you'd seen."

"And I told you that no one would believe you if you told them," Violet spat back. "Everyone knows you're just after my part."

"You did say that," I said, watching as the curtain at the side of the stage parted, and Ash came to stand behind Violet. "But one funny thing I noticed, you never denied making up the story."

"I didn't… I must have done."

I shook my head. "Not once. You just tore off your dress and told me no one would believe me."

"Violet?" Ash stepped on to the stage. "What really happened that night? Tell me again what you saw."

She spun round, pale and anxious as she started to stutter out her lies again. "I… I was at the White Hill Bakery, and I saw them together."

"Actually at the bakery? Or outside?"

"Outside. But I saw them through the window. They were sitting together…"

"And?" Ash asked impatiently. "What happened next?" A long, awkward pause. "Grace was right all along, wasn't she? You made up the whole thing."

Violet looked to me, then, and I think she knew the lies weren't going to stand up much longer.

"It was dark," she said quietly. "I... It was hard to see ... she had her back to me..."

Ash stared at her, his face almost grey under the stage lights. "You lied to me. You didn't see anything more than two friends talking, did you?"

"I just..." Violet's eyes were wide and scared now. "You're my friend. And ... and I knew she and Jasper were close. I didn't want her to make a fool of you."

"She didn't need to," Ash said, his voice hard. "You did that all by yourself." He looked at me. "I need to talk to Yasmin."

And I needed to talk to Connor. He was staring at me, those pale blue eyes expressionless. I needed to know what he was thinking.

"She's in the food tech classroom," I told Ash.

"There's no time now." Connor pointed down into the hall, where Mr Hughes had just walked in.

"Right!" he called, and the cast started gathering from around the hall. "Second half. Let's go!"

"You have to go for the theatrics, don't you?" Connor bit out, shaking his head as we moved backstage. "You can't help yourself."

"Look, I know you didn't want me to cause any drama. But you have to admit, I was right." I'd fixed things. Ash would talk to Yasmin, and everything would go back to normal again.

"You'd still have been right after the show." Connor pushed past, still frowning, and I stared after him. This didn't feel fixed.

But I didn't have time to worry about it just then. Connor would get over his sulk, we'd all get through the rest of the dress rehearsal, then it was showtime. The first-night high was bound to cheer him up. Everything would be fine. Right?

Back in the drama room, things were in chaos again, with most people only half in costume despite having the whole interval to get changed. Izzy was already there, thank goodness, and between us we got everyone sorted and sent them back out to the stage.

"What next?" Izzy asked, as the last one exited. She'd waited in the room for most of the first half, but the second half had more quick changes, so I'd need her backstage.

"Now we go and wait in the wings, ready to help with the last costume changes." I grabbed my script. "And I get to prompt them whenever they forget their lines."

"The first performance is in about four hours," Izzy pointed out. "Shouldn't they know them by now?"

"Yes. But it's the dress rehearsal. And you know what they say?"

"No."

"Bad dress, great show." I yanked open the door and headed out into the wings.

"So ... we want them to screw this up?" Izzy asked, following.

"No. But at least we have something to say that will make them feel better if they do." I flashed her a smile; Connor's grumpiness couldn't ruin my good mood. I'd let Ash and Yasmin make up, then everyone would know what Violet had done. Tonight would be a success and everything would be fine. "Besides, I wouldn't worry. They did great in the first half. And I have a feeling that the second half will be even better!"

But half an hour and countless prompts later, I had to admit I might have been wrong about that last bit. Izzy leaned in and whispered next to my ear, "I'm not sure some theatre superstition is going to help today."

I nodded. This wasn't just a bad dress rehearsal. This was the apocalypse of dress rehearsals.

Violet had barely managed a correct line since the break, and Ash seemed totally distracted, staring out into the hall as if willing Yasmin to suddenly appear and jump into his arms.

And Connor ... Connor just kept glancing over at me from the other side of the stage, and his looks made me want to curl up on myself. He thought this was my fault. And I was suddenly very afraid that he might be right.

Mr Hughes's expression grew grimmer as the afternoon wore on, until the curtain call, when it emerged that our future stars of the stage couldn't actually manage to all bow at the same time.

"OK, that's it." Mr Hughes sighed, obviously baffled as to what had changed between the first and second halves of the rehearsal. But I knew. "Look, you all know the saying. Bad dress, great show. So, no notes before tonight's performance. Just … go out there and give it all you've got."

The cast stayed loitering on the stage as he walked out, as if they weren't really sure what to do next. There wasn't enough time to go home, and Mr Hughes had asked us all to bring dinner with us. A few might pop out to the newsagent or the fish and chip shop, but otherwise, we had two hours before the call to obsess over everything that had gone wrong that afternoon.

That wasn't going to help anybody.

Looking up, I spotted Connor making his way towards me, and knew I had to act fast. If this disaster of a dress rehearsal was my fault, then it was up to me to fix it before the show, right? I didn't have time for

Connor to yell at me.

"Can you get them out of their costumes?" I asked Izzy, and she nodded.

"Where are you going?" she asked.

"To find something to cheer this miserable lot up," I told her.

"Grace! Wait." I slowed to a halt halfway across the yard to let Connor catch up.

"No time," I told him, starting to walk again as he got close. "I'm on a cheer-up mission."

"I need to talk to you." He drew level, and I could feel his warmth next to me in the cool evening air. I wanted to make everything right. But first, we had to get through this damn play.

"I haven't got time for you to say I told you so right now," I said, and picked up my pace.

"Where are we going?" he asked, matching my stride easily.

"The food tech classroom."

"Why?"

I flashed him a look. "Because everyone on that stage is miserable right now, and I know you think that's my fault."

"I didn't say—"

"You didn't need to."

He sighed. "I just don't understand why you had

340

to confront Violet then."

"Because she wouldn't have confessed at any other time. Sometimes, you need a little drama to make things work."

"And you think that worked?" Connor asked.

An uncomfortable feeling wriggled through me. "Maybe not entirely as planned," I admitted.

"You should have talked to me. I thought we were OK, that we'd agreed what to do. I thought that we could *talk* about things at least."

"I'm sorry. I really am. Is that enough? And I told you, I'm fixing it. I've never found a better way to cheer people up than with cake."

Yasmin looked up as we walked in. "You two, too, huh?"

"Two, too, what?" I asked. "Look, I need help. You guys up for it?"

"You just missed Ash," Jasper explained, from by the ovens. "Yasmin sent him packing." Of course she did. I fixed everything and she sent him away. Still, I could only handle one problem at a time, so Yasmin and Ash were just going to have to sort themselves out for now.

"What do you need help with?" Lottie asked.

"You might want to talk to him, you know," I told Yasmin. "We need cake, lots of it."

Mac, leaning against one of the counters, turned to Connor, "You able to keep up with their conversations yet?"

Connor shook his head. "I have no idea what's happening today."

"Give it time." Mac clapped him on the back. "You'll get it. What sort of cake and how much?"

"Whatever you can give me," I replied, ignoring his jibes.

Jasper winced. "Dress rehearsal went badly, huh?"

"Worse," Connor said, with a pointed look at me.

"Well, we've got a lemon drizzle, a batch of Red Velvet cupcakes and a tray of rocky road ready to go now. Will those do you?" Lottie started packing them up in a bag for me.

"That would be great," I said. "Will it leave you enough for tonight?"

"We can make more." Lottie passed the bag to me. "What else do you need?"

"Um..." I hadn't really thought beyond the cake. But now that she mentioned it... "Could someone grab the bunting we used for the Valentine's Day Extravaganza?"

"Do you want the leftover paper plates and napkins, too?" Yasmin asked, heading for the storage cupboard.

"That would be great. And I could really use someone to help me serve up…" I gave Lottie a meaningful look while Yasmin wasn't looking. Her eyes widened, then she caught on.

"Well, Mac and I need to be here to keep baking," she said.

"And I need to find Izzy," Jasper added. "You know, for the thing."

"The grand gesture," Lottie said. "Of course."

Yasmin came back with her arms full of bunting and party plates. "Looks like you're with me," I told her.

She frowned. "Can't Lottie go? I really don't—"

"Trust me," I said, handing the bag full of cake to Connor, and taking the bunting from Yasmin. "It will be worth your while. I promise."

It didn't take long to set up the Cheer-Up Cake Stall, as Jasper had taken to calling it. Hiding his grand gesture under the table when Izzy wasn't looking, he helped Connor hang the bunting, while Yasmin and I laid out the cakes. The stage was pretty much empty, with everyone off moping in corners around the hall or in the drama room. Behind the closed curtains, no one even knew we were there.

Well, almost no one.

"Yasmin?" Ash sounded uncertain, and with

343

good reason. For a moment I thought she wasn't even going to look up from the lemon drizzle cake slices she was laying out to acknowledge him. Then, with the last slice down, she sighed.

"What, Ash?"

"I wanted... I hoped that... Can we talk?" I almost felt sorry for him, standing there, his hands twisting around each other.

I'd half expected Yasmin to jump back into his arms, like he'd obviously thought she would. But then I remembered how he'd believed Violet over Yasmin and decided he deserved to suffer, at least a bit. The important thing was that he knew the truth. It was up to Yasmin what that meant for the two of them.

She sighed again, with more meaning this time. She was letting him know that if she said yes, it was just for him. She was fine without ever talking to him again, thanks.

"Can you manage here on your own?" she asked me.

"I think we'll cope," I told her.

"Fine." She looked at Ash at last. "You've got ten minutes."

As they headed off to the side of the stage, a clear metre between them, I straightened the last plate of cake, stepped back and admired my handiwork. The cake stall looked cheery, encouraging and – most importantly – delicious. Jasper had even drawn a brightly coloured sign with "Cheer-Up Cake Stall" on it to stick to the front. "Right. Time to open the curtains," I told Connor, and he moved to the side of the stage. "And where did Jasper go?"

"Not sure." He yanked on the ropes and suddenly the curtains fell aside, and the hall opened up before me.

I looked down at the cast and crew, who'd all turned to stare up at the stage – and me – when they heard the curtains open. Reflex, I assumed. You always watched the stage.

"OK," I called down, feeling self-conscious in front of a crowd for possibly the first time ever. Acting, I could do. I was less confident in my abilities as a motivational speaker. But Mr Hughes had been dragged off to some emergency staff meeting after school, and there wasn't anyone else to get these guys in the right frame of mind to put on the best show they were capable of. This was my responsibility now. And not just because Connor was blaming me – but because I might be the only person who could fix it.

Taking a deep breath, I walked to the edge of the stage and sat down, putting myself closer to their level so I didn't have to shout so much.

"Look, I know this afternoon's rehearsal was … wasn't great. But I also know you're going to rock it tonight. I know you can, because I've seen you all do it in other rehearsals. You just need to have a little faith in yourselves."

I stood up and stepped aside to point to the Cheer-Up Cake Stall. "This was the best way I could think of to perk you all up a bit. So, eat cake, cheer up, then go out there and do a great performance tonight. OK?"

We weren't taking money for the cake, so I didn't need to man the stall. I just moved to the edge of the stage to let them all come up the stairs at the side, as they ran for the cake.

All except two of them. In the middle of the aisle between the chairs we'd set out for the audience stood Jasper and Izzy. He gripped the stems of the flowers in his hands tightly enough that his knuckles were bone white, but he seemed lost for words now he finally had Izzy in front of him again, waiting to hear them.

"Go on, Jasper," I whispered, too quiet to be heard. "We practised this."

"Izzy, I…" He swallowed so hard I could see it. "I was an idiot. I should have known, from the first

346

time you showed me how to do a blanket stitch – or even the seventh time, when you did it with exactly the same patience. I should have known that you were the only one for me."

Izzy's smile was even brighter than the home-made dress she was wearing.

"You're weird – in a good way – and different and funny and clever and brilliant and an incredible seamstress. And you're the only one I want to be with."

"You're the only one I want to be with, too," Izzy said, her voice soft.

Jasper's smile rivalled even Izzy's. After a moment or two of just staring at each other, he seemed to remember about the flowers we'd spent two days making and thrust them forward at her.

"I made these for you. Well, I had help. But it was my idea. Sort of. I wanted to make you something special. Something you." Izzy tentatively took the unusual bouquet, touching the petals of one of the flowers with great care. "They're corsages, or brooches, or whatever you want them to be. We just put them on the stems for the look of the thing. There's one from every scrap of fabric I could find from every dress you've ever made, with a bit of help from Miss Cotterill and, well, your mum, too.

She was a bit confused until I explained… Anyway, do you … do you like them?"

Izzy beamed. "I love them." Then, still gripping her flowers, she flung her arms around Jasper's neck.

"Grace?" Connor's voice was too close, right behind me, his breath warm against the skin of my neck. "We need to talk."

Sighing, I turned. "I don't know what you want to talk about."

"Us." Connor put his hands in his pockets and stepped back, just a little. It was probably only twenty centimetres, but suddenly the distance between us felt like a mile. "Look, you know how I feel about you. But you made me a promise. And you broke it."

"I was wrong, I get that. But I had reasons," I said firmly. "I was trying to help my friend."

"And what now? You think everything is suddenly going to be OK?"

"Why shouldn't it be?" I waved a hand at the cast. "Ash and Yasmin will get back together, the show will be great tonight, and you and I can go back to how things were, too."

"Do you really believe that? That everything will suddenly be fine? Yasmin's told Ash she needs time to think about things," Connor said, and a heavy weight tugged at my heart. "He's off sulking in the back somewhere. If you'd just talked to me first, I could have helped you. We could have waited…"

"You mean you'd have told me to stay out of it, to avoid any drama," I snapped back. Because whatever he thought, I had found out the truth and cleared my friend's name. I'd done the right thing.

"Until after the play? Yeah. I would have." We stared at each other, and a horrible thought filled my head. What if I'd fixed things for Yasmin only to ruin them for myself?

"Grace!" The yelling came from behind me, and I turned, automatically, to see Sara racing across the stage towards me. "Violet's gone. You're going to have to go on as Beatrice tonight!"

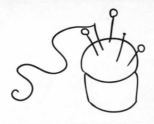

PATCHWORK QUILT

What you need:

7 different pieces of fabric, in complementary patterns
Plain backing fabric
Sheet wadding

What to do:

1. Cut fifty-six squares (eight from each piece of fabric),
   measuring 22 x 22cm each.

2. Lay your squares into eight rows of seven squares, in the
   order you want them to appear on your quilt.

3. Start with the top row. Take the first two squares and pin
   them down the side where you want them to join, right
   sides together, then stitch a 1cm seam.

4. Add on the third square where you want it to join the
   second square in the same way, and so on for the rest of the
   row, making sure your seams are all exactly 1cm.

5. Repeat with the other rows.

6. Line up the rows in order, then pin the first two rows
   together, lining up the seams exactly. Stitch in place with a
   1cm seam allowance again, then add the next row and so

on, until the end.

7. *Iron all the seams flat.*

8. *Measure and cut your backing fabric and wadding to fit the patchwork layer.*

9. *Lay out the patchwork and lining, right sides together, then add the wadding on top.*

10. *Pin all four sides, leaving a 30cm gap on one of the short sides.*

11. *Stitch all the way around, except the gap, removing your pins as you go. Turn inside out and hand sew the gap closed.*

12. *For a quilted effect, sew through all three layers along each of the seams between your squares.*

13. *Lay your quilt out, stand back and admire!*

For a moment, just a brief flying moment, my heart gave a leap.

This was it. The moment I'd been daydreaming about, planning for and half-expecting since the day the cast list went up. This was my chance.

But then I saw Connor's face, his thoughts printed as clearly across it as if he'd said them out loud.

"No," I said, reaching out and grabbing his hand. "That's not why I did this."

"I hope not. For their sake." He nodded towards the rest of the cast, and I followed his gaze, taking in the stricken looks, the fear in their faces. They were already beaten down by the awful dress rehearsal. Now their lead actress was deserting them, too.

My heart sank in my chest as I realized, for the first time, that I *wasn't* the best person to play Beatrice.

Mr Hughes had picked Violet. Violet was the one who'd rehearsed the part over and over, the one who knew all the tiniest moves. The one that everyone else expected to be on that stage with them. Their star.

And they needed her.

"Where is she?" I broke away from Connor, already crossing the stage. "In the drama room?"

"She was," Sara said. "But she was shoving things in her bag, she might have already gone…"

But she wouldn't be. I knew Violet. I used to be Violet. She couldn't leave without one last scene, one last drama playing out. "Keep everyone out of there, yeah?" I said. Sara nodded.

"Want me to come with you?" Connor asked, following me through the wings, towards the drama room.

I shook my head. "I can handle this." I flashed him a small, sorry smile. "I think I have to."

"OK." Connor stopped at the door, and my heart flip-flopped a little at the serious look on his face. "Fix this, Grace. Or we haven't got a show."

Biting my lip, I nodded. And then I headed in, alone.

Violet was huddled behind the screens we'd been using for changing, her bag half packed, her eyes red and cheeks blotchy. No wonder she didn't want anyone to see her; she wasn't one of those girls who could cry and look beautiful. Neither was I, but that wasn't the point.

"So. This is kind of undermining my Cheer-Up Cake Stall thing." I sat on the edge of the nearest table, swinging my legs and looking down at her.

Violet gave a muffled sob. "I thought this would be just what you wanted. Your chance to shine at last. Isn't that why you made me tell Ash the truth?"

"No. I made you tell Ash the truth to stop Yasmin from being miserable." I paused. Was that the only reason? "Also because you did a really lousy thing."

"And now everybody knows it. All I could think about, all through the second half of the dress, was how everyone knows what I did. They're all laughing at me behind my back. How can I go on stage with them tonight, knowing that?"

"Right now, I think they're all far too busy worrying about this show being a disaster to bother laughing at you." Not that they wouldn't, afterwards. Violet was right; too many people had been floating around, listening in. People knew now, which meant the whole school would soon. And, as Yasmin had learned, that was never fun.

Violet gave me a scathing look. "I bet this day is ending up exactly how you wanted it, isn't it?"

Jasper's grand gesture had been a success, at least.

People were eating cake, and telling me to go star in the show, just like I'd dreamed. But Ash was begging Yasmin to take him back, and I wasn't sure she would. And Connor and me ... I didn't have a clue what was going to happen there.

And if Violet didn't get up, pull it together and get on that stage tonight, the show I – and everyone else – had been working on for six months would be a disaster.

So, no. Not everything I wanted at all.

I slipped off the table and crouched down beside Violet. "Look. Confession time. You and me? We're not nice, sweet people. We're not Yasmin, or Ash. We want things, and we daydream about ways to get them. You think I haven't thought of a million scenarios in which I get to play Beatrice? I've been thinking about it all year. You were right, when you told Connor I was waiting for you to screw up so I could swoop in and save the day. I told myself that it would be for the good of the show, or that it would help Connor, even. But honestly? I wanted it for me. I wanted to be the star."

"I knew it!" Violet surged up, her cheeks pink. "I always knew—"

"But not like this," I said, talking over her righteous indignation. "I didn't want it like this. And

355

the difference between you and me, Violet, is that I never hurt somebody in order to get what I wanted. Until today."

"Today? You mean me?"

"I mean that I promised someone something, someone who matters, and I broke my word. I had good reasons, but … I went about things badly. And I hurt them." It felt good to confess everything. But Violet wasn't the person I needed to say this to.

"So, no," I went on. "This – you pulling out and me going on as Beatrice – it's not what I want. Even if I thought it was. All I want right now is for this show to be a success. And that requires you getting it together, washing your face, putting your costume on and walking on to that stage tonight like you own it."

Her eyes got kind of big at that. "But—"

"No. No buts. Yes, you screwed up. Yes, you're embarrassed. And yes, you were awful and everyone out there knows it. But the only thing to do now – and trust me, I'm speaking from experience here – is to get back up and try and be better next time." Just like I was going to promise Connor I would.

Violet looked like she might start crying again so, with a soft sigh that hopefully didn't sound too impatient, I stretched out my legs and sat beside her, my back to the screen.

"You don't have to be that girl any more, is what I'm saying. The girl who screws other people over to get what she wants, or who pushes other people out so she can be the star. You don't need the drama to be important. You can be important just by being yourself – and yourself can be anyone you want." I wasn't just talking to Violet, I realized. I was talking to myself. "But you have to be out there, facing everyone else, to do it. Otherwise, this is the only you they'll ever know."

I thought she was going to argue with me again, which would have been clearly pointless and a waste of time, but she didn't. Instead, she gave a sharp nod and said, "OK," in a slightly watery voice.

I jumped up and held out a hand to pull her up. "Then let's get you ready."

Fifteen minutes later we walked out on to the stage with Violet in her first costume and full make-up, 1920s headband in place, and the cast and crew cheered. It wasn't entirely clear which one of us they were cheering, but I chose to believe it was mostly for me.

After all, I had saved the day.

But to be honest? I needed to talk to Connor too

357

much to really care about applause.

"I fixed it," I said, approaching him at the side of the stage. Everyone else was too busy with Violet to pay us any attention, so at least I knew there wouldn't be a scene, whatever Connor's reaction.

"You did." He smiled, just a little, and relief flooded through me. "The door was still open, by the way. I heard what you said to Violet."

"All of it?" My heart clenched at the thought. I'd planned on spinning that confession a little better when I spoke to him about it.

"All of it," he confirmed.

"Oh." Then he knew everything. About how I'd lied to him about wanting Violet's role. How I wasn't the good, changed person he thought I was.

I thought about what I'd told Violet, about being whoever she wanted to be. I thought about Mum and Dad, and how they were doing their best but still just making it up as they went along, like the rest of us. I thought about Faith, trying so hard to be part of my family, even when I'd made it difficult for her.

And I thought about me. About who I was, and what mattered to me – my friends, my family ... and Connor. Not being a star, not the drama. Just the people I cared about. But that didn't mean I wasn't still Grace Stewart.

"I get that you're mad about me causing all this last-minute drama," I said slowly, still thinking through what I wanted to say. "And yeah, my timing wasn't great."

"It was terrible," Connor said, but he didn't look mad. "But I do get why you did it. For a moment, when Sara said Violet wouldn't go on, I admit, I thought that maybe you'd planned this. But then I remembered I know you better than that, and I had to trust that you were only doing what you thought was best, for your friends."

"I thought I was. And I wasn't just doing it for the drama, exactly. But Connor ... this is who I am. I'm always going to be a little dramatic, whether I'm backstage or on stage or even off stage completely. I'm not ever going to be calm and collected and just sulk quietly like you."

"I don't—"

"Yes, you do. But I like you anyway. Even when you're sulking." I gave him a quick grin to show I wasn't too serious. "I guess what I'm saying is ... I'm sorry. I shouldn't have lied to you."

"No. But I should have understood more what your friends mean to you. I guess ... I haven't had friends that mattered like that in a while."

"You do now," I told him, resting my hand

against his arm.

"Yeah, I do. And maybe good friends are worth a little drama." His fingers tucked under my chin, making me look up at him. His eyes were dark and serious, but he was smiling softly, like he couldn't help himself when he looked at me. "I know you now, Grace. I know exactly who you are. That's why I want to be with you."

"Yeah?"

"Yeah. What you said to Violet about the sort of person you are … sometimes I think it's only you who still believes you're that girl. The rest of us know better. Do you even realize how much more you've done for this play working backstage then you ever could have on stage? It's not just the costumes. It's everything. From running lines with Violet, to prompting, to helping me shift scenery, you did everything you could to make this show a success. Even if no one else noticed."

I stared up at him. Was he right? Had I really done enough, changed enough, for people to forget the Grace I used to be?

Was being myself all I had to do to get my happy ending and the applause at the curtain call? Because if so…

"The thing is, I can't promise that being with me

won't be a *little* dramatic sometimes. Think you can live with that?"

Bending close, Connor pressed his lips against mine, his arm snaking round my waist to hold me close against him. "If it means I get to be with you, I'll handle the theatrics," he murmured, between kisses. "It will always be better than being without you."

I smiled as I kissed him back, feeling his lips curving in response against mine. Maybe we didn't need to be like Mac and Lottie, all perfect for each other and everything, to be happy. We could just be us instead.

Just Grace and Connor.

From then, it was countdown to curtain-up. Mr Hughes turned up just as we finished clearing away the Cheer-Up Cake Stall. Jasper had finally let go of Izzy long enough to help Lottie and Mac with making replacement refreshments, while Yasmin was back helping me and Izzy to get everyone into their costumes. I'd talk to Yasmin later, once everything was over, and find out how she really felt about Ash. He'd been tricked by Violet, of course, but he should have trusted her anyway. Maybe they'd get back together, or maybe they wouldn't, but at least I'd done what I could to help her.

Right now, my focus was on the show – my first production as wardrobe and props mistress.

While Mr Hughes gave his last-minute motivational speech to the cast in the drama room, I snuck out front to watch the audience file in. I spotted Mum, Dad and Faith taking up their seats in the front row and waved. Faith waved back and beckoned me forward.

"How's it all going backstage?" Dad asked. "You taking charge back there and keeping everyone in order?"

"Something like that," I said with a smile. "I fed them cake, anyway."

"Always works for me." Faith grinned. "I'm so excited to see what you've done with the costumes. And look!" She held up a tiny bouquet of fabric flowers – leftovers from our mass flower-making session with Jasper.

"I've got some in my bag, too," Mum said. "I thought we could throw them on stage at the end."

"Like roses at the opera, but better," Faith added.

"That's a lovely idea," I said. But I had to admit, I felt a little sad to see the last of the flowers go.

"Don't worry." Faith wrapped an arm around my shoulder in a way she wouldn't have dreamed of a few weeks ago. "We can make more. I'm thinking that fabric bouquets would be perfect for the wedding, don't you? They last a lot longer, for one thing."

"And they'll go better with the new bridesmaids' dresses, too," Mum said, rooting through her bag. She held up a new pattern. Simple, sophisticated, and not yellow. It was everything I'd ever wanted in a bridesmaid's dress.

"It's perfect," I said.

"Oh good." Mum smiled. "Faith chose it. She said it reminded her of you."

I'd like to claim that my sudden excitement about the wedding had more to do with my growing closeness with my sister than the suddenly improved dress but, well, at best it was probably fifty-fifty. Which was a start.

"You'd better get backstage," Dad said, checking his watch. "They'll be starting in a minute."

I nodded, but then a thought occurred to me. "Actually, while Mum's working on the bridesmaids' dresses... Faith, I wondered if you might be able to help me with another project?"

"Sure," Faith said, looking surprised. "The flowers were tons of fun. What were you thinking?"

"I found one of our gran's last patchwork quilts in her sewing box. She'd barely started it when she died." I swallowed. "I thought we might finish it for her. Together."

Faith's eyes looked wet with tears. She'd never known Gran, I realized. I'd had my whole life with the family Faith hadn't even met. It was time for me to share some of that with her. After all, Gran had made all her other grandchildren a quilt. Faith deserved one, too.

"I'd love to." Faith wrapped me up in a hug. "Thank you."

"Well, I'll need something to keep me busy once the show's over," I said. "But first – Dad's right. I need to get back there. I'll see you all after the show."

They nodded, and I dashed back down the passageway that led to the wings of the stage. Glancing back over my shoulder, I saw Dad sitting with his arm around Faith, and Mum holding her hand.

Maybe we could all find our way through together, I thought. It had to be easier than doing it alone.

Out past the audience, tucked away in the same side room we'd used for refreshments the year before, I spotted Mac and Lottie, handing out cakes and drinks. They worked so smoothly together, like they could read where the other was and what they needed without any obvious clues. They were just in tune, I guessed.

I wondered if Connor and I would be like that, this time next year, only probably with a little more drama. I hoped so. But who knew? Connor had a whole summer of working backstage ahead of him, I hoped, and I had Faith's wedding, plus plenty of sewing projects I wanted to get on with. And maybe the youth theatre summer school Connor planned to be at would need an extra actress – or a wardrobe mistress, for that matter.

"Still wishing you were out there tonight?"

Stepping into the wings, I saw Connor watching me from the centre of the stage, putting the last prop for the first scene in place.

"No, actually." I moved towards him, drawn in like I always was when he was near. "I was thinking how much I'm looking forward to doing this again."

"The costumes?"

"Working with you."

I didn't think I'd seen the particular smile that spread across Connor's face at my words before. A special smile, just for me. Not quite proud, not just happy, not even pleased to be proved right … it was a mix of everything. Everything he'd ever felt about me, I think.

"I don't care if I'm on stage or backstage for my next show," I said, stepping closer to him. "It's not about being a star for me, any more. It's being part of something. And being with you."

"I can't wait. And until then…" Moving closer, Connor took me into his arms, and I smiled as I rose up to meet him in a kiss.

"A lot more of that," I said, knowing exactly what he'd meant.

"Definitely."

"Come on, you two." Mr Hughes stood at the side of the stage, smiling indulgently at us. I should have been embarrassed to be caught by a teacher, but I wasn't. He wasn't Mr Hughes right then, I could tell. He was Guy, Connor's stepdad.

"Time to start?" Connor asked.

"Yep. We're all ready back here."

Connor glanced around the stage, then at me again. "Here, too."

"Right then," I said with a grin. "Showtime."

And, with my hand in Connor's, we headed backstage. Exactly where I wanted to be.